Walking
still

Walking
still

Charles Mungoshi

BAOBAB BOOKS

Published by Baobab Books (a division of Academic Books (Pvt) Ltd, Box 567, Harare, Zimbabwe. 1997

The author notes that many of the stories published in this collection were published in Horizon *magazine in a different and shorter form.*

Cover design: Danes Design
Typset by: Fontline
Printed by: Mazongororo Paper Converters

ISBN 0-908311-99-0

Contents

The Hare

Later that evening, after Sara had left for Johannesburg with her friends of the combis, Nhongo had driven angrily back home to Chitungwiza, and packed a few of his clothes into a bag. He told the housemaid, Ella, to put the children into clean clothes and get them into the car. They were going home to the country, he said. They were going to see *Ambuya* Mangai and *Sekuru* Jumo. Ella said she would run the bath and spruce the children up a bit but Nhongo said they didn't have time. So the two girls, Sekai, six, and Netsai, four, were bundled into the car in their street-dirty clothes, their dusty faces creased into moon-grins.

Within ten minutes they were driving out of Zengeza, across the Manyame River over the new bridge towards the Mbudzi turn-off, where they would take the Simon Mazorodze Road south towards Chivhu.

Nhongo hadn't planned to go home but, watching his wife, Sara, as she waved to him through the window of the combi outside the Monomotapa Hotel earlier that afternoon, blowing kisses and laughing, she seemed suddenly to belong more to those friends of hers than to him, and he had had a sudden desire to taste *dovi* once more, sitting in his mother's pole-and-*daga* hut. A strange, irresistible nostalgia to revisit the scenes of his childhood had assailed him, to walk once more through the tall dewy grass, hunting for wild fruits such as *matufu, hute, nzviro* and *maroro*. It was mid-January, the season for wild fruits. But he had a premonition – the air was too dry and dusty and there had been very little rain since November – indeed, virtually the whole of the rainy season -- that there wouldn't be much fruit in the bush.

He pulled the car off the main road at the Eight-Mile Service Station and asked the petrol attendant to fill up the tank. He got out of the car and walked across to the kiosk to buy potato chips and soft drinks for the children. He wanted to have a beer but he was a very careful driver. His wife had often told him, with the merest hint of play in her voice, that if she were looking for faults, it was his sense of responsibility that she found oppressive; she said it could have provided her with an excuse to leave him.

His new shoes pinched and he felt hot behind the ears hearing them squeaking as he walked over the hard asphalt of the service station. He felt people were looking at him and he was forced to produce a vacuous apologetic smile that made him feel even more stupid as it wasn't directed at anyone in particular. For a strange -- exasperating -- reason, he felt as if they all knew that she had bought him those uncomfortable, flashy shoes. She had insisted that he put them on for the trip into town where she was going to board the bus to Jo'burg. And, in his anger, he had forgotten to take them off when he returned to their home in Chitungwiza. Now he would have to wear them all, the way to his parents' homestead. A bizarre childhood fear nagged him: his parents would ask him where he'd got *those* shoes from. Try as he might, he was finding it very hard to outgrow the thought that everything he did must first be approved by his parents. Uneasily, he sensed that Sara somehow despised him for this.

He handed the packets of chips to Ella to share among the children and herself, and the two little girls jumped up and down with glee. As always, seeing them happy because of something he had done, gave him a lump in his throat. And the way Ella spoke to the children, the way she asked them to behave towards … to treat … him!

Ella said to the girls, 'Say, Thank you, *Baba*.'

And the girls together, as if in a classroom, 'Thank you, *Baba!*'

He paid the petrol man and they drove off. Driving towards Manyame, Netsai said, 'Are we going home, *Baba?*'

'Yes.'

'Are we going to see Granny Zvauya?'

'Granny Zvauya doesn't live at Chivhu,' Ella said.

'Doesn't Granny Zvauya live at Chivhu, *Baba?*' Netsai asked her father. Her father knew better than Ella and who was Ella anyway? This was a family affair.

'Granny Zvauya is Mummy's mother,' Sekai said.

'No, she isn't!'

'Oh, yes. She is.'

'Is Granny Zvauya Mummy's mother, Dad?'

'Yes,' Nhongo said.

'What did I tell you?' Sekai bragged.

'You told me nothing,' Netsai said pouting, to hurt Sekai.

'And your mother is Granny Mangai?' Sekai asked her father, at the same time showing off to Ella and Netsai.

'Yes,' Nhongo said.

'I don't want to visit Granny Zvauya,' Netsai said.

'Do you hear, *Baba?* Netsai doesn't want to visit our Mummy's mother.'

'Girls, I don't want to hear this kind of talk. They are both your grandmothers. You must love them both equally,' Nhongo said. He felt uneasy as he said this. He was asking his children to do something that he himself found very difficult to do. Sara's mother was 'that woman', and his mother was 'my mother', and he couldn't change that. His body tensed each time he tried to see his mother-in-law as someone as worthy of his love and attention as his own mother.

'Our home is in Chivhu, isn't it, *Baba*?' Sekai asked.

'Yes.'

'I don't want to go to Gutu!' Netsai yelled.

'Netsai!' Nhongo bellowed.

And immediately regretted it. In the confines of the car he felt that his voice had been unnecessarily loud.

But it worked. The children fell silent, eating their chips. Sekai made faces at Netsai. Netsai hit her but Sekai didn't stop until Ella told both of them they were such good, grown-up girls and being such they would find it very silly and very stupid to laugh at other people.

Then the children began to sing, each her own song, each looking out of her own window.

'We are going home,

'Going home,

'We are going to see Granny,

'Granny,

'We are going to see Granny.'

Listening to the children singing to the smooth purr of the speeding car, Nhongo felt a little sad. When was the last time they had all driven home, as a family? When was the last time he had taken the children home to their grandparents? He seemed to remember that their last trip had been to Gutu, to see Sara's widowed mother. He wanted to be fair but he was sure the last trip had been to Gutu.

The sun went down before they reached Mupfure River, at Beatrice. There was a police road block just outside the little town. One of the officers signalled to them to pull over to the side of the road and stop. He came over and looked into the car through Nhongo's window. He smiled.

'A family?' the officer said.

'Yes.'

'Going home to see Grandmother?' the officer said to the girls.

'Yes!' the girls chirped brightly, together.

'What are you going to bring me?' the officer asked.

'*Dovi!*' Sekai said.

'We are going to Granny Mangai,' Netsai said.

'You seem to be driving into a storm,' the officer turned his attention to Nhongo, straightening up and pointing at the sky over Chivhu.

Nhongo was surprised. They were driving south but he hadn't noticed the heavy dark clouds ahead of them. The sky was grey and menacing.

'Drive carefully and bring the children back safely,' the officer said, signalling them to continue.

From the policeman's look, he must have thought Ella was his wife, Nhongo thought and glanced at Ella out of the corner of his eye. Then he quickly looked away, and put his foot hard on the accelerator.

At Rosarum, Nhongo switched on the headlights. The clouds seemed to be falling, swallowing the space between earth and sky. Memories of his ox-herding days suddenly overwhelmed Nhongo. Without realizing it, he found himself reciting the childhood ditties that they used to chant as they walked through the bush, covered in hooded jute sacks, after the cattle in the rain.

'*Muhacha ndipe hacha*
'*Mukute ndipe hute*
'*Muonde ndipe maonde.*'

The songs came from an almost forgotten childhood and he was surprised that he could have forgotten that there had once been a time when he had been happy and carefree. The low sky, so full of the promise of imminent rain, formed a kind of protective canopy over him and allowed past and present to merge in the strong smell of cowdung, damp soil, wet leaves, smoke.

'*Jaja Mandure*
'*Mandure mandure*
'*Jaja mandure.*'

Enclosed in the car, they were a family separated from the rest of the world, windows tightly shut, the sound of the engine lost in the rush of wind and swishing of tyres on the tarmac, the children clapping their hands and singing together with Ella – why was it that song, under certain circumstances and conditions, could transform even the most commonplace events – and the plainest of features – into something never-to-be-forgotten and never-to-be-repeated? Nhongo wondered, stealing glances at Ella who was now as absorbed in the story-telling and singing as the children. Ella contributed most of the stories and songs. Nhongo told one of his father's dark, dark stories of the crocodile and the girl, and surprised himself by singing the haunting crocodile's song – well, not quite note for note but well enough for Ella to compliment him and then to beautifully finish the crocodile's haunting song for him. Nhongo blinked back tears and hoped that Ella didn't see them. They were on the monotonous stretch of highway between Featherstone and Munyati River. The lights of the car formed a long shaft boring into the dark tunnel ahead of them, sometimes catching the trees along the road in grotesque shapes that rushed into and past them in a mesmerizing kaleidoscope of eery patterns.

It wasn't much of a thing. Just something, a shadow caught – again – in that sharp, magnifying corner-of-the-eye vision, like the furry-edged blur of a dream just as one falls asleep. He might have been falling asleep, it was that insubstantial, but he clearly heard Ella shout, '*Tsuro!*' Then a flash-and-bob of something fluffy-white, a slight fleshy thump, a squeal of tyres and a deep, deathly silence, the dusty shoulder of the road, the smell of burning rubber and petrol and, maddeningly, the roar of the engine and the lights ghostly bright, surreally lighting the trees ahead of them and etching unearthly silhouettes into the nightscape.

Nhongo experienced an instant of knife-like clarity. He had wished both to hit and to avoid the hare. He could feel his heart pounding in his ears. He switched off the engine and the lights. His hands were shaking. A car roared past them without stopping, horn full blast, echoing in chilling diminuendo up the dark night road towards Harare.

'Did you kill it, *Baba*?' Netsai asked sweetly.

For some strange reason, Nhongo thought that was the funniest thing he had ever heard in all his life. He began to laugh. Then the laughter began to feed on itself and he couldn't stop and they were all laughing safe inside the car – and yet they all seemed to be aware of something that was sitting out there, outside their laughter, something crouching in the darkness, ready to pounce the moment the laughter ceased.

Wiping tears from his eyes, relieved but still shaking, Nhongo opened the glove-locker, took out his torch, switched it on, opened the door and got out of the car.

The hare was crouched on the edge of the road a couple of metres behind the car. It didn't move when he picked it up. It just made a kind of hiccuping squeal and released a dribble of warm urine over Nhongo's fingers. He felt the tiny, delicate bones under the too-warm fur. Little electric spasms seemed to be passing through it. Nhongo cuddled it to his chest and carried it to the car. He realized that it must be in terrible pain although he couldn't see – or feel – any blood anywhere on its fur. The eyes were wide, wide open, dazed, stunned. Looking into those eyes, he almost dropped it to the ground. Something he saw was beyond him and all of a sudden he didn't want to have anything to do with it – but he was there alone and he had to do something. Something, at least, to show them that he still could.

He didn't do anything. He held himself carefully together, unlocked the boot of the car, and carefully placed the hare in the boot, on some old sacks that he always carried during the rainy season. He shut the boot. He smoked two cigarettes to rid himself of the shaking in his hands.

'When is Mama coming back?' Sekai asked suddenly.

'Did you hit it, *Baba*?' Netsai asked.

5

'Shut up!' Ella said, under her breath and Nhongo would never forget the shock it gave him. In normal circumstances, he would have fired her for talking to his children like that. But these were not normal circumstances. Later on, he would recall how very close to Sara's Ella's voice had sounded.

'I am feeling cold, *Baba*,' Sekai said.

Nhongo took the blankets from the boot of the car. The children seemed to go to sleep immediately after he'd covered them up. Ella was very quiet. Nhongo remembered that she was only eighteen and he rebuked himself for having wished her to be more adult than her years. He wanted to make up for it, to explain, to apologize, to say something – anything. He found nothing to say.

Later, when they were turning off the main road, ten kilometres from Chivhu, onto the dusty track towards Rugunhe, he said: 'One should never try to chase a hare crossing the road at night.' He looked behind him. Ella's eyes stared back. They looked strangely white in the darkness of the car. She held on to her stony silence. He didn't know why he'd spoken at all. Ahead of him, the bush track made such sudden twists and turns that he sometimes lost it under the wheels of the car. The lights made weird swings through the trees. He put pressure on the brake pedal. He asked himself: Where am I rushing to?

'Scared, are you?' Nhongo said without realizing it. There was just no way he couldn't talk. They were crossing a sandy dry river-bed. On both sides of the track a curtain of darkness pressed in on them. Ella didn't say anything but Nhongo sensed that she nodded her head twice. Fear communicates like lightning in the dark.

Then Nhongo became angry. There was no specific, immediate object at which to direct his anger but it seized him, a burning lump in his chest. The whole point was: *it isn't my fault.* He felt, vaguely, that this wouldn't have happened at all if Sara had been there. Somewhere deep within his tangled unexamined feelings: it was all Sara's fault.

Married now for sixteen years, with four children, the first two, a boy and a girl, away at a secondary boarding school, Nhongo had felt that nothing could ever touch his family. He had risen to the position of section manager in the textile company that he worked for in Harare. He was getting good money and he was a Party-card holder, a respected member of the community both at work and in Zengeza where he and his family lived. A careful, security-conscious, family man, he strongly subscribed to the old dictum: God helps those who help themselves. He was not one to take risks. He respected and honoured all elders, especially his parents. Sara thought he was too afraid of his parents to respect or honour them. She could think what she wanted to think: who was she anyway?

He had made her pregnant while she was still doing her Form Three at Gutu Secondary School. He had left school and been working for two years. His parents were already thinking that, as the first son, he was taking too long about getting married. They had been very happy when one day two women – an elderly woman and a girl – paid them a visit. They sat just outside their yard, the girl's head and face covered by a *zambia*. They could tell that the younger woman was very pregnant. They had been very pleased to receive Sara into their family and Nhongo hadn't disappointed them. He seemed to have been prepared. He had been saving money for just such an occasion. And in less than a month, Sara's people and Nhongo's people had become brothers- and sisters-in-law.

Only Sara's mother seemed not to approve. Sara was her last child. The other four boys and a girl had all married and remained in the village where they still looked to their widowed mother for help with their expanding families. Sara had been her only hope. Sara was to achieve what she hadn't achieved, what her other children hadn't achieved, what even her husband – who had died a poor village bricklayer and every-one's errand boy – hadn't achieved. In Sara, Kariwo, Sara's mother, would be re-created. And then Sara had become pregnant in her third year at secondary school. An unusually bright child, she had had promise, unlike the rest of her children. Kariwo never recovered from the blow.

Sara, quiet, obedient but with a subtle, stubborn streak that only a husband would discern, had understood her mother's dreams and had wept quietly, while making herself impossible promises. The pregnancy had been as much a surprise to herself as to anyone else. Still young, she did not understand how her body could have betrayed her. Yet no thought of abortion or suicide ever entered her mind. From an early age, Sara had learned to face her problems head on. But for a time she had lost her normal cheerful being, and withdrew so far into herself that she created a people-less space around her.

Nhongo had been working, saving and preparing so that Sara would be able to go straight from the classroom into motherhood and a full-time career as a housewife. He didn't want her to endure that anxious probational uxorial period so charged with over-doses, poisons, pesticides and traditional abortion concoctions that it had become a time which every mother dreaded as they watched their daughters growing up.

Sara soon became the envy of most mothers and girls in the village. 'How did you do it?' they asked her. She didn't know what they were talking about but she smiled and said, 'I didn't do anything about it.'

Sara didn't have to go down on bended knee to ask Nhongo to marry her. When she brought his hand to touch her changed belly he simply jumped from being a boy into fatherhood. And there had never been any doubt about her love for him, Nhongo thought. She hadn't spoken much about it, she was not the demonstrative type, but Nhongo could see it in her eyes, in her actions. Or had he been wrong?

He could swear, hand on heart, that Sara had never lacked anything in their married life. She had gone about her child-bearing business and her household chores cheerfully and he couldn't remember that she had ever complained about anything. Nhongo could also swear that Sara had never been unhappy with him. Or, at least, he hadn't seen her showing signs of being unhappy. But could he be sure?

One thing was certain, that when she came to live with him she was still too young to know what she wanted and if she had desperately wanted something, too shy, or afraid, to tell him. She had only been sixteen and he had been – what? Twenty-seven. Almost twice her age ... well, not quite. But she must have felt intimidated. She must have looked at him as one of her brothers: *I am not going to pay your fees this term if you don't work harder.*

Nhongo mulled things over: trying to come to terms with a new Sara. He had never denied her anything. After their first two children, she had done a secretarial course, had even passed her intermediate exams, but had then abandoned the idea of ever getting an office job because she couldn't stand the managers who 'look at my breasts all the time they are interviewing me'. Secretly, Nhongo had been relieved. It had solved a nagging problem without his having to commit himself. He had wanted Sara to have a job, to do what she felt she wanted to do. It was, after all, only what every woman was doing these days. But deep down, Nhongo was still a traditionalist, a tribesman, as he and his few friends liked to call themselves. What is a husband for, if his wife is going to work as well?

An example of what Nhongo and his friends believed lay in the story of Jokonya. Jokonya was headmaster of the primary school which Nhongo's children had attended. His wife was also a teacher at a nearby secondary school. Jokonya had sent his wife to University to do her BA and later her B.Ed. Now she was teaching. When she brought her first pay cheque home, Jokonya took it and tore it in half. 'I can manage my family very well without a second cheque in the house,' Jokonya had told his wife. This was a bit extreme, Nhongo and his friends agreed, but Jokonya was only making a statement. A man should be allowed to have pride in his own home. The burden of running the household, the financial burden, should lie squarely on the husband's shoulders ...

Fortunately for Nhongo, he had never been placed in a position where he had had to remind Sara of this ... and they had been doing very well ... that is until recently.

Nhongo hadn't been thinking of retiring from the textile company for another five years or more. He was a careful man who planned his life several years ahead – in detail. As long as he was alive and working as he was working, no one in his family would ever want for anything.

But then, one day, seemingly out of the blue, they told him that the company was going into liquidation. Nhongo, who had never been out of employment, thought this was a joke – at least he did at first ...

A year later he was home. A loaf of bread cost about three times what it had done, two years previously. The older children were still in school. Sekai and Netsai hadn't even started! He had bought a car a year before the liquidation, and he owed the finance house a suicidal amount of money. He had to be very careful with the little they had given him in terminal benefits. (It was criminal!) This wasn't the time to think of going into private business. He had had to shelve his plans to move to the low density suburbs. And they had to cut down on the amount of meat they ate every day and ... *No, Netsai. You had ice-cream yesterday!*

Could this constant nag-nagging about money have driven her into it? Or was it possible that she had always dreamt of doing something, biding her time, waiting until an opportunity presented itself?

She had started off innocently enough. Or rather, Nhongo didn't know exactly when she had started because he'd never really asked what she did when he was away at work. In their marriage, there had never been cause for distrust. Each of them knew where the other was at any time of the day. Or had he just thought he'd known this? Nhongo wasn't sure any more.

Anyway, what started her off, or what he thought started her off, hadn't been any-thing very much: just second-hand clothes.

As far as Nhongo could remember, Sara had never had any real friends, people who would visit them, spend time with them and vice versa. It wasn't that he had said anything about friends except, of course, about neighbours. Neighbours, as far as Nhongo was concerned, were the cause of most divorces or marital break-downs. But still, the only people Nhongo had heard Sara talking or laughing with were his neighbours' wives. Mostly it was open-air gossip as they hung the nap-pies to dry on the clothes-lines in their backyards. Nothing that they wouldn't want their husbands to hear. How well the children were doing in school. The best way to cook *derere*. Where you could get the best out-of-season tomatoes or vegetables. Two of their neighbours had become a little closer to Sara because one was a nurse at the local clinic, and she had helped Sara with tablets and anti-biotics for the children. The other had had a death in her family and Sara had sat up with her for two whole nights. Mrs Gundani and Mrs Zimbwa were all right, Nhongo felt.

Yet someone had told her about *mupedzanhamo*, the second-hand clothes market in Mbare – on the other side of town. And one day, Nhongo came home to find Sara going through a pile of women's and children's clothes. 'I would like to help,' she had said.

And he had said something – he had encouraged her, although he didn't really like the thought of his wife going from door to door selling *mazitye* – the popular name for this kind of clothing which came mostly from Zambia and Mozambique. Busy looking for a job himself, he hadn't paid any more attention to Sara and her business. Until one day when he returned home, he heard laughter in the house even before he reached the verandah.

'These are my friends,' Sara introduced the four women who were almost buried under mountains of clothes. Nhongo could have sworn that he had seen at least three of them around one of the downtown night clubs.

He had grunted a greeting and gone into the bedroom. There he had lain on the bed, hands locked behind his head, listening to their laughter and the pounding of his heart. He had realized that they had reached a very delicate phase in their marriage.

In the lounge, the women were talking at the top of their voices, and laughing so loudly that they must have heard it at Chikwanha's, three kilometres away. They were talking of Mozambique, Zambia, Botswana, South Africa. And even Mauritius.

Nhongo would hear of these countries for the next he couldn't remember how many months. Sara now had friends. Her buying-and-selling friends. And it seemed that a completely new world had opened up to her and she was like a little child lost within it. Lost in wonder. This world frightened Nhongo. When her friends were there, Nhongo could hardly get a word in edgeways. They dominated everything. It felt to him as if he had built his house on the banks of a river and a flood was threatening to sweep it away. 'Is it just the money?' he asked her once.

'Someone has to work,' she had said innocently.

Then she had showed him the passport. Her passport. She hadn't told him that she was getting a passport. She hadn't told him anything about anything at all and here she was, smiling, and showing him a brand new passport with *his* name and *her* maiden name in it. She asked him to guess how long he thought it had taken her to get the passport. 'Six months?' he hazarded. He had heard that some kind of brake had been put on the issuing of passports. Some unscrupulous foreigners were taking advantage of the lax Zimbabwean passport regulations.

'No. Two hours.'

'*Two hours!*'

'Some friends of my friends got it for me.'

10

'Man or woman?' The words slipped out of Nhongo's mouth and he immediately regretted them.

'What do you mean?' She had asked him defensively.

He had wanted to say sorry but he couldn't. In the silence that followed, he felt they were becoming strangers to each other.

After that Sara didn't try to explain anything to him. She simply told him that she would be going to Lusaka, or to Jo'burg, the following week or the following day. What struck him most, what stopped him from asking any further questions, was that she was quite cheerful about it all. She didn't seem to feel that she was doing anything wrong, doing anything that he might not approve of. The word Nhongo found himself obliged to use about her attitude was 'innocent'.

And this took place during the time when there were stories every day in the newspapers about the plight of the women border jumpers, or cross-border trippers. The stories were of arrests, nights spent in the cells at obscure border posts. Stories of murder, kidnap, rape and mugging. But Sarah always returned radiant and bubbling with energy; she seemed almost unable to sit still, until she could make yet another trip over the border.

Nhongo had always considered himself to be fair, to be reasonable, to be loving and considerate. He had always wanted to be the husband she would want to talk about respectfully, lovingly, to her friends and neighbours. He didn't think she could honestly accuse him of being jealous, least of all of being petty. He'd always felt that jealousy reduced people to non-people, it dragged people through the mud ... jealousy left people exposed to all sorts of ill-winds ...

But it was getting too much for him. It seemed to him as if they had begun to live their family life on their verandah, in sight of everyone. The worst of it was that Sara seemed to thrive. And he, Nhongo, felt helpless to do anything about it. (Was it because he had no money of his own?) Their laughter had become very loud. It jangled as if someone were suspending knives in the silence – the silence that was growing between them. Instantly Nhongo blamed himself. He had been so secure in her presence: Sara, the mother of his children, that he hadn't bothered to discover whether she might have preferred an adjustment to their lifestyle. He had never really thought of her alone, independent, without the children. Someone with her own individual needs. This new game, from which he was completely excluded, amounted simply to a new hand of cards, which differed from the ones he had dealt her only in that she was now the major player ...

Nhongo found he could only turn to the children on the days when Sara was away. Then he became conspiratorially friendly with them. And Ella, what could he have done without Ella? She had become both mother and elder sister to the young girls.

And whenever Sara was home, Nhongo couldn't help – but silently, and through his body language – to hold her up for the children to look at: *Look at her. Look at your mother. Please just look at the bitch!*

Yet other people, Sara's friends for instance, felt it was Nhongo who was behaving badly. They called it jealousy. A husband's jealousy because a wife is proving that she can beat him at his own game, providing for the family. Because, it seemed, that Sara had been born with an instinctive sense of business.

If she saw that her husband was jealous, she didn't show it. She had become a new woman: yes. But she hadn't lost her love for her family. In fact, her new freedom to leave the house, to be among other people, seemed to have given a new dimension to their life as a family. She had never had any money of her own to buy anyone in the family anything. Now she indulged herself. She bought fancy shirts and jeans for Nhongo – clothes he would never have dreamed of buying for himself. She bought colourful T-shirts for the kids and she occasionally took the family out to eat at some expensive restaurant in town, or some international hotel like the Holiday Inn, the Sheraton or the Monomatapa.

Nhongo became scared at the speed at which their life was travelling. Relatives and neighbours began to talk. And he could feel other men's eyes cutting through his wife's tissue-thin clothing like rapacious knives. 'Do you want to believe them?' Sara asked Nhongo. And he couldn't answer her. All he was aware of was the line of pale flesh above her knees, previously hidden from the predatory eyes of men by her old skirts.

Nhongo was also very aware of his dependence on her. Early in their marriage, he had told her that they shouldn't let money come between their love. He had been working then, earning money that was called money. Indeed he was so well-cushioned that he could afford to say that money didn't matter. Now, he realized, it was money that mattered all the time. The old song had it right – money made the world go round – and it was money that bound one human being to another. Nhongo longed to keep their old pretence intact: *our love is beyond money.* 'It's *your* money,' he was forced to shout one day after she had asked him if it would be all right if she bought her mother some clothes. 'Your money', 'my money'. 'Your mother', 'my mother'. Nhongo noticed that all these demeaning phrases had begun to infiltrate their conversations soon after he stopped working and Sara had begun the cross-border trips with her friends of the combis. 'It's your bloody money.' Sara had stood stock still. She had looked at him hard. And she had wept.

But she hadn't stopped going down south. Now it was mostly to South Africa. And then there was Mr Magaso. 'I got a lift from Mr Magaso,' she told him one day, as she came into the house at two in the morning.

'Has he got a wife?'

'Of course, he has. What can you be thinking of? He is much older than you are. He could almost be your father. Yet he is so understanding, and oh so full of stories ...'

'Why don't we go south together?' Sara suggested one day. Nhongo only gawked at her. Sara didn't seem to realize that there was a world of difference between people who crossed borders in combis and a former manager in one of the country's biggest textile companies.

Since then Sara had brought Mr Magaso home and introduced him to Nhongo. Still, even that didn't rub out the big knot of bile which Nhongo felt each time Magaso drove Sara to the house at two in the morning after they had returned from Jo'burg – a trip they always did in one day, or so they said.

Mr Magaso would give two short blasts on the horn of his BMW, and Nhongo, unable to sleep whenever Sara was away, would think: I'm damned if I'm going to unlock the gate for them. But then the children would clamour:

'Mummy's back!' 'Mai vauyawo-ho!'

And there he would be, opening the door for her one more time.

And there she would be standing in the doorway with her bulging bags, all smiles, tired but jubilant, smelling of a new perfume – and she would turn back to Mr Magaso and the others in the car: 'What time do we leave on Sunday?'

'Be ready by one o'clock. By six we must hit Beitbridge!' As always, she would be loaded with goods for resale and clothes or toys for the children. And always a tie, a shirt or underpants for Nhongo. And it was on this last trip that she had bought him these fancy shoes. Very expensive by the look of them.

Nhongo had been too embarrassed to put them on for days. His children had yammered at him: 'Try them on let's see, *Baba*'.

But he simply stared at the shoes sitting on the coffee table as if they were a pair of cobras.

'Please, *Baba*! Please!' the children cried.

'Some other time,' he had said, unable to tell them why he wouldn't try them on, why it wasn't easy for him to accept them: he belonged to a proud tradition that said the hunting is done by the man of the house. This incident made him suddenly aware of his own helplessness.

For several days after she had given him the shoes, Nhongo seemed to keep coming across the word 'castration' each time he picked up something to read. Walking down the street, or entering a room, he felt people turning to look at him. He was overwhelmed by the feeling that they could see everything that was inside him. And he would become aware of his whole body assuming a defensive posture – physically manifested by a slight forward stoop and his right hand dangling in front of his fly. He became obsessed with his feeling of his nakedness.

In secret, he found himself looking at and comparing himself with the men that Sara travelled among. Either they were younger than he was: the muscular, sporty types; or they were older in an unpleasantly worldly-wise way, and they seemed to pity Nhongo. Their laughter, when they laughed, was between themselves, although it included Sara, and it seemed to hide something that they didn't want Nhongo to know. A child, they seemed to be saying: he would only hurt himself if he knew. And when Sara waved at him through the window, she too seemed to feel sorry for him.

And then there were his cousins and friends from home. It was unheard of that a married woman, somebody's wife, had male friends and left her husband at home to go on business trips to foreign countries with them. The way they pronounced the word 'business' made Nhongo's heart sink. They asked him if he were happy, only they didn't use these words. They were very much concerned with the *happiness* in his family. They even dared to ask who made the rules in his home.

What they meant, he knew, was: *did he still have his balls on him?* With lots of people from home talking about him, he *knew* that word had reached his parents.

They turned a bend in the road, the thick bush fell away and they were out in open country. The lights of the car fell on the whitewashed wall of an old abandoned store. In front of the store was the gate into Marondamashanu Communal Land.

Another ten-minute drive and they were home. Four grass-thatched huts: his parents' living-room and bedroom, the *hozi* or granary, and his own hut. He still had to build his own bedroom and *hozi*.

As soon as the lights swept across the buildings his father's elderly mongrel, Major, began to bark. His parents came rushing out of their living-room, despite their ages, and were standing in the full glare of the headlamps when the car came to rest at their feet. They lifted their hands to shield their eyes from the harsh light.

Major had stopped barking. He too was there to greet Nhongo when he got out of the car, jumping up and placing his paws on the man's chest, trying to lick his face, tail wagging. Nhongo was always amazed at how the dog remembered him, even after a three-year absence.

'*E-e, veHarare,*' Nhongo's father greeted him, stretching his hand out to Nhongo.

'*Titambire,*' his mother said, clapping her hands and peering into the car. 'Have you come alone?' Nhongo's mother asked. 'A-a, the whole family – no. It's *Mainini*

Ella! And the children,' his mother said as Ella got out of the car. The two women threw arms round each other.

'Had you forgotten us,-*Mainini* Ella?' Nhongo's mother said.

'Wasn't I here only two months ago?' Ella replied.

'Two months or too weeks — it's too long for us,' the old woman responded.

'One day I shall come forever,' Ella said, in a low voice. But Nhongo overheard her, it sounded odd to him but in the flurry of unpacking, he didn't think any more about it.

'And, how are the children?' his mother said quickly as if to cover up what Ella had said.

'They're in the car. Asleep.'

'Hey, hey, wake up!' *Va*Mangai, Nhongo's mother, leaned into the car and gently shook Netsai and Sekai.

'A-a, *Muroora*,' *Va*Jumo, Nhongo's father, responded to Ella's greetings as she knelt, clapping her hands to Nhongo's father.

For a second, Nhongo found himself comparing Sara with Ella. It wasn't a fully conscious act. He just noted that Ella had wrapped an ankle-length cloth round her lower body. Sara would have been in a pair of jeans and she wouldn't have knelt right down in the sand on both knees as Ella had done.

'A-a, my wives,' *Va*Jumo said as he hugged Netsai and Sekai. 'How are my wives?'

'Your beard is prickling my cheek,' Netsai said and everyone laughed.

'*Baba*, I want to sleep,' Sekai said.

'Say hello to Granny and Grandpa,' Ella told the children.

'*Mainini*,' *Va*Mangai addressed Ella, 'take them to bed. We will see them in the morning.'

Ella herded the two girls in the direction of *Va*Jumo's bedroom. *Va*Mangai picked up some pieces of wood from the firewood stack and went into the kitchen. Nhongo and his father remained outside by the car. 'And where is the girls' mother?' *Va*Jumo asked.

'She has gone to Jo'burg.'

'Jo'burg?'

'Yes.'

'Who is in Jo'burg that she's gone to visit?'

'No one.'

'No one?'

'No one.'

'Ho-oo?' *Va*Jumo said and fell silent.

Nhongo's mother called out for them to come into the house. She had already put a kettle on the fire and she was sitting on her side of the fireplace. Ella came in a little later and joined VaMangai on the goatskin mat on the women's side of the fireplace. Nhongo and his father sat on an earthen bench along the wall of the room, opposite the women.

After some small talk about the rain and the weather, VaMangai said, 'And where have you left the girls' mother?'

'He tells me she has gone to Jo'burg,' VaJumo said.

'Jo'burg?'

'That's right. Jo'burg,' VaJumo repeated ominously.

'She finds time to visit her relatives in Jo'burg and no time to come to see her own husband's parents?'

No one said anything. Nhongo looked down at the floor between his feet. The floor seemed very far away.

'Mother,' Ella said, getting up onto her knees, 'is there anything you would like me to do?'

'Go into the chicken coop. There is a useless old rooster. You know what to do: the water is about to boil, the knife is on that shelf over there.'

Ella went out with the knife and a basin.

'Whenever she comes here she doesn't give herself a minute's rest,' VaMangai said, nodding towards Ella. 'She will make some lucky mother a good daughter-in-law.'

'Why let her leave this home?' VaJumo said roguishly. 'She would make some lucky man a good second wife.'

'Whatever would you do with her?' VaMangai asked.

'Whatever do I do with you?' VaJumo winked at his son.

'Your father refuses to grow up,' VaMangai said, laughing. Something knotted in Nhongo's guts. This conversation sounded too familiar. He felt as if he had heard it before, but not from them.

Ella came in with the cock in the basin, its head chopped off, the bloody stump of the neck still jerking in memory of its death spasms. She lifted the kettle of boiling water off the fire and poured the hot water over the cock. Then she turned it over and left it to soak. She put more water in the kettle and put it back on the fire. Then she sat down in her place.

'Do you have any groundnuts, Ambuya?' Ella asked.

'No, Mainini. You can do that tomorrow. It's late now.'

'I would like to make peanut butter for the children,' Ella said. The old couple exchanged glances before quickly averting their eyes. Nhongo felt like a stranger in his own home. VaMangai stood up and took a wicker basket from the wall and went out of the room. She came back a few minutes later with the basket full of groundnuts. She placed the basket between herself and Ella. Then she sprinkled some water on the nuts to soften their shells, and she left them to soak for a while.

Nhongo's father began to talk of his days in Jo'burg. He called it Janana in a voice that made it sound like a place where people went and were never heard of again. It was only men, he said, and not just any man with nothing between his legs, who dared to go to Janana in those days – when he was still a young man. Most of the people who attempted the journey died in the jungles, from hunger, disease or wild animals. Those who got to Janana perished in the gold mines, the compounds or the streets. And those who finally made it back home brought nothing except their battered bodies, demented minds and crushed manhood. So, *Va*Jumo sighed, laughing, now it was the women's turn to go to Janana was it? For what? The old man spat into the fire. 'I hope to dear God in his Heaven you know what you are doing. I know nothing any more,' he said, heavily. Ella began to pluck the rooster, starting with the big hard feathers.

'What do you mean you don't know any more?' *Va*Mangai confronted her husband, 'Why don't you just tell the boy that you are having none of it? It's your cattle that paid for her bride-price. Listen, Nhongo. When your wife comes back from Jo'burg, tell her I want to see her here. I would like to ask her why a dog shows its teeth but can't laugh. I want to know if her aunts – her people – asked her to treat us like this.'

'She has only gone to Jo'burg, Mother. She'll be back,' Nhongo said, feeling that his mother was being unfair to Sara. Actually, he didn't want to hear his mother's views because she only seemed to confirm his own suspicions. He desperately wanted someone to tell him that he was wrong.

'So she has only gone to Jo'burg, has she?' *Va*Mangai said, looking at Nhongo with that pained look that made all sons wish they were still babies in their mother's laps.

Ella was dressing the rooster for the pot. She cut off its crop. She opened its belly, pulled out the innards and let them spill into the basin. Then she stood up, took a clean pot from the shelf and began to cut the bird into smaller pieces for the pot. When she thought she had enough for the number of people in the household, she put the lid on the pot and placed it on the open fire. She covered the rest of the rooster in a clean basin and stored it away.

'Have you brought us any onions and tomatoes, *Mainini*?' *Va*Mangai asked Ella.

'Yes. But *Baba a*Sekai doesn't like tomatoes or onions in fresh chicken. He says when he wants to eat chicken, he wants to taste chicken so he knows he is eating chicken.'

Everyone laughed. Something tugged at Nhongo's loins and he felt something welling in his throat. Ella's words were true – and innocent enough. But Ella's soft voice, self-consciously reduced to almost a whisper, shamelessly invoked a midnight bedroom scene in Nhongo's mind. His head swam as he felt himself melting.

The old couple quickly exchanged glances. VaJumo coughed, VaMangai unnecessarily pushed a piece of wood further into the fire.

Ella busied herself with preparing the meal. Nhongo, now very much aware of, and registering each of Ella's movements, sat gratefully in the presence of his parents, helping to shell groundnuts. VaMangai began to talk about one of Nhongo's cousins. It appeared that this particular cousin's wife had returned home after two years away from her family. Her husband, Nhongo's cousin, had given her up as lost and useless, but the children, especially the first two sons and their sister, had gone out to Chivhu and brought her back home. She had been living with another man in Chivhu.

'Her sons beat her up horribly,' VaJumo said.

'Beat up their mother?' Ella was scandalized.

'Beat up their own mother so badly that for days she couldn't eat. Her jaw broken,' VaMangai said with a vengeful inner satisfaction.

'But it is not done,' Ella said. 'You can't beat up your own mother.'

'Chizema's children beat up their own mother,' VaMangai said. 'This is one beating that I would forgive any child. Maybe this is one beating that the father hadn't given the mother. It's the one thing she wasn't getting from her husband. Of course, the children had to pay her for beating her up. Paying her for doing to her what their own father should have done to her years before they had been born.'

'I never beat you up,' VaJumo said.

'And I never did anything that would have made you want to beat me up, did I?'

'Women,' VaJumo said, shaking his head, 'Because the woman is a daughter-in-law, a stranger in the family, she must be beaten to tame her. They conveniently forget that they, too, are daughters-in-law in this same family.'

'But – beating up your own mother?' Ella repeated; she couldn't get over it.

'It was wrong,' VaMangai said. 'But she is back with her family now and seems quite happy. Really, I blame Chizema. He gave his wife too much freedom. Anything she wanted to do, she did. He wouldn't say no.'

'But he doesn't sleep with her any more, does he?' VaJumo said in a voice that seemed to remind VaMangai of something she seemed to have forgotten.

'What do they want? Sleeping together at that age!'

'We still sleep together.'

'She was stupid, running away from her children. Now her sons will look after her. And when she dies, they will be there to bury her.'

Sadza was ready. *Va*Mangai asked Ella to divide it into three portions: one for *Va*Jumo, one for herself and the third for Ella and Nhongo. Ella protested: she couldn't eat from the same plate as Nhongo. Tradition forbade it. *Va*Mangai told her that every once in a while it didn't matter. After all, brothers and sisters ate from the same plate. What was there to be ashamed of? Unless of course – and here *Va*Mangai looked directly at Ella – unless, she said, Ella herself had something on her mind, or had done something that made her feel ashamed to eat from the same plate as Nhongo?

Both parents looked from Ella to Nhongo and from Nhongo to Ella. Neither Nhongo nor Ella looked at each other nor at the elderly couple. *Va*Mangai looked at her husband. *Va*Jumo returned his wife's look.

Nhongo washed his hands and began to eat. Ella also washed her hands and began to eat. Both ate, careful not to look at each other. As they ate, *Va*Mangai would look up now and again to check if Nhongo and Ella still had food on their plates. 'Want some more *huku, Mainini* Ella?' *Va*Mangai offered.

'No, we still have enough,' Ella said. But at one point *Va*Mangai simply ladled some pieces of chicken onto Nhongo and Ella's plate.

'But, Mother,' Ella protested.

'But nothing. I don't want it said that we didn't feed you when you came to visit us.'

The two women laughed.

Nhongo washed his hands and said he was going to sleep. *Va*Jumo got off the earthen bench and sat on the floor, his back resting against the bench and his legs stretched out in front of him.

*Va*Jumo snored heavily and loudly. Then he broke wind. *Va*Mangai nudged him with the cooking stick and told him to leave the room and go to sleep. Ella laughed without showing it, then hid her embarrassment by collecting up the plates and putting them in a dish. She started to do the washing up.

*Va*Jumo made a groaning and grunting effort, then stood up. He looked at Ella for a long time as she worked on the plates.

'See you tomorrow, *Muroora*,' *Va*Jumo said.

'It is tomorrow, *Baba*,' Ella responded softly, head bowed. In his bedroom, Nhongo heard the sound of the plates and above them, his mother and Ella talking and laughing. Once more, he was surprised at how easily Ella got along with his mother. And it struck him again how little he knew about the lives of his own people. He realized he didn't know this Ella who could talk and laugh so loudly and freely with his mother. He had heard Ella talking to Sara and now that he thought about it, although she wouldn't be this loud, she had shown that she was quite at ease with her too. He had heard what they were talking about once, Sara and Ella. Money. They talked like two grown-up women, seriously, like equals. They also talked about the health of the children. He had never heard them talking about other people.

Now, what would Ella talk about with his mother? He found himself becoming suspicious, like someone guilty of something. He didn't know why but he had a feeling that they talked about him. And Sara. Once he thought this, he felt it was true and he began to agonize over it. Who was Ella to talk so freely about Sara whom she hardly knew? And again he was assailed by the fact of his own ignorance. Maybe she knew something that he didn't know about Sara. Maybe in those long idle hours that they had always shared – Ella had been with them for four years – maybe in those hours when he had been at work they had discussed all sorts of things? Sara might have revealed things she would never have told her own husband. Ella had been recommended to them by Sara's sister who lived in Gokwe. All that Nhongo knew about her was that she desperately needed a job. She had stopped going to school after her father had got a second wife and now she needed money to help her mother keep their large family alive. That was all he knew about Ella. And now here were his parents, forcing him to think about Ella. He knew that since his arrival all their talk had hinged on making him aware of the presence of Ella. Ella. And he suddenly felt that Ella knew about all this. She hadn't been just a dumb innocent player. He was suddenly convinced that his parents had discussed the issue with her. There had been plenty of time to do that. Sara hardly ever visited her in-laws. Instead, she sent Ella at the end of every month with groceries or money ... There had been more than enough time for Ella and his parents to ...

Ella. She had been nothing when she came to live with them. She had just been part of the house, as far as Nhongo was concerned, just like the furniture. He had hardly even talked to her, or at least he couldn't remember ever having had a real conversation with her. But now he realized that even if he hadn't talked to her, she knew about him all the same: knew him in such detail that Nhongo had been shocked into looking up and at her. If he didn't remember talking to her, she had talked to him. *Baba a* Sekai *doesn't like onions or tomatoes in fresh chicken.* This was the kind of intimate detail that only Sara was supposed to know – and utter. What else did Ella know? And did Sara know what she knew? Maybe, the two women ... ? Nhongo shut his mind to the possibilities of the women's relationship concerning him.

It had not been long ago that Nhongo had begun to see Ella in a new light. She had grown bigger, prettier, but in a way that your sister grew bigger and prettier. As he continued to think about her, Nhongo realized that his heart had quickened. Ella had come to his house in rags. Sara had given her some of her old dresses. The old ankle-length dresses which he had bought her.

Now Ella was buying her own dresses and they all seemed to be replicas of dresses Nhongo used to buy Sara. Nhongo felt wide awake. As Sara began to buy her own dresses, they had become shorter, knee-length, sometimes – shockingly – the hemline was even slightly above her knees.

Nhongo felt justifiably angry — even vindicated – whenever Sara found herself forced to pull her skirts over her knees as she sat down in the presence of other people. It seemed he had identifed the reason for the vague amorphous irritation he had begun to feel towards Sara. He hadn't been able to place or trace it before – the new Sara embarrassed him. The length of her dresses against her age. The pale pink paint on her lips and fingernails.

The change hadn't been anything sudden or revolutionary. No: it had been slow, and almost imperceptible: the bath tub left unscrubbed one day, then again on the second day, until you stopped paying attention to it, so that by the tenth day it seemed normal. Or his underpants which she wouldn't let anyone else wash except herself, no matter how late or tired she might be. Until one day she had asked Ella to collect them from the clothes-line. And on another, she had left them soaked in the washbasin and (Mr Magaso's car was idling outside) she had called out to Ella to rinse them for her as she had run out of time. And now Ella washed his underpants as well. Nhongo couldn't believe it. Had his parents noticed all this – over how long? As Sara's dresses had become shorter and more liberated (she'd even begun to wear trousers), Ella's had become longer, more housewifely, and more motherly.

The difference – revealed in people's eyes when the three of them went walking together – became clear to Nhongo. And as Sara's trips to South Africa and Botswana became more frequent, Ella had begun to assume the role of mother. And people, the neighbours, frequently began to see Nhongo and Ella in each other's company – with the children, of course. The process had been so slow, so apparently natural, that Nhongo hadn't noticed.

He couldn't believe it. He wanted to protest but he knew no one would believe him: Was everyone else right and he wrong about Sara? What about the children? And the clothes that she bought him? And the shoes? And everything she did to make them a happy family? The cheap pictures and coloured prints she brought home, to cheer up the place they lived in? Wallhangings, she called them. Nothing artistic or imaginative about them. He knew a bit of modern art, he read books, her wall hangings embarrassed him -- but, strangely, he would never have thought of pulling them down. They touched him more than they embarrassed him. He let her hang them on their walls. They were all reproductions of what he saw in the homes of other mediocre couples just like them: GOD BLESS OUR HOME: THE HOUSE MAY BE SMALL BUT THE

WELCOME IS BIG. He tolerated them in that he felt she wanted to improve their lifestyle. They seemed to mean a lot to her. And to him, they meant that she meant, even wanted, to stay. It's only what we have become, he thought, members of the new Zimbabwean lower-middle class, a class that will swallow us all. He had aimed higher but that was when he had had a job. He had even had plans to buy a new house, a plot, and build a new home, elsewhere, some distance out of the city. But now he was unemployed. And the fields were dry, as his father had told him.

'How are the crops?' he had asked.

'Are you joking?' his father had retorted. Could they all be right and he wrong? He tried to recall Sara when she talked of, say, Mr Magaso. Or could it be that Sara and Ella ...? Nhongo couldn't sleep. He got out of bed and left the room. He looked up at the sky; the dark clouds seemed to have lowered above him, blotting out the stars. A dry wind had risen from the north-west. His memory of growing up on this land told him that the clouds would float on, leaving the soil as dry and parched as it had been before. In the kitchen, he heard Ella and his mother *still* talking. He heard the soft oily sound of the grinding stone. Either his mother or Ella was making peanut butter.

He walked out into the bush. He couldn't see much in the dark but he felt challenged to see if his feet still knew the old childhood paths. He followed the sandy track down to their old fields, once so full of water that they had even been able to grow rice occasionally. These fields were now so dry that only burrs, thistles and stunted acacia bushes grew in them. Ahead of him, he could see the dark looming shape of the Rugunhe Hills. Further to the right he saw the luminous arc of light that was Harare over a hundred and fifty kilometres away. Now and again cars flashed past on the highway to Harare and beyond.

Accidentally, he hit his left foot hard against a rock, and was surprised to feel his heart pounding. He tried to laugh it off but the old feeling persisted: If you knock your left foot against something it means bad luck. In the distance a thin crackle of lightning flashed like a brief glimpse of electrified spider's legs. He had totally forgotten about the barbed wire fence until he found himself on his back in the darkness. He must have been walking very fast, for him to hit into it with such force that it felled him.

In his youth, this fence had been reduced to one strand, a broken one at that, and most of the strands had been pulled out by the local people. The fence must have been mended since then. *Waya yaBaba Cripps*. Father Cripps's fence, the local people called it. Father Cripps, the eccentric English missionary priest, who had preached the gospel of Christ, had bought this land from the Southern Rhodesia Government (representing the British Crown) to resettle the indigenous people who were being evicted from their traditional homes by the land-grabbing settlers.

22

Nhongo moved his fingers across his chest. There was a scratch. A little blood. He turned and walked back the way he had come.

Returning to his room, he noticed a light through the cracks in the soap-box-board door. He heard water splashing, someone bathing and singing under their breath. He knocked on the door.

'Who is it?' Ella whispered from within.

Nhongo had meant to spend two or three days with his parents but after a sleepless night, he told them that he had to get back to Harare that morning. His parents protested but he was adamant. He had to attend an interview the following day and he needed time to collect his thoughts.

His mother looked at him hard. He scratched the floor with his shoe. Ella came in with a pail of water on her head and another hanging by its handle in her hand. After putting the pails down, she left the room. Nhongo's mother looked after her, then at Nhongo. Nhongo looked at the floor between his feet.

'You would be a fool to lose her,' his mother said in a very low voice. They were the only two in the room. Nhongo could hear his father whistling happily somewhere in the yard outside.

'Did you ask her to come to my room last night?' Nhongo asked, without looking at his mother.

'Why would I do that?' VaMangai seemed genuinely surprised. 'Did she come to your room?'

'Mother,' Nhongo said in a voice that he thought would stop his mother, 'I love Mai Sekai.'

VaMangai looked at him and said, 'Did I say anything about your Mai Sekai?'

Ella came in with some pieces of wood and stoked the fire into a blaze. She went out again after placing a twenty-litre bucket of water to heat up on the fire.

'We know these things, my son. You are still young but what will you be like when you are old?'

Ella came in with a pot and some plates. She took the chicken left over from their supper and cut it up for the pot. She seemed to belong to his mother's house, she could have been married to him for the past ten years.

Nhongo left the room. Outside, he saw Sekai playing nhodo in the sand by the car. 'Good morning, Sekai,' Nhongo said. Sekai didn't answer. Nhongo bent to stroke her hair but Sekai ducked her head, stood up, opened the door of the car, went in, slammed the door shut and locked all the car doors from inside.

Nhongo found his father working on a plough in the toolshed. Soon after an exchange of good mornings, *VaJumo* began to talk about the importance of a home and a herd of cattle in a man's life. The city was all right if you were still young and had a job. But jobs in the city were not life. The blackman's wealth is a home out in the country among his own people. But a home, a family, meant a good hard-working wife.

Here *VaJumo* paused in his talk and looked towards the living room where Nhongo could hear his mother talking to Ella.

When *VaJumo* was certain that Nhongo had understood what he meant, he went on, without a wife, a hard-working wife, there was no home; a faithful wife is what makes a man a father. Any man can be a man but very few were fathers. He should strive to be a father, not just a man. And he couldn't be a father without there being a mother.

'Think very hard about this,' his father told Nhongo. Ella came out of the living-room towards the toolshed. She knelt down in the gritty sand on both knees. Nhongo could almost feel the pain of the sand grains biting into the flesh of her knees, through the thin material of the cloth she had wrapped around her from waist to ankle. Ella told Nhongo that his bath was ready. Nhongo suddenly felt great remorse. He could sense the sacrifice she was making, the desire to be accepted. And after she had been accepted?

'No,' Nhongo said, 'I don't need a bath. It's only an hour's drive to Harare.'

'But I have already ...'

'You clean up the children and let's go.'

They had breakfast in the living-room. They were all very quiet, subdued, as if they were accomplices in something that they couldn't bring themselves to talk about. *Va*Mangai made it a point of *not* looking at Nhongo and Ella, addressing everything she said to her husband as if seeking approval and support for something very important she wasn't certain she could do alone.

Nhongo and Ella hardly said anything. Sekai wouldn't eat breakfast. It was clear she was accusing somebody of something but she couldn't say who or what it was.

Netsai was having fun feeding Grandfather *VaJumo* porridge. He would pretend to be blind and each time Netsai brought the spoon to his mouth, he would make her miss it.

After breakfast, *Va*Mangai packed some groundnuts, cobs of maize, cucumbers, two pumpkins (from the last rainy season) and a tin of peanut butter into a plastic bag. She presented Ella with a live chicken, its legs tied together with a piece of string.

'Next time it will be a nanny-goat.' *Va*Mangai said.

'And after that, a cow,' *VaJumo* added. They all laughed except Nhongo and Sekai.

'Don't forget us,' *Va*Mangai said.

'Thank you for your kindness, *Amai*,' Ella said, clapping her hands, on her knees as she received the proffered chicken.

Nhongo thought she was about to cry.

'What kindness? I am only doing what any mother would do for her daughter.' VaMangai said, with a look at VaJumo. VaJumo nodded: it was the only proper thing to do.

VaJumo asked Sekai to come to him. Then, with the girls on either side of him, his arms round their waists, he said, 'And when are my wives coming back to cook for me?'

Netsai laughed and said, 'I am not going to be the wife of such an old man as you.'

Everybody laughed. Sekai remained pointedly quiet. After prayers to the God of the Christians and to their Ancestors, they all went out of the room.

As he opened the boot of the car to load in their things, Nhongo's heart stopped. The hare lay in the bottom of the car trunk. It was dead. He dumped the plastic bag into the trunk and closed it.

Nhongo's parents and Major, the dog, watched as they all climbed into the car. The children got into the back seat and Ella sat in front with Nhongo.

'You come and sit with us in the back,' Sekai said. 'That's Mama's seat.'

'Yes,' Netsai chanted, 'that's Mama's seat.'

'Do you want me to kick you out of the car?' Nhongo said.

Sekai looked down at the floor of the car and fell silent. Netsai looked at Sekai, seemingly betrayed by her silence.

They said goodbye. 'Come back and see us soon, Mainini Ella,' VaMangai said, earnestly. They drove off. Nhongo saw them in the rearview mirror, waving, Major, the dog, rubbing itself against VaJumo's leg and wagging its tail. This was always the hardest moment for Nhongo. The loneliness he felt his parents must feel, alone, with just the dog, cut him to the quick.

Ella lifted her arm and put it along the back of Nhongo's seat. A whiff of strong perfume wafted through the car. Nhongo felt tears stinging his eyes. 'You stole Mama's perfume,' Sekai said ruthlessly. Ella removed her arm from the back of Nhongo's seat self-consciously. She held her hands tightly together in her lap.

'I saw you walking out of Mama's room this morning,' Sekai said again. The car grazed a tree by the side of the dust track. Nhongo quickly brought it under control.

It began to rain as soon as they got onto the Masvingo-Harare highway. Within ten minutes, the rain was coming down in a thick sheet. Visibility was almost reduced to zero but Nhongo kept driving. They passed other cars distorted to extra-terrestrial beings parked by the side of the road, hazard lights on. Nhongo drove on as if someone were holding a gun to his head.

From the corner of his eye, Nhongo saw tears rolling down Ella's cheeks. He put out his hand and laid it on her knee. Ella bent down and laid her forehead on top of

Nhongo's hand. A sob as big as the world caught in Ella's throat. Her shoulders shook.

Sekai looked over the top of the seat and saw Ella's head resting on her father's hand which was resting on Ella's knee.

She made a cluck-cluck-cluck sound of contempt and pulled a face. Nhongo heard the sound and looked up and saw the dirty-word face in the rearview mirror. Nhongo removed his hand from Ella's knee.

'I saw you,' Sekai said. 'I saw your hand on Ella's knee.'

Nhongo drove onto the left shoulder of the road and stopped the car. He turned round in his seat and faced Sekai. The child pulled her head into her shoulders, put up her hands to shield her ears and shut her eyes tightly.

Nhongo raised his left hand, and with the back of it clapped Sekai on one side of her face and as his open palm was about to repeat the same on the other side of her face, Ella quickly grabbed Nhongo's hand in mid-air.

'Don't! Not in my presence!' Everyone jerked up to look at Ella. Her face was set in such a hard, determined way that Nhongo's immediate thought was: she is years older than I am. Instinctively, he quailed. Ella's grip on his arm, just below the wrist, was vice-like and so steady his own arm shook and ached up to the shoulder socket.

Nhongo felt like pleading: *Please you are hurting me.* And the children saw it, too. Their eyes opened wide, in wonder – and admiration at Ella's strength. They looked as if they couldn't take their eyes off her. They had watched enough wrestling movies on TV and knew what this meant.

For a moment, the silence that fell inside the car was louder than the throbbing rain outside.

Then, slowly, Ella seemed to realize what she had done and whom she had done it to and who she was to do it to him, and, slowly, very slowly, her fingers relaxed and her hand slid down to the seat. Then, quickly, without looking at anyone, Ella opened the door and slid out into the rain and began to walk along the road.

Nhongo's arm was still in the air, in the position Ella had caught and held it. It seemed as if he didn't know what to do with it.

Then Sekai's door swung violently open and she was out and away, running after Ella, the rain pelting on her as she shouted: 'Mummy! Mummy!' And Ella stopped. But she did not look back. Nhongo saw her standing out there, in the rain, still like a pillar of rock.

And to him, she seemed to grow taller and taller and he felt as if she was falling on top of him.

And as his head slumped against the steering wheel, he heard Sekai's voice echoing in his mind: 'Mummy! Mummy!'

26

The Homecoming

Old Mandisa was too surprised to say anything when Musa suddenly came home. The last time he had been home, six or so weeks previously, he had brought his school trunk with him. Old Mandisa had only seen the trunk by accident. She wasn't meant to see it. He had wanted her to go on believing that he was still attending boarding school, six kilometres away, across the Mwerari River.

Old Mandisa had heard about Musa but she hadn't thought that it was as bad as this. Although she felt she had lived too long and seen too much to be shocked by her grandson's behaviour, she was very disappointed because he was her only heir, the son of her late daughter, Muchaneta. She felt sad that she had allowed herself to be duped by fate into believing that things had taken a turn for the better.

When Old Mandisa realized that the boy had been lying to her all along and that he had now been expelled from school but didn't want her to know it, she didn't ask him to do anything and she did not reveal that she knew. She just offered a silent prayer to her daughter, the boy's mother: if you hear me, Muchaneta, tell me what to do now. She wouldn't bother her deceased daughter with lists of the things that the people in the village – his playmates as well as elderly people, including Headman Mapara – accused Musa of doing. Everyone in the village seemed to agree that Old Mandisa was too old to bring up a sixteen-year-old single-handed. What the boy needed – the villagers didn't hide what they thought – what the boy needed, was a severe caning – daily if necessary. Of course Old Mandisa agreed with them, although she didn't tell them that Musa didn't do what they said he did on his own. She wondered what they were doing to their own children when they misbehaved. But she also knew that most of the village people meant well and that most of the time they were telling the truth. Musa was growing up wild. Once he had spent a weekend in the cells at the local police station. He had only been released after she had made a personal plea to the chief constable. Then some village youths had threatened to put out his eyes if he didn't stop stealing chickens. Headman Mapara had personally come to talk to her about it.

'I am afraid I will be forced to let the police lock him up – to save him from having his eyes plucked out by the village boys,' Headman Mapara had said. And Old Mandisa knew that what he said was true. Indeed, he was saying less about what might happen than what could happen – and she didn't want to think about this. The last thief in the village, a boy barely ten years old, had been locked up in a hut which had then been set on fire. No one had been arrested or brought to the courts. 'You know once the people decide they have had enough, there is nothing anyone can do to stop them,' Headman Mapara had said. And Old Mandisa knew things were really going badly wrong for her grandson.

'You are experienced in these things. Tell me, what I should do with him?' Old Mandisa had asked the Headman. And he had spread his empty hands before him to show her just how empty they were. He said, 'If I knew how to handle children, would I still be poor?'

So, Old Mandisa had listened to the whole village.

'He needs someone to give him a good beating.'

'There should be a man in the house.'

What they said sometimes worked, of course. But she was old, and a woman, and now she had the burden of bringing up a hot-blooded sixteen-year-old and turning him into someone who did his work and respected his elders. Somehow she had to find a way of doing it. Either that or they would have to ask her to leave the village and take her incorrigible grandson with her. They probably felt as bad as she did over the whole matter.

Old Mandisa only regretted her age: certain things, places, people and events had been misplaced or displaced by her mind. She was, however, certain that if she sat down for a few days and gave the problem her whole attention, a way forward could be found.

It was very important that something be done to help the boy. He had no other relatives except herself. Both his parents had died in his infancy. Muchaneta, Old Mandisa's last child, was the last of her eleven children to die. And she had left her mother the infant Musa to nurse and bring up. She had managed, somehow, to send him to school. She had a few head of cattle, some goats and chickens. Also, she could brew the best seven-days' beer in the whole region.

Most of her customers were teachers at the school Musa attended. They knew her very well. But she could tell that they were not willing to discuss Musa with her. Still, she hoped they would do their best for him. She understood that her own time had been different. But she wanted to give him the best that she could in terms of education. Musa didn't seem to understand this. And so he had brought his trunk home, and tried to hide it so that Old Mandisa would not see it. But then he had hung around longer than he should have done and Old Mandisa had been forced to ask him if the school holidays had started early. He didn't bother to answer her but she had to know certain things.

'Where do you go to every day, Son?'

'Where I want.'

'And what do you eat there? You are growing as thin as a needle.'

'I eat dung.'

'You don't have to answer me like that ... You still have a home.'

'Where is my home?'

'Here. Please don't sulk as if it's my fault.'

It was as if the boy had been waiting for her to say just this. His outburst went beyond anything Old Mandisa would have thought possible.

'So, it isn't your fault? Then tell me, whose fault is it? What are you, an old woman, doing still hanging about on this earth? Where are your children? What did you do to your children? How could they all die? All of them! You must know something about it. And now you are onto me. I know you watch every cent you spend on me. I'm going to pay it all back one day. All of it. Every cent of it. I'm going to give it all back to you. Sooner or later. Why otherwise would you want me around you like a fly over rotten meat, or a louse in your rags? You only want me to pay you back!

'Some people here, in this village, even think I sleep with you!'

He had said all this, in the open yard, where everyone could see and hear him.

He had gone away that evening and he didn't return home. Old Mandisa discovered that he had broken into the tin in which she kept the money for his school fees. She heard about him for two weeks — although she didn't want to listen to what people said — and then she heard no more. She didn't even bother to ask if anyone had news of him. If it was fated that he should go away, then he would go away just like the rest of her children and grandchildren before him.

She had stopped asking about the workings of the Earth. And soon after the boy had disappeared, Old Mandisa had taken to her bed. For a month or more she hadn't left her mat: the pain was in her heart, her limbs and her back. She had felt, with great concern, the intense still heat building up in the air and she had smelt the rain on the occasional breeze that blew in — with the dry dust — through the door which she kept open, day and night. She had worried less about the pains than her firewood which was still on the mountain, and the first hole that finally appeared in her ages-old roof under which she had brought up all her eleven children.

Seven of them had died under the roof, still unmarried. The other four were buried elsewhere in the world together with some of their own children. But, to her, they had all died under her roof because she had grieved and mourned for them beneath it.

Now a hole had appeared. Someone had to go up and mend it before the heavy rains fell. There were many people in the village who would do it for her, she only had to ask them. She only had to send word and in less than a day, half the men in the village would be throwing bundles of thatch from hand to hand, mending the hole. That was the least of her worries. What mattered most to her was who got up on the roof to mend the hole. The village people could help her all right: cut the grass, fetch firewood, bring her water – even ask their daughters to take turns to prepare meals for her, but the village people were not her own flesh and blood. They couldn't inherit her dilapidated little huts and the rat manure in her dozen clay pots.

It was when she was in the middle of thinking about all this, that Musa suddenly turned up, unannounced. He just walked in through the open door as if he were coming from … well, just around the corner, as if he had gone to borrow some salt from one of the neighbours. And suddenly, the old woman didn't know what to say. She warned her heart not to rejoice prematurely. And she told herself to be careful with the words she used, when she spoke to him. Who knew what went on inside his head?

She had had more than enough time to think about what he had said to her the last time he was home. She didn't think those were his own words. Those were too grown-up for the boy's mouth. Either a bad spirit was sitting inside him, or someone, somewhere wanted to get at her, through the boy.

In her day, she might have used her whip on the boy but now – how could she tell if a whip was the right thing to use on a child whose insides were so murky, so turbulent? So she let him come in, just as he had always come in while he was still attending school across the river. She was careful not to act as if anything had happened to change their old relationship. She even decided that she didn't know that he was no longer attending school. In fact, he was coming from school, on one of his weekends off to visit his old grandmother who was also mama to him.

'You asked for permission to come?' she asked him, feeling more and more convinced that as far as they were concerned he was still in school, his trunk was still at the school, and there hadn't been anything said between them about anything. 'You are sure you won't get expelled?' She carefully avoided looking at him as she said this – did he notice? – something she had never done on other happier occasions.

'Yes I have permission,' he said. 'I always have permission when I come home.'
'Good. Keep it up. Don't start thinking that you are cleverer than your teachers.'
'I have been there three years now – have you ever heard anything bad said of me?'
'There is a saying: "When a skin drum is loudest, it is about to crack"!'

'There are still ten nights of song and dance in this skin drum,' he replied quickly.

She looked at him with her watery eyes which could no longer see very clearly. She was grateful to him for playing along with her. She didn't know how else she could have handled the situation. She said, 'I'm glad you've come. The cicada is noisy. Heavy rains will fall any day now and my firewood is still up on the mountain. Once it gets wet, it's hard to burn. I should have brought it down long back but this pain in my knee joints ...'

'I know,' he said. 'But I'll have to do that next weekend. Today I have to hurry back.'

At this, Old Mandisa stole a glance at her grandson. Dare she hope? He did not give any indication that he knew they were only pretending. She desperately wanted to know where he stood; this way, she would know where she stood. She said, 'You are sure the rains won't come before then?'

'Quite sure. I'll bring a friend along, to help me.'

'As you wish,' she said and was silent for some time.

Then she said, 'There is a hole up there in the roof. Can you see it?'

Musa looked up into the soot-blackened cone of the roof: 'No.'

'It is there, I saw it last week. It must have been there for quite some time although I didn't see it until recently. It fooled me.' The old woman fell silent, then said, 'This house is falling down.'

Something in the old woman's voice chilled Musa and he quickly looked up into the dark cone of the roof. He said, 'There is nothing there. You must have been seeing double.'

'You think so? Maybe, but I'm sure I'm not that old yet. Anyway, it's only natural, this house has defied wind and rain for a long time. But it can't go on forever.'

'All right. Next week we'll fix it.'

'Yes,' the old woman said, thinking of something else, then she began to mutter, almost inaudibly, 'It's strange how a house will assume a soul. I feel as if someone I know was very ill, a very close friend: someone who, after laughing at time and ruin for a long long time, finally bows down to the same fate.' Then, raising her voice a little, she said, 'Do you know that this house is older than your uncles and aunts and much, much older than your mother at the time she died?'

'You have told me that before.'

'Yes, I wouldn't like it to fall on top of me while I'm asleep and I still have you to look after.'

'It won't fall on you while I'm still around,' Musa said softly and the old woman looked up, hopefully, then decided to change the subject.

31

'You've come for the beer?'

'Yes. But not so much as to see you.'

And money, of course. She said, 'You needn't worry. Nothing ever happens to me and needn't happen for a long long time yet.'

'You have been ill.'

'It's been my condition since birth. Normal condition of any healthy person. The secret of a long life.'

Musa said nothing.

'Have you brought a container to carry the beer in?'

'I'm sorry. You will have to give me one of your calabashes.'

'What happened to the one you took the last time you were here?'

'Someone stole it.'

'Just like you, Musa. Now, how many calabashes have you lost or broken because of your carelessness? And this last one was your mother's. I didn't want to give it to you. It was the last one I had here. The last calabash that belonged to your mother.'

She held her breath: had she raised her voice too high?

'What about that canvas bag?' Musa asked.

'What bag? That? I am not going to part with that one. It was your grandfather's.'

'I need it more than you do, Mama. I am going to put beer into it while you just keep it for rats to lay their dung in.'

'You heard me, Musa.'

'I remember the days when my mama used to give me anything I wanted. I only had to ask and it'd be fine. Now I don't know what's got into my mama: is it old age or brine?'

Both of them laughed and both of them understood that this was no longer pretence.

'You needn't say that to me. I know you. It's all right with me if you lose the calabashes and remain in school.'

'You should never be afraid for me.'

Old Mandisa raised her head and looked at Musa anxiously.

'Is what I hear true?'

'What do you hear, Mama?'

'That you are not allowed to drink beer at the mission?'

Musa knew he couldn't fool the old woman but he couldn't lay himself open either ... It was a weak defence, he knew that even before he opened his mouth, but better a weak defence than ... He said, 'No. It is not true. They do not stop us from drinking beer if we want to. They only punish you or suspend you for a few weeks or days if you make a nuisance of yourself in public. It's nothing, really.' And he had to suffer once more as he watched the eternal shadow of pain flicker across his grandmother's face. It hurt him to know that she knew that he knew he was lying to her. And she would never ask him about it, she would act as if she didn't know he had lied. That was what hurt.

'I shall be all right, Mama,' he said lamely.

'I hope so. I just hope you will be all right. You don't know how much I ... anyway, I talk too much. Now, you must go back to school while the sun is still in the sky. Let me fill up that bag for you. Bring it back when you come back next time. It was your grandfather's.'

She struggled to her feet, holding onto Musa's shoulders for support.

'Let me do it for you, Mama.'

'No, no. I have been planted here for too long. No good ever came out of a rotting pumpkin.'

'It cannot even beat away the flies that shit and vomit on it,' Musa added, remembering the saying.

'It's true. I have been rotting here for the past I don't know how many days. I even asked God to finish me off, but you know how he is when people our age desperately need his help. It's like talking to the clouds. Or, if he hears you at all, he doesn't do what you asked for. He gives you another day, another year to walk, to hope...'

'It must have been terrible.'

'It was. Without anything for your hands to do, your mind takes over. It drags you all over the place, through all sorts of mazes. It reminds you of everything you've done wrong. A gossiping mind is worse than idle hands or a rotting pumpkin.'

'I don't believe it's you talking like this, Mama.'

'No one is asking you to believe it. You are on your way to the same place ... unless you kill yourself on the way, as some do.'

She went out of the room. Musa shook his head as he watched her tottering towards the *hozi* where she kept the beer in big earthen pots. She walked without the aid of a walking-stick and Musa remembered what she had told him once; 'God would have given us three legs if he had wanted us that way.'

'Musa!' the old woman yelled.

Musa went out to the *hozi* and stood below the steps to the door.

'You called?'

33

'Come and help me with this bag. It's dark in here and I can't see.'

Musa climbed up the four stone steps into the *hozi*. Old Mandisa was sitting. Something about the way she sat told Musa something was terribly wrong. She had spilt some beer on the floor. Just the beer on the floor would have been enough to tell Musa that something was terribly wrong.

'Here,' she said, 'I'll hold the bag for you. Fill it up. I can't see.' She handed him the gourd.

'Careful. Don't spill,' she kept on repeating as Musa carefully dipped the ladle into the beer pot and brought it over and carefully allowed the beer to trickle through the small mouth of the canvas cooler bag.

'A single drop of that on the floor is so much sweat wasted,' she said.

'Full,' Musa said when he saw the beer shoot up through the narrow bamboo neck of the bag and spill just a little. Libation for a poor ancestor or two. There was a little beer still left in the ladle. Musa turned 180 degrees away from the old woman and gulped down the beer in one throatful.

'You haven't forgotten what I said, I hope,' the old woman said, quietly.

'Not to drink before I cross the river.'

'Don't drink before you are across the river.'

'But this beer. It's so good, it's hard not to ...'

'Cross the river first,' the old woman said. Silence fell between them then she said, 'Is there anything else you want? Peanut butter or salted nuts?'

Musa hummed and hawed. When he spoke, even Old Mandisa didn't recognize his voice. 'If you have, I don't think you would have ...' He was too embarrassed to go on.

'It's money, isn't it, Musa?'

'Forget it,' Musa said.

'How much? How can I forget it? Who else will give it to you if I don't?'

'You wouldn't have twenty dollars, would you? They need it at school for ...' he was sinking.

'I know. You've never lied to me,' Old Mandisa said as she reached for an old powdered milk tin in which she kept her money in the *hozi*.

Musa swallowed and looked away and when she handed him the money, he felt as if there was nothing of him left, his hands felt clammy. The joke, if it had been a joke, at all – had transcended all bounds. It would have been easy for him to stop. To stop and tell the old woman: enough! But instead, he found his arms outstretched before him, as if of their own volition. Old Mandisa placed the money in Musa's palms.

'Good. Now, go before the sun goes down. They tell me of crocodiles seen on the river lately,' Old Mandisa said.

Musa's throat was too swollen with emotion for him to trust himself to say anything.

'And, remember: the firewood, the roof and your grandfather's cooler bag. Of all things he salvaged from the whiteman's world, he thought that cooler bag was a work of genius. Only second to the sheath.' Old Mandisa laughed.

'The sheath?' Musa asked, puzzled.

'The loin sheath into which men put their third leg so that the ants don't get at it!' Old Mandisa laughed again.

Musa immediately looked down, unable to look his grandmother in the eye.

Musa slung the bag over his shoulder and climbed down the steps of the *hozi*.

As he reached the bottom, he heard the little noises of pain. He looked back quickly and saw the old woman in a heap on the floor of the *hozi*, her legs folded under her.

'Are you all right, Mama?' Musa's voice was really concerned.

'I am quite all right, thank you. I'll just rest a bit.'

'Mama?'

'I am all right, I said. Haven't you got ears?'

They were quiet for some time, and then, as if waking up from sleep, the old woman said, 'All of a sudden everything seems to be moving away from you, slipping through your fingers like water through a sieve.'

'Mama?'

'The biggest problem, the most frustrating thing of course is the loneliness – the impossibility of communication. No one hears you no matter how loudly you shout.'

'Mama?'

Old Mandisa seemed to hear Musa for the first time, looked up and waved her hand at him as if to warn him not to pay any attention to her. Then, she seemed to remember something and brightened up, saying, 'Did I ever tell you how beautiful your mother was? How quiet? How she was never angry no matter what anybody said to her? How hard-working? She would stay up all night grinding corn and would be up before third cock-crow preparing peanut butter. I wish you had had a little more time with her. I wish both your mother and your father had had a little more time with each other. Time. That's what every one in this family has never had with each other. Time. I've not even had it with you and maybe that's why you always leave me and why you think the people you meet are your own people. I am the only one left of your own people.

35

'I am sure there are others somewhere – on your father's side. I don't know. I never had time to talk to him. He hadn't been long married to your mother when we heard the mine he was working in at Chakari had fallen in. He was one of those who were trapped and died inside it. And – it might have been the shock – six months later, your mother, my beautiful Muchaneta, followed him.'

The old woman was silent, then she said, 'I must tell you a little about her, and about this family, for the little good it will do you, so that wherever you go and whatever you do, you won't be haunted by the thought that you are a helpless orphan. Your uncles were good sons to me. They hunted and worked on the land. So did your aunts, all good and obedient daughters to me but your mother – now, your mother was something else. I had her when I was tired and old and she was, so people said, the spit image of me. And for a short, very happy time after the others had gone, she had me hoping, fooling me that she was here to stay … I would have gone in her place. Even now, I would be very happy to go but I have got you. I am not allowed to go yet because I still have to see you …' Abruptly she stopped, then said, 'Curse these eyes!' because her eyes had begun to water again. 'One day,' she said, 'remind me to tell you about your great-great-grandfather.'

She tried to rise but fell back heavily. There was a terrible stench of rotten eggs in the *hozi*.

'Can you lift me out of here?' she said.

Musa put his right arm under both her armpits, and the left in the hollow behind her knees and lifted her up. He fought hard with himself not to gag at the stench.

He carried her down the steps of the *hozi* into her living room. 'You see?' she said, visibly and painfully embarrassed as Musa put her down on her mat and covered her with a blanket. He felt there was something he wasn't doing right, but he couldn't tell what it was.

She said, 'Everything suddenly goes out of control and you are helpless, at the mercy of other people, even strangers.' Tears were rolling down her cheeks. 'It is the same when you become blind or lose one of your limbs … Suddenly you can't do on your own what God created you to do on your own … You become something people don't want to touch, something that they don't want to see … '

Musa didn't say anything. He was looking at his soiled arm and hand. He was arguing with himself whether to wipe the mess off or not, whether the old woman who was looking at him, wouldn't think it rude of him to …

'Go on, wipe the shit off,' Old Mandisa said but all of a sudden Musa found he couldn't move a finger. An unbearable desolation, an infinite loneliness, swept over him. When he had lifted the old woman in his hands, he had hardly felt anything.

That had frightened him. Now she looked at him and he couldn't bear it. She looked listless, lost, wronged; an almost naked look came into her eyes.

'Well, now you know what it is to be like me, what are you still waiting for?'

Lost for words, confused, not knowing how much she knew, or whether what he was doing was the right thing or not, Musa slung the beer bag over his shoulder and left the room. As he came out into the last of the day's light, his eyes stinging as if someone had thrown piri-piri into them, he kept on repeating to himself: *No, no, no, no.* He felt that no person should ever be allowed to see of another person as much as he had seen of Old Mandisa.

As soon as Musa left the room, Old Mandisa slowly rose to her feet, came out of the hut and stood in front of the open door, looking after her grandson's receding form until he had become a blur and disappeared. As soon as he had disappeared, her body tensed and she closed her eyes, waiting for the blow that she was certain was coming. While waiting she saw, in her mind's eye, Musa walking towards the river. She would have loved to have watched him until he had safely crossed it and was climbing the little hill on the other side. She kept looking in the direction that he had gone and hoped that it wouldn't grow dark too soon, grow dark before he crossed over to the other side.

She didn't know how long she had been standing there looking into the gathering gloom, waiting for something that wouldn't come, when she heard his voice close to her ear. 'I have come home to stay, Mama.'

'I have been expecting your friends.'

'I have told them to go home, Mama.'

There was a heavy silence in which Old Mandisa slowly sank down to her knees.

Musa unslung the beer bag from his shoulders and put it down. He brought out the twenty-dollar note she had given him and held it out to her.

She looked at the money, then up into his eyes.

She said, 'You know I don't need it, Musa. I am past the age when people have use for money. You keep it.'

'No. You keep it for me,' Musa said as he quickly turned his eyes away from hers although he knew that in the gathering darkness, she wouldn't be able to see anything in his eyes.

Then, after a brief pause, Musa gathered all his strength, put one arm under the old woman's armpits, the other behind her knees and lifted her up and carried her into her room.

'Mind, you don't drop me!' Old Mandisa giggled. She didn't realize what she meant by this. All she remembered was that a long time ago before Musa was born,

37

a long long time before any of her children were even dreams, her big elder brother, Mugadza, would carry her in his big safe arms across the slippery stones at the crossing place of another, bigger, far- far-away, river which she now seemed to remember as a bright silver thread winding its way through her darkening memory.

———————————— ⚫•⚫ ————————————

The Singer at the Wedding

This is my song to you who would not read the meaning in my heart; who would not see the depths in my eyes; who would not hear the silent music of my limbs: you, who turned your back on my smile and a deaf ear to my plea. This is my song to you who robbed me of my youth and hung it on a dry tree for the vultures to peck at, bleeding with love for you. But what did you see in her? Yes, she is beautiful … educated … sophisticated, but …

Take that egg, the day you paid the bride-price. It stood on the table, alone, pure, white … vulnerable. I remember it, I think about it: the seed and the death. And you, sitting outside, waiting for the verdict of the aunts. The Aunts! Who doesn't know about our Aunts? And when you heard their shouts and ululations, the blood rushed to your head and deafened your ears to my thinner wailing: The egg is cracked. But you preferred to listen to the Aunts: She is a virgin! Words!

… Now let me stop awhile and let the dancers rest. This is the first night of your wedding. While the drummers tighten the skins on their drums, we shall drink *maheu* and wait for the dark to get darker. There must be silent darkness and the glow of a fire for me to sing well, for the song to travel deep into the night. Perhaps with the darkness you will see and hear better. Perhaps you will remember where you come from: the great dark womb… Maybe my presence at your wedding embarrasses you? Maybe you thought that like the proverbial rat I'd just melt into the soot clinging to the thatch? The two years we have spent together, you and I, cannot just be cast aside without tearing something out of me. Although I was yours only at night and you were hers during the day. I thought that perhaps you would hear the warnings that are crowding into my heart. I allowed myself to think that perhaps you would hear them …

But: you first. You are in a sky-blue suit and white shirt with brown pencil stripes, a blue tie, blue socks and black square-toed leather shoes. There is a bright imitation gold ring on your finger. She is in a white, white – the egg and virgin that she is – flowing wedding gown that defies all shadow in its rich folds – how false I find things that defy shadow! On her head she has a paper crown – imitation silver. But what hurts me is your innocent smile and the nervous twitch in your hand gently holding hers – her little white smile is also without shadow. But there's a fly – don't you see it? – a tiny greenbottle that she keeps having to wave away from her tiny powdered nose! How the little fly vexes her! Is it true that a greenbottle can smell carrion twenty years and a hundred miles away?

Of this fly I sing. And of the village women whose smiles are tight, sorrowful and protective with the pain of the snapping cord, and of her mother who knows so much – her daughter's three abortions? – who is dressed in mourning; her smile is tremulous, shadowy, secret. She knows, as all the Aunts know, that the egg cracked, and she is fighting, labouring, to hold that crack in her innermost soul against the predatory men of both families – and you cannot see it, just as all the men in the village cannot see her pain. They just strut about looking important, making impotent decisions and counter-decisions, or sit around the fire, fooling and joking about the ecstasy of the newly-weds' first night. Like the boys that they are, that is all they can see in a man taking a wife. So I sing of the sadness of these men who cheer you, who wink at you so obscenely, so openly, so jealously – as if you were a conqueror, a hero. Maybe you do feel like a hero? In your vain stupidity you carry yourself in your blue suit and square-toed shoes as if you had indeed just washed off the grime of battle: you hold her as if she were the reward of a hard won contest.

Or am I wrong? I wish you would answer me. I am not certain of what I see. Speak to me. My heart desires certainty. I desire an audience, Sango ... I live on the clap of your hand, the glint in your eye, your carefree gestures ...

The night creeps in on soft padded claws. It has swallowed the valley. The sky, deep and distant, holds a handful of stars like maize grain scattered across a large field. Several fires have been lit outside and the men sit beside them talking and drinking – always drinking – and sometimes singing wedding songs in hoarse discordant voices. Some of them are asleep, their heads on logs, knees pulled to their chins: close, warm, drunk, fraternal.

As I have done for her and her family for the past five years – and I hope this will be the last time – I bring you tea and bread in a huge bamboo basket. Two other girls help me serve the wedding retinue. You sit like strangers at a funeral in the dim glow of the weak candle. You are sitting next to her but you are not talking to each other. You constantly look at her but she is smiling at the best man who is telling a joke. It is a poor joke but the six of you laugh as if you were drowning. You do not see your huge shadows written like your fate on the ceiling. At the sight of the tea you are relieved. After pouring it out, I retreat from the table, to wait in the darkness of the room, away from the light, for the empty cups and the dregs ...

After tea, there is rice and chicken. Once more I stand in the shadows, to wait for the bones, for the remains of the rice ...

The endless meal over, her aunts take her to the room they are going to share with her tonight – her last night in her home before she can share a bed with you. She leaves the table and deeper emptiness descends on me. You yawn. Your friends try out another couple of jokes but the candle is low, it's been burning for too long and you want to sleep before it burns out. Well, good night, my love, and sweet dreams. Perhaps in your dream you might remember a familiar face ... turn your pillow over, if you do. Goodnight. But I shall not go to sleep, not yet, not tonight. I long to see a new day breaking. Dawn: possibility, promise, hope. Goodnight. I shall go out into the yard with the other girls and we shall sing for you and your new wife until the day breaks. We shall sing song after song until our voices are hoarse. We shall sing and hope that dawn finds us awake, for we are still girls and we must watch for the new day ...

Now day is breaking the night into patches of light and holes of darkness. The timid stars scatter before the sharp spears of bright sunlight. Day arrives and night is broken into pieces and driven deeper into the hollows of the valley and western cups of the mountain where it crouches, cowering. The tops of the great hills in the east rise out of the darkness like hippos out of water and a faint mist shrouds the mysteries of the valley. We are still singing. The drums beat louder. We have survived the night. How have you weathered the darkness, my dear? With all that eating and drinking yesterday – did you not dream of distant pools? Did you not wake, your parched throat crying for cool water? You come out of your bedroom in wrinkled clothes. You slept in your wedding suit!

Oh, are you looking for her? Yes, she too is awake, dressed, and looking strangely contented. She responds well to her aunts' teasing. They tease us too – our aunts – her aunts: 'See? Your friend has gone away well. She has listened to her mother and obeyed her words. She goes to her man a virgin and the pride of her parents. Will you too be able to do as much?' We, of course, have no answer, we look down at the ground, as we know we are meant to do, caught up in the conspiracy. We are also mothers and we must learn to protect each other, our menfolk, our families, our homes ... I leave the women to bring you water to wash your face, your hands ... I am ashamed of the sleepless hunter's look on your face. Long shadows. Your eyes are dying embers wanting kindling. Where is the blaze that should be in them? Your mouth is self-pitying, your lips are grey with the salty residue of a sweaty night: the banks of a river after a flood... I hold out water to you and you take the basin out of my hands. You don't notice that my hands remain outstretched. My arms aching with the load of something you do not wish to relieve me of.

Night is here again and I am here with it by your side. What more is there to say? Time is running out. There are tears, many tears, as she says farewell to mother,

41

friends, home and childhood toys. She already looks old – no, dead – in the dimming bloodwashed sun. We feel it, all of us – men, women, her mother, although she is the only one who has not shed tears. Maybe her life has been one long wail, who knows? Deserted by her drunken husband, left single-handed to raise five daughters none of whom has been successful. Who knows what she is thinking?

The cutting of the cake is the very last thing to be done before the wedding moves to the groom's home. Let me sing of the cake ...

It sits on a big white platter. Everyone -- mother, aunts, uncles, relatives from near and far, village elders, friends are all here to share the cake. It pains my heart. No, I will say nothing. You wouldn't understand. You would simply dismiss my words as those of a jealous woman. We sing a hymn. I am leading the singing. The room is heavy with something we can't explain. Darkness seems darker although the night is still young. Somewhere in the darkling trees a dove coos. A rooster crows. We are singing but there is silence: can you feel it? Her uncle, Sarapavana, guardian and caretaker, dabs at his eyes with a spotless white handkerchief and waves us to stop singing: 'Time is running out,' he says. I couldn't agree with him more. He asks everybody to sit down. Then he asks you to stand up. You stand up and accept the knife from the uncle.

Three times her uncle asks her to stand up and three times she stands, falters and falls back into her chair. There are murmurs in the gathering: 'You aren't going to your death.'

'A husband is a kind of death, you know.'

I hold my breath. 'She should feel like this on the third day,' my aunt says. 'This is the second day.'

Finally, trembling, she manages to stand, holding onto your hand for support. You look wonderful, standing so straight, almost defiant, as if challenging a ghost while coaxing a little sister not to be afraid of the dark. You hold out the knife to her. She lets her hand be taken in your calm one. Both of you hold the knife over the white cake. We hold our breath. The knife hesitates an instant, her hand is uncertain, as if afraid to touch the cake in all its wholeness, its snowy whiteness. Then slowly, the knife descends. As its edge touches the nape of the cake, you wince – how cruel the action seems as the blade sinks through the soft texture. A gasp and the room breaks into ululations, whistles, applause. Everything swims into darkness before my eyes but only for an instant. You smile shyly as if you have ... but why say it?

I remember the violence, the never-to-be-repeated peace of that first day up on the mountain, the stars so close you could stretch out a hand and reach them, the realization that the stream had been flowing forever. Why say it? And as the knife cuts through the heart of the cake, it's as if you too are cutting away from all that you have known. I can only watch as the walls of my heart crumble, break and for a moment I sit down on the floor in the middle of the gathering.

It is a rich cake with a yellow heart. It looks as fresh as a melon. People begin to laugh, relieved laughter, as if they were afraid you would bungle the job. 'Give it to her!' A voice shouts – the meaning is very clear but it's lost the usual vulgarity. 'Give it to her!' And you take a small piece of cake and hold it out to her mouth, almost as if it were a sacrament. The piece is a little too big for her small mouth, which she hasn't opened very wide, and you push it, almost force it in, and she chokes, splutters, gasps. Someone calls out for water and everyone is laughing and clapping their hands: 'That's it! That's it! Too much for her, huh?' I look away and smother a sob with a cough. Someone somewhere in the room, one of the old women perhaps, starts a hymn. It is one of my favourite songs. I can't sing it.

I am choking on the words. There is a storm in my heart. And, as people go on singing, the room is suddenly dark. The mountains in the west have shut out the sun. They look like monsters crouching just beyond the yard, advancing, threatening to swallow this home. And suddenly, without any warning, the song falters and fades away. Everyone begins to button up their coats and jackets against a cold wind which hasn't yet quite reached them …

Tears flow like rain falling from the heavy clouds menacing the skies of my heart for the past – I don't know how long – but I refuse to sit down. And as the wedding guests file out of the room I sit at the deserted wedding table and stare at the remains of the wedding cake. I pick up the broken pieces, the remains of the plate she dropped. Abstractedly, I piece them together, as if in a dream. Except for the seams, the jigsawed plate seems whole again. You can't even see the cracks in the close darkness of the room … Inside me, your child kicks for the third time this week … An omen? Three days at least, my aunt said. If she is right, tomorrow I shall be singing again with other girls, singing as I probably shall never sing again: at her funeral.

— • ● •• —

Did You have to Go that Far?

One late afternoon, after school, Pamba walked into Seke Dam on Manyame River, and was drowned. I wasn't there when he was drowned. I didn't know that he'd drowned until well after midnight on the night he died.

Pamba was my best friend. He lived with his parents at Number 63, Bise Crescent. I lived with mine at Number 65. We were in the same class, Grade Six, at Pfumo Government Primary School in Zengeza.

Pamba and I were the terror of Bise Crescent.

Pamba is King of the Hill
Who says 'No' he will kill
Damba is Cock of the Roost
'No?' Kick up dust before you roast

I would make up the songs – tunes and lyrics. I came from a musical family. Uncle Gina Mudzonga played keyboards and did vocals in one of the most popular bands in the country. And Uncle Zanda was a trombonist in the Police Band. So I made up the songs and Pamba, a kung-fu fanatic, would marshall all the kids in the neighbourhood, line them up on our street and teach them these songs. We would then march them along the streets singing at the top of their voices.

If we weren't marching and singing on the streets, or playing the mini-soccer and pinball machines at Gavaze's bottle store, we were searching for 'treasure' in the rubbish dumps at the edge of the location across Tsoka Crescent. The dumps were in an open space, a kind of no-man's-land, that stretched from Tsoka Crescent down to Seke Road. Beyond Seke Road was a tract of land thickly covered with trees and bush right down to the edge of Seke Dam. If you were walking through the bush and didn't know of the existence of the dam, it could give you a nasty jolt or a pleasant surprise as you came out of the bush right at the water's edge.

There were many anthills and hillocks in this bush. We had our secret place here, a huge flat rock where, sometimes, we would make a fire and cook or roast whatever we had filched from the small fields nearby: maize cobs, *mbambaira*, *nyimo* or groundnuts. There was also a hole in the rock where we would hide tins of beef, beans, fish or whatever we had lifted from the tuckshops that were scattered all over Zengeza

45

One. It was there that we also did our kung-fu exercises and played the cowboys–and–Indians games we saw on TV.

Seke Dam. We hardly ever got as far as the water's edge, except to fetch water to cook our stolen food. But there were always people fishing in the water along the dam. Pamba and I didn't care much for fishing.

Next door to our house, at Number 67, lived an old childless couple. I think that the old man's death was due to the awful pranks that Pamba and I played on the couple. After the old man had died, his wife lingered on for a month or two, then she too just disappeared. At first we thought she had died and her body was in the house. So we broke one of the windows and went in to check the place out. The floors and walls were completely bare. There was a strange old-people-smell which Pamba and I thought was the smell of death. (Later, Pamba's own death would tell me how wrong we were.) We took off our shorts and planted little mounds of excrement throughout all the rooms. *Pamba and Damba were here,* we wrote and signed our names in shit on the walls.

Pamba and I would be the first on the streets to go to school every morning, but we would be the last to get there. We were always late for assembly. And when the bell went at the end of the last lesson, we would be the first to run out into the streets.

We would run home for our mid-day meal. On most days I shared my food with Pamba. My mother didn't mind. Pamba told me that his father always bought all the groceries for their house: both breakfast and supper. But there was no mid-day meal unless his father was home during the day. After eating, we would change out of our school uniforms into our street clothes and we were back on the streets even before most of the other children had left the school grounds.

And we were always the last to leave in the evening. Our mothers had to literally drag us off the streets if they wanted us home early. Pamba's father and my father were drinking friends. They had become quite close in spite of their differences in character. The Party had brought them together. Pamba's father was the Chairman of our ward, Chaminuka, and my father was the Political Commissar. They used to call for meetings every Sunday morning, and spent half the day grilling in the hot sun at The Rock – the place where political meetings were held. At mid-day, after lunch (every household had a mid-day meal on Saturdays and Sundays because the men would be home) they would go to the local beerhall until around ten-thirty, when it closed. On Saturdays, they would frequent any one of the shebeens in Zengeza One or Katanga and continue their drinking until two or three in the morning. During working days, our fathers would leave for work well before we were up, and come back long after we were in bed. It was very strange. We hardly saw our fathers during the week. We only heard their voices when they went out in the morning or came back at night. They were like radio DJs: only heard, not seen. So we really had ourselves to ourselves. Of course, we had only our mothers to deal with. And, because our mothers had the rest of the family – the little ones (who are not part of this story) – to look after, they were glad not to have us around the house, messing up the wax-polished floors with muddy or dusty feet, cutting holes in their cheaply upholstered sofas with pieces of wire, or just causing general mayhem around the house. They would only think of us in the evenings after they had prepared the meal.

'Pamba-a!' Mrs Dengu, Pamba's mother, would shrill from one end of Bise Crescent. 'Pamba! come back to the house right now or I'll tell your father when he comes back from work!' And my mother's words would echo from the other end of the street, 'Damba-a! Come home this minute if you want your supper!'

They were empty threats, we knew, and they knew we wouldn't come home until the last game of pinball – or mini soccer – had been played to the bitter end at Gavaze's bottle store, where we were holed up. I'd like to think that they also enjoyed being out on the streets in the later, cooler part of the evening, taking a break after spending the whole day cooped up in the house attending to their endless women's household chores.

Sometimes we would hear them getting closer to Gavaze's and we would go on playing, even starting a new game, knowing that they would never make it to the bottle store where they could clearly hear us yahooing, cheering and cursing, depending on the progress of our game. We would hear their voices growing nearer, and then there would be a conspiratorial silence, and next we would hear them calling from further away as they trudged back home.

We loved to play pranks on them. Some days we would hide in an open ditch or in a hedge near them as they turned home. This was how we discovered that they were on the streets, not really to look for us, but as an extension of their daily gossip.

'He threatened me with a second wife,' we heard Pamba's mother saying one day.

'And what did you say to him?' My mother asked.

'What are you saying, Ronia?' – that was my mother's name –'I told him that if he tries it, that will be the last he sees of me.'

'What would you do?'

'Are you joking, Ronia? The moment she walks in through that front door, I jump out the back window.'

'*You* leave *him?*'

'That's too easy for him. I would kill myself!'

'Kill yourself?' My mother was surprised. 'Kill yourself? For what? He's got only one carrot and two tomatoes like any other man. Why make him feel as if he has a dozen ...'

I didn't hear the rest of my mother's speech because at that moment, Pamba, who was giggling uncontrollably, poked me in the ribs and said, 'They're talking about my old man.'

'Why? Is your old man thinking of marrying another wife?'

'He talks about it all the time. Mother once swallowed some pills. They had to pump them out of her at the hospital.'

One day, we heard them talking about us.

'You know what he did?' Pamba's mother said.

'What did he do?' My mother asked.

'You know that pair of jeans I bought him at Mupedzanhamo last month? The brat took a pair of scissors and cut off the legs then did some fancy lace trimming to the shortened legs. I screamed, Ronia. I swear I could strangle him. He takes after his father.'

Not to be outdone, my mother responded, 'That's nothing to what Damba did.'

'Tell me. What did he do?'

'I left twenty dollars on the kitchen table ...'

And before Mother could say another word, Pamba's mother jumped in, '*Twenty dollars?*' Her voice was so high she could have heard 'Murder!'

'Well, Pamba might take fifty cents or even a dollar – and he would be sure to tell me what he needed it for – but twenty dollars! Why, Ronia, that's a whole week's earnings. Really, Ronia, you must do something about that boy of yours. I just hope Pamba doesn't catch it from him ...'

'Well, it wasn't twenty dollars exactly,' my mother tried to defend herself.

Why did they find it necessary to lie about us? It wasn't twenty dollars I had taken off the kitchen table. Just some loose change out of twenty dollars.

Sometimes we thought they would really come to blows over us. One day – we had been playing at the rubbish dump – I dug up a hardly used pair of sneakers and Pamba claimed that he had seen them first. We argued over them. He hit me in the eye with his dirty fist. I struck him back with the piece of iron I'd been digging with. A little blood spotted his head. I would have given Pamba the sneakers but he wouldn't take them. He went home howling that I had wanted to kill him.

His mother brought him to our house that evening.

'You tell Damba never to hit my son with an iron bar again!' Pamba's mother shouted so loudly through the lounge window that I could see people beginning to gather on the street in front of our house.

But my mother retorted, equally heatedly, '*Iwe* Grace. Are you telling me that my son would just pick up a piece of iron and hit your son for nothing? My son may be bad but he is not a murderer!'

'So, whose son are you calling a killer?'

And while they quarrelled I brought out the sneakers and cut each one into two pieces so that Pamba could see that they were not important.

Living as neighbours for such a long time, we knew, of course, that our mothers would never come to exchanging blows. They were just two harassed women who were forced to turn to each other for company yet half the time they couldn't really stand each other. I didn't – or we didn't know that then. The following day we would be digging for treasure in the rubbish dump or playing pinball at Gavaze's and they would be gossiping again as they walked along the street, calling us in to supper.

In fact, most of the time, our mothers were forced to team up, to defend us against hostile neighbours. Every house in Zengeza had a fruit tree or two in the yard. Either a peach tree or an avocado pear tree. Pamba and I would go on fruit hunting sorties. We climbed fences into other people's yards to get at the ripe peaches or avocado pears.

And so we always had visitors.

'You have to do something about these two boys of yours. This is no longer a safe neighbourhood. They beat up our children, steal their toys, and there is hardly a tree they haven't stripped bare – even of the unripe fruit!' they would shout.

'Somebody poisoned my dog yesterday,' one would say, pointing a finger at us.

Some people wouldn't talk to our mothers at all. They would wait for the weekend when our fathers were home. Now, with my father, you could never tell how he would respond. He was as likely to beat up the complainant as to beat me up, depending on his mood or on whom he thought was wrong. But most of the time he had no patience with tell-tale neighbours.

'Do you want me to keep my child on a leash? Haven't you got children yourself? Do you want my children to play in my pocket so that you don't see them?'

My father was very different from Pamba's father, although they drank together and, as Party office-holders, sometimes held kangaroo courts to disipline errant members and disputing families or couples in our ward.

Pamba's father said my father was spoiling me. He was too lenient with me.

'But the boy is sometimes innocent, you know,' Father would say.

'Innocent? Show me a boy who is innocent at that age and I'll show you a woman who is innocent!' Pamba's father would almost spill his beer.

49

Let me explain what I mean about my father. Rose was a girl on our street. For just a toffee or a biscuit she would let us touch her budding breasts. She lived with her stepmother who didn't care where she went or what she did. Her father only came home once a week; he drove out-of-town trucks.

One Sunday morning Rose's father brought her into our house. I knew why. On the previous Friday, I had touched and pinched Rose's breasts in front of her stepmother at their table in the vegetable shed at Gavaze's market. Rose wouldn't have cried if her stepmother hadn't seen us. Pamba had just touched her and the stepmother hadn't seen him doing it. But when I pinched her, a little too hard, I must admit; she jumped and pointed at both Pamba and me.

'They are touching me!'

And now her father had brought Rose to our house.

'Would you please ask your son what he did to my daughter on Friday afternoon?' Rose's father said to my father. My father was having his breakfast of *sadza* and stew, a bottle of beer at his elbow.

'You want a beer?' my father asked Rose's father.

'I don't drink,' Rose's father said, apparently offended.

'Even water?' my father said and I relaxed. I knew he was in his neighbour-taunting mood. I had slipped into the kitchen the moment Rose and her father came in. I meant to sneak out if things got a bit hot, but until then, I was curious to hear how it would go.

'What did he do?' My mother, who had now ensconced herself on one of the sofas, asked Rose's father.

'Isn't he here? Call him in and ask him what he did to her.' Rose's father said.

'Damba-a!' my father called.

I went into the lounge and sat beside my mother on the sofa.

'What did you do to his daughter on Friday?' my father asked me.

I looked at Rose sitting beside her father on one of the sofas. She looked down and started pulling at a thread in our already threadbare carpet with her toes. She had left her slippers just outside our door. I looked at her hard. She tried, but she couldn't look me in the eye.

'Well, haven't you got a mouth?' my father was getting impatient.

'I didn't do anything,' I said boldly, to silence Rose, although I knew she wouldn't say anything. We were old friends in many ways, at school and on the streets.

'There you are,' my father addressed Rose's father. 'You heard for yourself. What does your daughter say he did to her?'

But Rose's father was almost too angry to answer. He fumed, 'Well, your son and that Dengu bastard are regular little lying thieves!'

'I suppose that makes your daughter a regular little truth-telling angel?' my father said politely.

Rose's father rose and grabbed Rose's hand and dragged her towards the door.

'You will see!' Rose's father said at the door before he went out. Rose had just enough time to pick up her slippers with one hand as the other was held tightly in her father's.

That was my father, it was one typical way in which he dealt with situations such as this.

Five minutes after Rose and her father had left our house, we heard Mr Dengu, Pamba's father, shouting at Pamba. And then we heard Pamba howling. I went to the door and looked out over at Pamba's house.

Rose's father was dragging Rose as they went out of the gate, Rose casting glances back over her shoulder at the Dengus' house from which I, too, could hear the slap of the belt and the noise of heavy furniture being dragged across the floor. I knew Pamba must be trying to duck his father's belt.

'Whatever did you do to her, Damba?' my mother asked me when I went back into the lounge.

'Nothing she didn't ask for, I'm sure,' Father said.

'Don't say that in front of him. You encourage him,' Mother said.

'Encourage him? That man doesn't attend Party meetings, that's why he is so stupid,' Father said.

'I don't see what the Party has got to do with this,' Mother said, rising to go into the kitchen to get breakfast ready for the rest of us. My father only looked after her, shook his head and drank from his bottle.

This story is just to show that my father didn't always react to everything that people said I had done in the same way that Pamba's father did. We, however, seemed to want to exploit all this. I went on to do other things because my father would always be on my side. Pamba went on to do other things because it was all the same to him: whether he had or hadn't, his father would always belt him.

At times I thought a demon possessed Pamba. One day we broke into the old next-door couple's house and shat all over their bare furnitureless lounge. For this my father caned me raw. I still have the scars where his green *musasa* stick cut into my flesh.

On another occasion the headmaster brought us home himself. We had stolen some books from the school storeroom and sold them for pinball money. My father threatened to stop me from going to school and he caned me again.

But we seemed to thrive on these thrashings. We would boast about them to our mates. And many boys wanted to be friends with us so they could escape the 'protection fee' we made the other school kids pay us.

It got to a point where everyone, every parent in our ward, didn't want to see us. They thought we were poisonous and they discouraged their children from playing with us.

Then the old man in the house next door died, and as I said, soon after that, his wife disappeared and Mrs Gwaze and her son, Dura, came to live in the house.

There were only the two of them: Mrs Gwaze and her son, Dura. No Mr Gwaze. The women on our street – and anywhere else for that matter – didn't like women with children without visible husbands. I guess it was our preoccupation with pinball, but Pamba and I didn't realize that the house next door had new occupants until we heard our mothers talking. They were standing at our gate and they didn't see me listening at the lounge window. It was early in the morning and they were sweeping out their yards.

'I hear her husband died mysteriously,' my mother said.

'Mysteriously? She has a disease. That's what killed him,' Pamba's mother said.

'You mean the new disease?'

'Look at that son of hers, do you think he will survive?' Pamba's mother said. 'He looks very sickly ... '

'What are we going to do ... I mean our children will naturally want to play with him.'

'Well, we just tell them the truth.'

When I told Pamba this piece of news he suggested that we investigate. So, we began to watch the house next door.

The first thing we saw were men replacing the window panes in the broken windows – after the old woman had disappeared, Pamba and I had used the remaining window panes for target practice. Then a very beautiful woman emerged from the house and began to laugh and talk with the workmen. It was an hour after school and Pamba and I had just changed into our street clothes and were lying on the lawn in our yard, watching through the hedge.

'If my Old Man sees her, he is going to lick his lips ...'

'Look!' I pointed out a frail boy – but one almost our age – in thick glasses and a very smart school uniform. He was carrying a satchel and had just walked through the gate.

'Ah, Dura!' The woman called sweetly, going over to the boy. She kissed him on the cheek, took his satchel and said, 'How was your new school?'

We didn't hear the boy's reply, because they disappeared into the house.

'That must be the son our moms were talking about,' I said.

'He does look as if he is going to die soon, doesn't he?' Pamba responded.

52

'That uniform – he goes to Shingai Primary School.'

'I think his mother must have lots of money,' Pamba said.

'Why do you say that?'

'I don't know. Well … kissing him – that is a very expensive habit. People who do it have money.'

I didn't see how Pamba arrived at that conclusion but I agreed with him.

Then my mother came round to where we were and said, 'Damba. Come into the house this minute. I've got something for you.'

I left Pamba lying on the grass and followed my mother into the house.

'Sit down, Damba,' my mother said when we were in the lounge. I knew there was something serious she wanted to tell me from the tone of her voice. She unwrapped her *zambia* and then re-wrapped it more tightly so I knew that whatever she had to say was very serious indeed.

'Now I want you to listen to me very very carefully, Damba,' she said, sitting down on the sofa facing me.

'Do you know what AIDS is?' my mother said.

'I have heard about it.'

'What have you heard about it?'

'People die from it.'

'People die from it, right. Young or old, they die from it. Now listen very carefully. Keep away from the new people that have come to live next door. Do you hear me? Keep away from them.'

'Have they got *AIDS!*'

'I didn't say that. But just keep away from them if you don't want to die. Especially the son. You can see how thin he is?'

And Pamba's mother told him the same thing. Pamba's mother *actually* said they had AIDS, and ordered Pamba not to go near the boy.

We must have kept away from them for about a week. But during the second week I heard my mother talking to Mrs Gwaze – we had, at least, found out her name.

Mother was hanging things to dry on the clothes-line at the back of our house while Mrs Gwaze was doing her washing in the wash tub behind her house. I was having my after-school meal in the dining-room when I heard laughing. At first I thought Mother was talking to Pamba's mother and I went out to the back and stood at the door. Mother was talking to Mrs Gwaze. I dropped my plate in astonishment and Mother whirled round.

'Damb-a!'

I quickly retreated into the house.

I wanted to kick myself. I wanted to know what they'd been talking about.

I told Pamba about this and Pamba said it was high time we found out for ourselves.

We knew that Dura always returned from school an hour or so after we did. Shingai School was just down the road from us. So, one day we decided to fetch Dura.

At the end of the morning, we went down to Shingai School and waited by the school gate. It wasn't long before we saw him, alone, very smart, satchel in hand walking towards the gate.

'Hello, Dura,' Pamba said, stepping out into Dura's path, his hands in his pockets. I saw he didn't stretch out his right hand in a customary greeting.

'Hi, Pamba,' Dura said, stretching out his right hand.

'You know my name?' Pamba was surprised but he didn't take Dura's hand. Dura withdrew it in some embarrassment.

'Hi, Dura,' I said, stepping forward.

'Hello, Damba,' Dura said but this time he didn't stretch out his hand. I didn't act surprised at his mentioning my name. If he knew Pamba's, he was bound to know mine.

'How do you know our names?' Pamba asked.

'How do you know mine?' Dura answered, not rudely. He didn't look the rude type behind his glasses, smiling at us. But I thought he was worse than rude. I thought he was looking at us as if we were some things from the lavatory that had landed in his glass of milk.

'Where is your father?' Pamba asked.

Dura looked puzzled and surprised at the same time. He looked from Pamba to me and back again.

'Do you have a father at all?' Pamba said, grabbing Dura by the collar of his shirt. I was horrified. I tried to signal Pamba with my eyes: '*AIDS*, man, he's got *AIDS*,' but Pamba was in his element now. And, afraid that he might think me coward, I said, 'Maybe he doesn't know what a father is?'

Dura suddenly looked at me, sadly. *Sadly*, yes. He didn't look surprised or afraid at all, which made us even angrier.

'A father is the man who sleeps with your mother in their bedroom at night,' Pamba said.

'It's not always your father but *any* man who sleeps with your mother,' I said, remembering some houses on our street.

Dura began to cry. We could never stand boys who cried without provocation. What had we done to him? We looked at each other. Pamba pushed him in the face and Dura fell on his bottom into the dust.

Surprisingly, we didn't hear any more of it, from Dura or his mother. We didn't know whether he had told her or not. Probably not, because the following afternoon we were lying on our lawn and we again heard my mother talking and laughing with Dura's mother.

Then we got a song going:

Dura's mother, Dura's mother.
Bring back Dura's father.
Dura is crying, Dura is crying –
Where did you put Dura's father?

We sang this song in the morning on our way to school, we sang it in the afternoon after school, we sang it in the evening as we came from Gavaze's store. We became so daring that we would sing it over our hedge and into Mrs Gwaze's yard. I am sure she heard us yet whenever we ran into her, coming or going out of her house, she would give us a charming smile and say, 'Good morning, boys. How's school?' The greeting and the cheerful smile struck us dumb. Is she normal? we wondered. We wanted her to scream and shout and stamp her foot – to do *anything* to show us that we'd got to her. But she only smiled: 'Good evening, Damba. Evening, Pamba. How are the books?' And she continued to talk and laugh with my mother in the backyard as they hung the washing out.

And Dura. Dura was even worse than his mother. We were certain that he hadn't told his mother about what we had done to him outside the gate at Shingai Primary School. It stumped us. We just had to find out how tough he was. And we'd discovered that he was a grade ahead of us; and the kids who were in his class said he was a genius. There was nothing that Pamba and I loathed more than geniuses in the classroom.

So, we decided we'd get him – one way or another.

We approached him with our 'protection fee' plan and it didn't seem to bother him to part with his tuck money daily. We faked disappointment over one thing or another, cut his rubber ball into strips, took away his colouring pencils, ripped the pockets from his school shirt, poured cooking oil on one or two of his school books but all he ever said on our way to school was 'Good morning Brother Pamba!' with his terrible smile while his eyes seemed to be laughing at us behind his thick glasses.

'Good morning, brother Pamba,' Dura would say, cheerfully.

'I'm not your brother!' Pamba would snap back.

And in the evening, standing at the gate into their yard, he would see me entering our gate, he would call out softly, 'Good evening, brother Damba!'

'Do you know what a brother looks like?' I called back at him.

The truth was, instead of us getting at them, Dura and his mother had begun to get at us. We forgot everything else in our obsession to break Dura and his mother.

So, one day, Pamba knocked off Dura's glasses and one of the lenses cracked. He was about to bring his foot down on them as they lay on the ground but I held him back. My father had glasses and I knew they cost quite a lot of money.

I picked up the glasses and handed them back to Dura who was now standing pitifully alone, arms outstretched as if he was afraid of knocking against a tree or running into a wall. His eyes were screwed into slits as if they had sand in them.

'Sorry, Dura,' I said. 'That was an accident. He didn't mean to knock them off.'

'It's all right,' Dura said. 'They're due for a change any way. I am going to my optician and he will probably recommend a change of lenses.'

And all we heard from Dura's mother was, 'Good evening, Pamba. Evening Damba. What subject do you like best in school?' Nothing, nothing at all about her son's glasses.

This was too much. We just had to see them from the inside. If we saw the stuff that they had in their house, we thought maybe that would give us an idea about how to deal with them.

We also realized that we were not the only ones who were riled by the aloof cheerfulness of Mrs Gwaze and her son. Pamba's mother must have been watching the developing relationship between my mother, her friend and old neighbour, and the newcomer, the AIDS victim, Mrs Gwaze.

We were returning home one evening when they were standing at the gate into the Dengus' yard. They hadn't seen us, so we crept closer and squatted against the hedge.

'You are becoming very precious these days,' Pamba's mother said. 'What has she given you?'

'What do you mean?'

'Don't ask me that, Ronia. She got you, admit it. You stand at your lines talking and laughing so hard that they can hear you over at Chikwanha's ...'

'We don't talk about you, if that's what you are afraid of ...'

'What do you talk about then? She hardly nods at me when I greet her. But you ...'

'People are different ...'

'You mean I stink ...'

'Listen, Grace ...'

'Don't "listen Grace" me. I would like to know what you talk about, that's all. Does your Claver know that you spend hours and hours gossiping at the back of your house with her?' Claver was my father's name.

'What's got into you, Grace?' my mother's voice grew higher.

'Well, if you're talking about me, I'll hear about it one of these days. But let me warn you, Ronia. You're playing with fire.'

'You're imagining things, Grace. She doesn't have time to talk about any ...'

'Then what do *you* talk to her about?'

My mother was quiet for some time, then she said, 'All right, Grace. I will stop talking to her. Are you satisfied?'

Pamba's mother shifted her weight from one foot to the other and coughed. She said, 'Well, I've heard things about her and I wouldn't tell you if you weren't my best friend. You see, I like you, Ronia, and I can't bear the thought of standing by and seeing your marriage and life ruined ...'

'Oh, Grace, please!'

'The woman is a witch! A witch!' Pamba's mother was almost screaming. She was talking so loudly that my mother looked around nervously.

She couldn't see him but at that moment we saw Dura standing at the gate to their house. Dura was looking straight at the Dengus' house. He must have heard every word that our mothers were saying ...

'You see how thin that son of hers is? He shares his food with a huge python she keeps in a trunk in one of the rooms. Why do you think she doesn't take in lodgers like the rest of us? There are only two of them and what do they need a house as big as that one for? She moves about alone. She doesn't go to meetings. She doesn't complain about anything. Do you know why, Ronia? Do you know why? Do you know where she lived before she came here? Do you ever think about all that, Ronia my friend?'

At that moment Dura coughed from their gate. He was so close, the two women were startled.

'He's been listening,' my mother whispered.

'Oh, my God, do you think he heard me?' Pamba's mother whispered back. 'Do you think he is going to tell his mother?'

So, we were not the only ones who had begun to be afraid of Mrs Gwaze and her son, Dura. After that talk by the Dengus' gate, my mother also seemed to lose her enthusiasm for Mrs Gwaze. Her friendship wilted as if it had been nipped in the bud. Mrs Gwaze would call out, 'Hi, there!' and my mother would mumble back something I could hardly decipher, maybe a 'Good afternoon' or 'Good evening' but it sounded more like a push in the face: *Don't bother me.*

And we watched Mrs Gwaze retreating into herself. Even with us, her greetings were reduced to scant nods. But the smile, that bright smile, was always there as if she was saying: *Not now. Busy. See you later.*

Dura would stand by their gate and say, 'Good evening brother Pamba. Good evening brother Damba' and we would either return his greeting or not, depending on the mood we were in at the time.

Then slowly, we noticed, Dura began to come home later than usual. And when he did, he had a train of kids with him. They would go into the Gwaze house and we would lie on the grass in our yard and hear them laughing and shouting happily inside the house as they played music or videos. We felt as if we were being excluded from a party to which we had every right to be invited.

But what irked us most was that the kids followed Dura willingly. He didn't bully them or anything. And we realized that we were losing to him. Dura, however, still greeted us, 'Good morning, *Mukoma* Pamba. Morning, *Mukoma* Damba.'

One day we were working through the rubbish dump looking for 'treasure'. We heard a lot of noise and looked up. There was Dura with his retinue of kids singing a strange song in Shona:

'*Tinoadhaura mashizha*
A he–e nd'o zvinoapatisa.'

It was a good tune, and I kicked myself for not having made it up myself. Then Dura saw us and called out: 'Come and help us bury this thief!'

We didn't respond. We went on with our digging. Who was he to come to our area, take all our people and start giving us orders?

We pretended not to notice that they were there. But I gave them a sideways glance and noticed that one of the kids was carrying a sack, and another had a hoe.

Dura raised a hand and they all stopped singing. He started walking about on the empty lot beyond the rubbish dump. Then he stretched his hand for the hoe and he started digging. He dug for some time then gave the hoe to another kid to dig.

Each of them took turns to dig and when the hole was deep enough, they threw the sack in and began to cover up the hole.

'What is it?' I asked Pamba. I was really curious. And I could see he, too, wanted to know what it was.

'What do I care what it is? Kid's stuff.'

When they had filled up the hole, Dura made a cross out of sticks and stuck it at one end of the mound of earth and then they started singing as they marched back into the streets:

'*Tinoadhaura mashizha*
A he–e nd'o zvinoapatisa.'

After they had gone, Pamba said to me, 'Come on. Let's go and see what it is.'

'They have buried it.'

'Let's dig it up.'

It was a dead cat. We dropped it and ran. We didn't look back.

'Hi brother Pamba, brother Damba,' Dura was standing at their gate one late afternoon as we passed by. Pamba beckoned to him – Dura came.

Before I realized what was happening, Pamba smashed a fist into Dura's face, smashing his glasses into his eyes. Dura just yelped – and put his hands to his face. We ran. We ran past Pamba's house, right to the end of the houses and on to the rubbish dump, across Seke Road and into the bushes beside Manyame Dam.

We headed for our rock. We sat down on the rock. Although we had been running, I suddenly felt cold. I thought we had gone a little bit too far. I suddenly felt homesick, as if I had already left.

'Why did you do that?' I asked Pamba.

'Who does he think he is?'

I looked at Pamba and away. We were very late getting back home that day. We expected to find Mrs Gwaze waiting for us either at Pamba's or my house. She wasn't there.

'Is everything all right?' my mother asked me when I entered the kitchen.

'Yes.'

'You look as if you've killed someone.'

My heart skipped a beat but I didn't say anything

'I think your friend Pamba will get you into trouble one of these days if you don't watch out. Dura seems all right to me. And he's bright. He could help you with your lessons,' my mother said.

Again my heart skipped but I didn't say anything.

The following day I didn't go out of the house until I saw Mrs Gwaze leave for work. There was a car parked outside her gate. Then she came out of the house, holding Dura's hand. I lowered my head, so they wouldn't see me at the window of our lounge. Mrs Gwaze looked neither towards the Dengus' or our house. They got into the car and drove off.

Dura came back that afternoon with a new pair of glasses. I had just come back from school and was standing at our gate, looking the other way, so I didn't see him approaching.

'Hi, brother Damba,' I heard his voice. I whirled round and he opened the gate to their house.

'Oh, hi, Dura,' I brought the words out but I nearly choked on my saliva.

Dura gave me a cheerful smile, pointed at his new glasses, and went into their yard, shutting the gate behind him.

'I don't like it,' I told Pamba as we lay on the grass in our yard some days later. We had waited for Mrs Gwaze to come and see our parents but she hadn't. We had avoided her at first but we had to know. So, when she came back from work one evening, we were standing at the gate to our house.

'Hello boys. How is school? Think you will get a prize in English, Pamba?' Mrs Gwaze called out to us as she opened the gate to her house. Pamba had told her that his favourite subject was English.

When she had entered her house, we looked at each other. Once more, Mrs Gwaze had given us her smile.

'Do you see anything in that smile?' Pamba asked me.

'What? Am I supposed to see anything in it?'

'Don't you see the dark shadow in it?'

'Oh, come on, Pamba.'

'Well, my mother told me about it. That's a witch's smile.'

'Pamb-a!'

'There is only one thing we can do.'

'What's that?'

'Make them leave this place.'

'Pamba.'

'I know some medicine ...'

Pamba's medicine was some dog shit, ground together with black cinders, tied up in a red and black cloth. This had to be placed somewhere where Mrs Gwaze would see it easily, but late at night when everyone else was indoors.

The following morning, at five o'clock, I was at our lounge window. That was the time that most women, including Mrs Gwaze, swept out their yards.

I took my books and sat on the sofa below the window and pretended to do my homework. Mrs Gwaze was already up, singing as she swept in her yard. She was still sweeping at the back of the house. The medicine was out at the front, near the gate.

'Hello,' my mother said as she came out of her bedroom, wrapping her *zambia* round her waist, as she got ready to sweep out our yard. 'Is everything all right?'

'I am doing my homework,' I said.

'Really? And is my mother going to rise from her grave and talk to me? Since when have you started waking up early to do your homework, Damba Mudzonga?'

'Everything has a beginning, Mother,' I said. I had heard someone say this, I couldn't remember who. My mother flopped on a sofa and began to laugh. She laughed so hard she woke my father up.

'What's all the noise?' Father called from the bedroom.

'Your son is up! Doing his homework, he says.'

'Well, everything has a beginning, hasn't it? He is growing up,' my father called back.

And suddenly I remembered where I had heard the expression before.

'Well, I won't disturb you, my son. Let's hope it's not a passing whim,' Mother said as she stood up and went out.

Mrs Gwaze was moving closer to the *muti*. I knelt on the sofa and hid behind the tattered curtain, looking out. My heart beat so fast I thought I would collapse.

Mrs Gwaze didn't stop singing as she finished sweeping out her yard. She collected the rubbish and put it into a black plastic bag and dumped the bin just outside her yard for the municipal rubbish truck.

'It will take some time to work,' Pamba said unconvincingly three days later when Mrs Gwaze seemed to show no signs of leaving.

'Who gave you the recipe for this medicine anyway?' I asked.

'My mother. She knows all sorts of things.'

It was by now almost a month since we had strategically dropped the *muti* in Mrs Gwaze's yard, and she was just as cheerful as ever. We were playing with a plastic-and-rag ball in our yard. It was late afternoon. Dura hadn't yet come home but his mother was there. We could hear her singing as she went about her house.

Then, I don't know what came over him, Pamba hit the ball high and wide. It flew over the hedge into Mrs Gwaze's yard and hit one of the window panes. Pamba ran out of our yard and into his house. I stood there, open-mouthed. I looked at the window pane. It hadn't broken.

Mrs Gwaze came out of her house. She picked up the ball and held it over to me across the hedge. 'Is this yours?' she asked, smiling.

'Yes.'

'Well, I can't throw it to you. It's bad manners to throw things at people. I can't give it to you over the hedge either because handing things over a fence or a hedge is not a good thing to do. Only thieves do that. Would you like to came round and collect it?'

I should have run away, like Pamba, I thought.

'It wasn't ...' I began.

'I know it wasn't you. Come and get it anyway. I am not going to bite you.'

I went round and through Mrs Gwaze's gate. She was waiting for me at her door.

'Would you like to come in? I want to show you something.'

Before I could say 'No' Mrs Gwaze turned and entered her house. There was nothing I could do but follow her in. I looked across the hedge towards Pamba's house. I saw him duck his head behind a curtain at their front window.

I followed Mrs Gwaze into the house. Immediately I entered, I regretted having come in. It was one of those rooms -- her lounge – where everything in it, from floor to the ceiling – seemed to throw your reflection back at you. My clothes were dusty, my feet were in torn sneakers that stank.

'Sit down, Damba. Would you like something to drink? An orange drink or a lemonade?'

I swallowed saliva. My voice wouldn't come out.

'No,' I said. 'I am all right.'

'People who come into my house are not allowed to say "No" to a drink. Especially when they have almost broken my window pane. What shall it be? Orange or ...?'

'I will have a Coke,' I could barely hear my own voice.

Mrs Gwaze went through an inner door – to get the drinks probably. I looked around. Glass. One side of the room was all mirrors – and glass – a huge display cabinet with glass and silver and china things, a TV *and* a radio set – which growled as deeply as the grumblings in the belly of an elephant – as I heard my father say once. I can't remember what else was in the room because my mind kept jumping to my smelly sneakers, which I was trying to hide under the sofa. This was not a room in which people were meant to be comfortable.

Mrs Gwaze came back with two glasses one with a light brown liquid – that looked like beer – and my Coke. She took a sip from the glass, saying, 'That's what we do where I come from. It shows I haven't put poison in it,' then she handed me the glass. I clapped my hands first before I took it, Mrs Gwaze seemed to be impressed by my manners. She smiled more brightly than before.

Then she sat down opposite me and began to sip from her glass. She was looking at me attentively. Then she said, 'Damba, I would like you to help me, I would like you to be nice to Dura.

'He has got a problem with his chest and the slightest thing you do to frighten him could make him seriously ill. It could even kill him. It isn't his fault. He was born like that: weak chest, weak eyes, knock-knees -- but ...' Mrs Gwaze raised her index finger, and fixing me with her dancing eyes, tapped her head, 'he is very sharp up here. Sharp as a razor.'

She drank from her glass, her eyes on me. She went on, 'I know what happens when you are playing. I know that sometimes you fight -- that's natural among boys your age. I used to fight a lot too. And I have told Dura that I don't want to hear about your fights. It is not healthy for any of us – you or him or me or your parents. So I don't want fights, or stories of fights, in this house. I just want you to help him so he doesn't get into too many fights. Will you do that for me?'

I didn't know what to say. I was confused. I remembered everything we'd said and thought of them – Mrs Gwaze and Dura – and I couldn't look her in the eye.

Then I finished my Coke and stood up.

'Thank you for the drink. I am going now.'

'Aren't you forgetting your ball?'

'It's just a rag-ball. We will make another one.'

'No! Wait.'

She put her beer down on the coffee table and stood up and went through another door. She came out holding a football. The real thing. One of those huge leather things you put air into.

'You can have this.'

I looked at her very hard. I wanted to cry. I have never in all my life wished for somebody to understand exactly how I felt as I did that day.

'Don't you like it?'

'Mrs Gwaze, you know I like it but you know I can't accept it,' I said and ran out of her house.

'Why didn't you take it?' Pamba was angry with me when I told him about my invitation into Mrs Gwaze's house and the football.

'Well, why did you run away?' I retorted.

Pamba looked away, sulking. We were quiet for some time. Then he turned to me, smiling, and said, 'Do you think you ... you think you ... she will invite you into her house again?'

'I don't know.' Something told me not to tell him what she had said about Dura.

'How don't you know? You were in there. You stayed in there for so long I didn't think you were going to come out. You are lying to me, Damba. What else did she give you? Money? Yes. She gave you money and you are hiding it away from me. Come on. Turn out your pockets let's see.'

But before I could even turn out my pockets, Pamba had knocked me down and was searching my pockets. He found the two-dollar note I had pulled out of my father's wallet while he was having his bath that morning and he waved it into my face.

'I knew it! I knew it! Liar! Liar!'

'No, Pamba. That's mine. Pamba!'

I tried to get it away from him but he pushed me so hard that I hit my head against the wall of our house. I sat down against the wall, crying. Pamba ran away.

I sat there crying for a long time, although I didn't really know why I was crying. Then, I raised my head and saw Mrs Gwaze looking at me across the hedge. When she saw that I had seen her, she moved away. I stood up and went into the house. As I went into the house, I was thinking that I would never, ever, play with Pamba again.

That evening Pamba's mother came to our house. She called Mother to the gate. I went to the front window so that I could hear what they were saying.

'What did I tell you?'

'What did *you* tell me?'

'Look at this. Just look at this. What is this?'

Pamba's mother was holding out something towards my mother. My mother took it and said, 'It's money. It's two dollars. I don't under ...'

'Your son,' Pamba's mother said.

'My son? What about my son?'

'He got it from Mrs Gwaze's.'

'Got it from ... listen, Grace. I'm not joking. There are mosquitoes out here and I am not going to stand here listening to your ...'

'Listen to my what? I came here to help you and you sneer at me. Call your son out here right now. You always accuse my son of ...'

'Please, lower your voice. Damba is in there. I'll ask him ... '

'You know, you are still green. Very green. Ever heard about *kurasirira*? Do you know that expression?'

'I know what it means. Still ... anyway, who told you that Mrs Gwaze gave him the money? And how come *you* have got it yourself? How did you get it from him?'

'Pamba got it from him. They were going to play those machines and your son brought out the money and Pamba asked him where he got it from and your son told him that he had been given it by Mrs Gwaze.'

'Mrs Gwaze just opened up her purse and said: Damba, here is two dollars?'

'That's what I want to find out from you. That's why I am here. I told you that your Mrs Gwaze is going to destroy you if you are not careful.'

'Damba!' my mother called out.

'*Mha!*'

'Come out here, quick!'

There was nowhere to run to, so I went out.

'Where were you this afternoon?' Mother asked.

'You are wasting time with him,' Mrs Dengu said. 'He is going to lie to you. Did you go into Mrs Gwaze's house this afternoon?' Mrs Dengu asked me in a way that said she knew all about it.

'Yes.'

'You see?' Mrs Dengu turned to my Mother.

'What did you want there?'

'Pamba and ...'

'Don't bring Pamba into this,' Mrs Dengu said.

'Let him finish what he is saying.'

'We were playing ragball here, in this yard, then ... then ... the ball went over into Mrs Gwaze's yard. It hit one of her windows – but the pane didn't break – and Mrs Gwaze told me to come and collect the ball.'

'And you went?' Mrs Dengu asked.

'Yes.'

'And where was Pamba then?' my mother asked.

'He ran away.'

'Why didn't you run away too?' Mrs Dengu asked.

I couldn't answer that one.

'And what happened when you went to collect the ball?' Mother asked.

'Mrs Gwaze asked me into her house.'

'She asked you into her house? Why?' Mother asked.

'She said – she said – she wouldn't give me the ball unless I went into her house.'

'And why didn't you refuse to enter her house?' Mrs Dengu asked.

I couldn't answer that one.

'Did Mrs Gwaze give you anything?' my mother asked.

I shook my head.

'Haven't you got a mouth?' Mother's voice was dark.

'She didn't give me anything.'

'Are you quite, quite sure she didn't give you some money?' Mrs Dengu asked.

'No,' I said.

'Damba, tell the truth,' Mother said, her voice getting darker and darker.

'No. Mrs Gwaze didn't give me any money.'

'Where did you get this two-dollar note from?' Mother asked.

I kept quiet.

'You see?' Mrs Dengu said. I could have strangled her.

All of a sudden I didn't care what they would do to me and I said very quickly, 'I took the money out of father's wallet when he was having a bath this morning. And Pamba grabbed the note from me saying that Mrs Gwaze had given it to me.'

'He's lying,' Mrs Dengu said.

'I am *not* lying,' I shouted so loudly at Mrs Dengu that my mother put her hands on her ears. I heard a window open and Mrs Gwaze put her head out. My mother and Mrs Dengu turned their heads and saw Mrs Gwaze at her window.

I shouted, 'Mrs Gwaze didn't give me any money. If you want, if you think I am lying we can go right now into her house and ask her!'

'Don't shout so loudly!' my mother said, twisting my ear. I howled.

'Well ... I ... I thought I should make sure,' Mrs Dengu said as she walked out of the gate and slip-slopped to her house in her old shoes.

Mrs Gwaze banged her window shut.

My mother grabbed me by the hand, almost wrenching my shoulder out of its socket and dragged me into the house.

In the house, Mother said, 'You father is going to kill you for this, do you know that? I should really kill you myself because he is going to think I took the money when I didn't. Do you want your father to kill me?'

That explained why I hadn't heard Father complain about the two-dollar and five-dollar notes I had been filching from his wallet for some time. But I hadn't heard him shouting at Mother about the money either.

Mother didn't say anything about me going into Mrs Gwaze's house when we were alone. I felt, somehow, that I owed her something and I told her about the Coke and what Mrs Gwaze had said about Dura. The idea that father might kill her because of the money I had stolen made me feel very bad.

After I had told her everything, Mother, said, 'From now on, I don't want to see you playing with Pamba. Leave him alone *nengozi dzekumba kwavo.*'

I am sure Mother never told Father about the two dollars I had taken from his wallet. He never asked me about it.

But it was hard to get away from Pamba and keep him away from me. I tried to avoid him by going to school earlier than usual, or by pretending to be doing my homework when he came to find me in the afternoon, but he was persistent. He would just hang around our house and make noises to tell me that he was out there, waiting for me.

He tried to make up for knocking my head against the wall. He brought me useless little things he'd dug up at the rubbish dump. He moaned about how I didn't want to play with him any more because I'd been bewitched by Dura's mother. I realized that besides me, Pamba had no one, no one at all, to play with. He must have complained to his mother because one day she said to me, 'So, you don't want to play with Pamba any more? Ha?' I didn't answer but she gave me such a scowl that I nearly peed in my shorts. She could be that ugly when she wanted to be.

Mother, too, seemed to have cooled towards Mrs Dengu. But she didn't turn to Mrs Gwaze either. She just kept herself to herself and she had pulled out her hand-sewing machine from under the bed, dusted it and resumed sewing things for little children – something she hadn't done for years.

Whenever Mrs Dengu came in, Mother's sewing gave her an excuse for not going out and Mrs Dengu would sit around, talking and talking and talking while Mother stitched away. Eventually, Pamba's mother would get tired of talking to someone who wouldn't answer her and she would leave.

I also began to realize that something was going on in the Dengu household. I was used to hearing the slap of the belt and the sound of furniture being dragged around and Pamba howling. But I hadn't ever heard Pamba's mother screaming as the belt slapped *her.*

At least twice a week, we would hear Mrs Dengu crying, and shouting: 'Kill me! He's my son, not yours! Kill me!' This would be late at night, after Pamba's father had come in from the beerhall. There was a pattern to it. Father would open the door, Mother would wake up to warm and put the food on the table before him.

Then just as Father had begun to eat, a piercing scream from the Dengu's house would startle us. We would hear the voice of Pamba's father, just once and that would be followed by slapping, screaming and Mrs Dengu talking as she cried.

'Whatever is going on in that house?' Mother asked one day.

'Why don't you ask her? Isn't she your friend?' Father said, but he wasn't angry. He just didn't want to be bothered with what went on in other people's homes.

'Well doesn't he tell you what the matter is when you're drinking your beer?'

'Dengu doesn't talk about his family when we're drinking.'

'But don't you think you should ...'

'I should nothing. And don't you put shoulding into their business.'

Sometimes Pamba wouldn't go to school the day after one of these episodes. Instead he would hang round our house, looking bruised and woebegone, and I would share my afternoon and evening meals with him.

Then one day Mrs Gwaze came over to our house – for the first time since she had started living next door to us. She asked my mother if she would let me join Dura and his friends the following Saturday. It was Dura's birthday and Mrs Gwaze said that she wanted me to be there. Dura had especially asked her to ask my Mother if I could come.

Mother was quiet for some time, then she said, 'Well you will have to ask his father

'I thought you could do that for me,' Mrs Gwaze said.

'I will see,' my mother said.

'Do you want to go to this party?' Mother asked me after Mrs Gwaze had left.

'Oh, yes,' I answered, eagerly.

Mother stopped her sewing and looked at me as if I had done something she didn't like.

'You are not going,' she said.

'Why?'

'You steal. I don't want Mrs Gwaze coming over here dragging you behind her, shouting that you have filched twenty dollars which she had left on top of her TV or whatever.'

I was quiet for a long time, then I said, 'I don't steal any more, Mother.' And, at that moment, I wanted so much to be believed that I could have died.

Mother gave me such a piercing look that I almost looked away, but I didn't.

'We'll see about that,' she said enigmatically and went back to her sewing.

Mother let me go to Dura's birthday party. It was the last Saturday that I would ever see Pamba although I did see him during the first part of the following week. For the whole week before Dura's birthday party, things had been going terribly wrong in the Dengu household. The slap-slapping and screaming went on every night. And it was during that week that Father started coming home early. He would buy his beer at Gavaze's bottle store and bring it home to drink by himself.

The Friday just before the party was the worst. Crockery crashed, doors banged, and Mrs Dengu screamed until midnight. Then I heard Pamba sobbing outside our gate. He was there for a long time, probably making up his mind about whether to come and knock on our door or not. I didn't get up but I couldn't go to sleep either. Finally he stopped crying.

Early on Saturday morning Mother found him huddling in our hedge on some dirty cardboard boxes. Then he disappeared until the afternoon when I saw him beckoning to me outside Mrs Gwaze's gate. The party had already started and all the kids – lots of them – were jumping about, shouting, and dancing to kwasakwasa music. There was a sprinkling of women, mainly Mrs Gwaze's friends from her work. My mother had also been invited, but she only stayed long enough to drink a coke and chew a drumstick.

I saw Mrs Gwaze talking to her and they laughed long and hard. I liked the way they looked in each other's company. I wished they had been friends for longer than this. Then I looked out and there was Pamba, standing at the gate, urgently signalling me to join him. I went out.

'Listen, there is something I want to show you. Come on.'

'No. I am helping at the party.'

'You can come back. Let's go.'

'They want me to ...'

'I have got my own party. Come and see.'

I was curious. I slipped out of the gate after making sure that neither Mrs Gwaze nor Dura were looking.

We went past our house and into the Dengus' house. No one else seemed to be at home. I knew Pamba's father would be at the beerhall and wouldn't come back until maybe after midnight. After last night's goings-on, he might even stay away from home all weekend. He had done this several times before, although he had turned up for the Sunday meetings at The Rock.

We entered the Dengus' house and made straight for Pamba's room. Pamba shut the door and locked it. In the centre of the room was a little stool on which there was a big bottle of Coke: a parcel wrapped up in newspaper lay on a plate.

Pamba said, 'Sit down on the bed.'

'I have to get back.'

'Oh come on. There's plenty of time. You can go later. Sit down.'

Reluctantly I sat down on the creaky old bed which must have once belonged to Pamba's parents. Everyone in the family must have used that bed. It sagged in the middle where the mattress was so worn away that there was almost nothing there at all. When you sat on the edge, you kept sliding backwards towards the hole in the middle.

'What is it?' I asked Pamba as he began to take the oily wrapping off the parcel. I felt anxious and suspicious. I didn't like this at all. The huge silence throughout the house and Pamba's movements didn't feel right.

Pamba removed the last wrapping and a whole chicken lay in a bed of dirty sooty wrapping. The chicken was charred charcoal black and the wings were just stumps. They had been completely burnt away.

'Roast chicken,' Pamba said proudly. 'My own party.'

'Where did you get it from?' I whispered.

'My mother gave it to me.'

'Roasted like this?'

'Well ... no. I went down to our place at the dam and ...'

I was at the door, struggling with the key.

'Where are you going? I can't finish this chicken all alone!' He was moving towards me.

'Don't touch me, Pamba!'

Pamba stopped. He stood still. I wanted to get out. I didn't want Pamba to touch me. I didn't know what I would do if he did. Pamba suddenly looked scared.

'So,' he said, 'you go to his party but refuse to come to mine?'

I unlocked the door, went out and shut the door behind me.

When I got back to Mrs Gwaze's house the party had begun to move outside, for dancing space. More kids seemed to have arrived during my short absence. I helped Dura and Mrs Gwaze's friends to carry the music system into the garden.

'What did he want?' Dura asked me in a very low voice as I watched him uncoiling and plugging in the power cords into the wall sockets.

'Who?'

'Pamba.'

'Oh. He wanted to show me some things he'd dug up at the rubbish dump.'

Dura was quiet for some time, then he said, 'Why was he crying last night? Did you hear him? He stood outside your gate for a long time, crying. We were all out in the yard where Mother and her friends were preparing the food for the party. Didn't you see the huge fire in our yard last night? I thought you would come. It was such a lovely fire.'

'I saw the fire.'

'You saw it?'

'Yes.'

Dura stood up and whispered into my ear, 'A dog stole one of the chickens.'

My heart kicked violently. I hoped Dura wouldn't hear it beating.

'Oh?' I responded weakly.

'Yes. But don't tell anyone. My mother would skin me alive ...'

'Well, if it was a dog ...'

'No dog ever came here last night. There are no dogs in Bise Crescent. There were no footprints in the yard this morning. I looked for them.'

My heart was pounding. Tell him? I decided not to.

'Do you know something,' Dura said to me in a mysteriously low voice.

'No. What?'

'I could let him die, if I wanted to.'

'Are you going to let him die?' I was suddenly scared.

'Do *you* want him to die?'

I shook my head, 'No.'

Dura clicked his tongue and shook his head in a way that made him seem much older than his real age. And I thought I would rather be friends with him than Pamba.

Dura didn't say anything more for the rest of the party. But as I was leaving, after everybody else had gone home – I realized my mother hadn't once called me to come home – Dura took me to the gate and said, 'You're not going to tell him or anyone about this, are you?'

'No.' I meant it.

Dura stretched out his right hand for me to shake.

'You're my friend.'

I didn't say anything as I shook Dura's hand. Then I left their yard and entered ours. I was aware of Dura standing at the gate, watching me go. A stone smashed into and broke one of our window panes and a voice hissed, 'Sell-out!'

I rushed into our house, scared that a stone might hit me.

My mother was standing at the broken window, picking up pieces of broken glass from the sofa.

'That must have been your friend, Pamba,' Mother said.

'He is not my friend.'

I was surprised at my mother's calmness as she picked up the pieces of glass and put them into the dust pan.

'Don't sit on the sofa until I have got rid of all the glass,' she said.

On Monday morning Pamba was waiting for me outside our gate as I left to go to school.

'How did the party go on Saturday?' he asked.

'Fine'.

After walking in silence for some time, he said, 'What did Dura say?'

'About what?'

'Oh, anything. Did he mention me?'

'No.'

'He didn't?'

'No, he didn't.'

'Are you sure?'

I looked at Pamba. He looked away.

'Did you throw that stone that broke our window last night?' I asked.

'No. By the way. That chicken. I couldn't finish it all by myself. We can finish it off after school.'

'Hi *Mukoma* Pamba. Afternoon Damba.' It was Dura. We had just come out of school and he was waiting for us outside the school gate with a group of his friends. I recognized most of them from the party on Saturday. They all smiled and greeted me.

Pamba was impatient. He hurried on ahead of us. 'Come on, Damba,' he urged. 'Let's go.'

'Wait for us, brother Pamba,' Dura said before I could make up my mind whether to hurry and join Pamba or remain behind with Dura and his friends.

'I have to rush home,' Pamba said, slowing down. I could see his heart was divided. He really wanted to join Dura and his friends but he had his pride.

'There's plenty of time,' Dura said. 'We're all going home.' Pamba slowed down a bit and we caught up with him. We walked on in silence, then, out of nowhere, Dura said to his friends, 'You remember that cat we buried at the rubbish dump?'

'Yes,' they answered.

'Do you know how it died?'

'You said it had stolen some meat your mother had taken out of the fridge,' one of the kids said.

'Yes,' Dura said.

I saw Pamba stumble but he continued to walk beside us, if a little more slowly.

'You see,' Dura continued, 'My mother has got some poisonous medicine she sprays on meat before she stores it in the fridge. When she takes it out, she soaks it in water first, then sprays another *muti* on it to neutralize the poison of the first medicine, before she cooks it. This cat ate this meat before it had been washed and neutralized.'

There was a deathly silence in the group. Pamba began to kick at stones and tins lying in the road as he walked on, his head down, not daring to look at anyone. I felt my heart threatening to burst.

'But that's terrible,' one of the children said. 'What if someone comes to visit and your mother is away and they just cook the meat without ...'

'It's simple, really,' Dura said quickly. 'The poison takes three to four days to start working. So, if you eat the meat, say, today, and Mother discovers it, she gives you the other medicine to drink and nothing happens. You won't even feel any pain at all.'

'So, if that cat had told your mother that it had eaten the meat, your mother would have given it some other *muti* and it wouldn't have died?' one of Dura's friends asked.

Everyone laughed and the boy looked around rather stupidly.

'Well, what's wrong?'

'Cats don't talk!' Dura said and everyone including the boy who had asked the question, laughed again.

'So, if this dog comes and tells your mother about the chicken and your mother gives it this neutralizing medicine, it won't die?' I asked for the sake of Pamba, who, I could see, was swallowing very hard. He must have wanted to vomit but he couldn't do it in the presence of Dura and his gang.

'Let me see,' Dura said, counting on his fingers.'Tomorrow or Wednesday, the dog will begin to feel pain. On Thursday, it will die.' He said these last words with such conviction that I almost shouted to Pamba to confess. Dura did not even once look at Pamba as he said this.

Then quickly changing the subject Dura asked, 'What shall we do? Go to the rubbish dump or go and watch some videos?'

The boys all shouted that they wanted to go and watch videos.

'Are you coming with us, brother Damba?'

'No,' I shook my head. I would have loved to accompany them but I felt it wasn't right. Not yet. Pamba was also watching me.

'Brother Pamba?' Dura asked.

Pamba shook his head and said, 'Mother told me that I should come home straight.' And he started walking very fast down the road.

I dithered a bit, walking a little faster than Dura and his gang but slower than Pamba. I would have liked to go and watch videos with Dura but – well – I thought it was still too early in my friendship with Dura, and I was worried about Pamba.

I found Pamba waiting at the gate to our house. Dura and his gang passed us and turned in through Mrs Gwaze's gate.

'Do you think it's true?' Pamba asked me when we were alone.

'I don't know. But you saw the dead cat, didn't you?' Pamba thought for a little while, then asked, 'Do you think I'm going to die?'

I acted surprised, 'Did you steal the chicken?'

'Don't talk so loudly,' Pamba winced. 'I was hungry. I hadn't eaten a thing the whole day.'

'But you said your mother gave you the chicken.' Pamba was quiet for a bit, and then he said, 'But I didn't finish the chicken. Do you think I'll still die even if I didn't finish it all?'

'I don't know,' I said, rather impatiently.

'Look,' Pamba was scared. 'You go and tell Dura that I saw the dog and chased it until it dropped the chicken. I can give him the rest of the carcase. I didn't eat it all.'

'Why don't you go and tell him yourself? You will still have to see his mother about the medicine.'

Pamba scratched his shoe in the sand. He said, 'If she tells my father he will kill me.'

'So, what are you going to do?'

'Will you go with me to get the chicken? I hid it in a hollow of the rock at our place near the dam.'

'No. I have to help Mother with some things in the house.'

73

'You don't want to go with me?'

'I want to go with you but ...'

'You want me to die?'

'Look, Pamba. I didn't steal the chicken.'

Pamba looked at me imploringly. He said, 'I thought you were my friend.'

I didn't say anything to this.

'You don't care if I die,' he said walking away. I looked at him as he left. He stood at the gate of his house, then he walked past it. He walked a little distance and then turned back, walking quickly towards me.

'Are you sure you don't want to go with me?' he asked when he got back where I was still standing by the gate to my house.

'No, Pamba. I'm busy,' I said.

'I will tell them you ate it too,' he said.

'But I am not going to die, see? It's you who is going to die and that will tell them who ate their chicken.'

'I am not going to play with you again, ever,' Pamba said finally and hopelessly.

I didn't say anything. I couldn't look at him. I wished he would just go away and leave me alone but he remained standing there. There was nothing more to say and yet he went on and on standing there. I opened the gate to go into our house. Pamba rushed at me and grabbed me by the arm. He said, breathlessly, 'Listen, Damba. I lied when I said I had hidden the remainder of the chicken.'

'So? What did you do with it?'

'I threw it into the dam.'

I stared at Pamba, dumbfounded. I just stood there and looked at him, without saying anything because I, too, was frightened and I didn't know what to say.

'Talk to me, Damba! Don't just stand there. Talk to me,' Pamba was dancing on the same spot, jiggling my arm up and down.

'Am I going to die? Please, Damba. Am I going to die? But I didn't eat all of it, I swear. I didn't!' He was crying.

'You shouldn't have thrown that left-over bit into the dam, you know,' I said, getting some secret pleasure at seeing him dance with fear.

'Damba, please! How could I know? You should have told me ...'

I turned from him and walked through the gate into our yard. Pamba followed me and then stopped, his hands on the bars of the gate.

'Damba!' He called out. 'Am I not your friend?'

I didn't turn back. I could hear the 'Oohs!' and 'Ah's!' and clapping of hands and stamping of feet in Dura's house. I wished I had gone to watch videos.

I went round to the back of our house and sat down on the backdoor steps. The noises from Mrs Gwaze's house seemed to be coming from an infinitely far away and much happier country.

As I sat there, alone, I was half expecting Pamba to appear and ask me to go hunting for treasure in the rubbish dumps. How could I have known that I would never see him alive again?

At around eleven o'clock that night Pamba's mother knocked on our door. Pamba hadn't returned home yet, she said. She wondered if he might have put up at our house. We were all in the lounge, Father, Mother, myself and Mrs Dengu.

'I last saw him this afternoon,' I said.

'He has never stayed out this late on his own,' Mrs Dengu said.

'Maybe he has found new friends and he will turn up,' Mother said.

'No, Ronia. I feel something has happened to my son,' Mrs Dengu said.

'What could have happened to him? We haven't heard of an accident on the streets today,' Mother said.

'Or he might have decided to run away,' Father said, not very kindly. He had been drinking and was rather annoyed at being awakened in the middle of the night, as he called it. Mother gave him a reproachful look.

'He hasn't run away before,' Pamba's mother said.

'Well, everything has a beginning. And I'm going to bed,' Father said very firmly.

'*Baba* aDamba,' Mother said.

'What?'

'Why don't you accompany Mrs Dengu to the police station?'

'Now, now, now, hold it. There is no need to panic. He's probably hiding in a friend's house. Have you looked carefully in all the hedges and ditches?'

'Why don't you go to sleep, *Baba* aDamba?' Mother said getting annoyed with Father.

'Well, isn't it true that he sometimes sleeps in the hedges?'

'Could you please let Damba accompany me to the police station?'

'Damba has to go to school in the morning,' Father said. 'Where is Pamba's father?'

'He isn't home yet.'

'Well, why don't you wait until he comes back?'

'I can't sleep.'

'I'll go with you,' Mother said.

'Women!' Father said. 'Get me my coat, Damba.'

Mother and Mrs Dengu exchanged glances.

Father put on his coat grumbling to himself and went out with Mrs Damba.

Mother and I went back to bed but I couldn't sleep. But after a time I drifted off, and then woke with a start. I thought I saw Pamba looking in through the window.

Two hours later Father returned from the police station, with an almost hysterical Mrs Dengu. The wailing and shouting woke me up. At first I thought it was a nightmare. I woke up, got out of bed and went into the lounge. I saw Mother standing at the open window, curtain pulled aside. I went and stood beside her. There were other voices coming out of the Dengus' house, besides Mrs Dengu's. I heard Father's then Mr Dengu's. But there also seemed to be others.

'Something has happened,' Mother said, as if to herself.

'What?' I asked, my heart in my mouth. The lateness of the hour made everything mysterious and frightening.

'I don't know what but your father and Mrs Dengu have come back with three policemen.'

I stood beside Mother and tried to catch what they were saying in the Dengus' house. But I could only hear Mrs Dengu's voice almost hysterically repeating: 'If he is dead ...' Then a door opened and the voices spilled out into the yard.

'There is nothing we can do right now, Mr Dengu. It's the middle of the night. If your son has drowned, he is now beyond help and no amount of searching, however quickly done, will bring him back to life,' one of the policemen was saying. I heard the gate open. And shut. Then Father and the three policemen were walking towards our house.

My father said goodnight to the policemen at the gate and one of the policemen chuckled and said it was already morning. Then they went away and Father entered the house.

We turned towards him. He stood by the door which he took a long time to close, then he leaned against it. He stared straight ahead and would not look at us but I could see he was really looking inside himself.

'Trouble?' Mother said.

'Trouble.'

'How big?'

'We don't know yet,' Father said. They spoke in very low voices. Next door, Mrs Dengu was wailing.

'Damba,' Father said.

'*Baba*,' I answered him my heart pounding afresh, afraid he was going to ask me a question about a crime I had committed but had somehow forgotten.

76

'You are quite, quite, quite sure you were not playing with Pamba this afternoon?'

'Pamba left on his own soon after we came back from school.'

'Is anything the matter?' Mother asked. 'Have they found him?'

'There has been a report at the police station. Some people who were fishing on Seke Dam this afternoon saw a boy wading into the dam ...'

Father didn't finish what he was saying because there was banging at the door.

'Who is it?' Father called out angrily.

'I want to talk to your son.' It was Mrs Dengu.

'Our son is asleep. You will talk to him tomorrow.'

'No. Tomorrow is too late. I want to talk to him NOW. NOW!' Mrs Dengu's already hoarse voice, was rising.

' I thought the police told us ... '

'Are the police going to bring back my son?'

'Mrs Dengu, we are not yet certain that it was your ...'

'Oh? So you are not yet certain? You want to see if it was him first? You aren't going to be happy if it wasn't him? Your son ...'

'Will you please leave my son out of it?'

'Leave your .... Ronia?' Mrs Dengu was shouting.

'Go to sleep, Mrs Dengu,' Father said.

'Go to sleep? Ronia! Are you asleep, Ronia? Can you sleep when ...' Father banged the door shut in Mrs Dengu's face. He turned the key in the lock and turned to face us. He sighed, leaning against the door.

'Is he dead?' Mother asked in a whisper, her hand on her chest.

Father shook his head. 'We don't know yet.'

Mrs Dengu was screaming and banging on the door again.

'The people who gave the report to the police said they saw him, or whoever it was – wading into the water. They didn't pay much attention to him. But then, when they looked up later, they couldn't see him.'

'Open up and tell me what you have done with my son!' Mrs Dengu screamed.

I heard the squeaking of a gate and looked out of the window. Mr Dengu was coming into our yard. He came to our door. I heard him talking quietly to his wife. But Mrs Dengu screamed: 'No! No! No! I am not going anywhere until he tells me what he has done with my son!'

There was a loud clap and Mr Dengu hissed, 'Don't be a fool!' Then he must have put his hand over Mrs Dengu's mouth because I heard her muffled scream as if she had been gagged. I heard them struggling. There was another clap and Mrs Dengu suddenly became quiet. Then I heard feet shuffling away and a noise as if something were being dragged along the ground. Our gate squeaked open and shut. Then I heard the Dengus' gate opening and banging shut.

'What did the police say?' Mother asked.

'They said they will have to call in divers tomorrow,' Father said weakly. He moved away from the door and went into their bedroom. Mother followed him in, saying, over her shoulder, 'You go to sleep, too, Damba,' as if she were afraid that I, too, might just slip out of the house and never come back.

Sometime around eleven o'clock the following morning, I asked my class teacher if I could be excused to go to the lavatory. But I didn't return to the classroom for the last two lessons of the day. I went home. There were groups of people on the streets. Some people were coming from the the dam, others were walking out towards it. The colour of the light on the streets was strangely soft and sad, as in some of my dreams. I gathered from the conversations I overheard that the police were still searching the dam for Pamba's body. I heard that his shirt had been found in the hollow of our rock. His parents had identified it as his.

There was no one at home. I retrieved the front door key from under the stone where we kept it and entered the house. Then I quickly changed into my street clothes, went out and locked the door behind me. After putting the key back under the stone, I ran towards Seke Dam. There were people everywhere going and coming back from the dam.

People were standing in a line almost half a kilometre long beside the water's edge. In the water, I saw several figures in diving gear. There was an unusual silence hanging over the crowd. Somewhere I heard Mrs Dengu wailing. Her voice was now hoarse. I walked towards her but I don't think she would have either seen or recognized me, even if I had stared her in the face. She was a mess: one eye was so swollen it was almost closed, there were welts and swellings on her face which was already swollen and distorted from crying, her clothes were torn, and her feet dragged on the ground. Mother, Mrs Gwaze and other women from our street were with her, holding her back as she made as if to throw herself into the dam. A little further up slightly detached from the line of people on the bank stood my father, Mr Dengu and men from Chaminuka Ward. They were silent, their eyes fixed on the police divers working in the dam.

78

I walked along the line of people until I reached the group of children. They were telling each other larger and larger lies about drowning, comparing it with other drownings some of them claimed they had seen, in real life or in the movies. I looked around until I spotted Dura and his gang and I walked over to them. They were solemnly quiet. I went and stood beside him. He must have sensed my presence. He turned and said, 'Hi, brother Damba.'

'Hello, Dura.'

'Is it him?' I asked in a whisper, aware of the heavy, depressed silence around me.

'They found his shirt tucked in the hollow of that huge flat rock where you play,' Dura said.

My heart gave a violent kick and I thought my knees would give way under me. I looked down into the water and then quickly up and away from it.

I heard myself talking as if in a dream, as if I wasn't responsible for the words that came out of my mouth.

I said, 'He must have been trying to retrieve the chicken that he threw into the dam.'

'I don't know,' Dura said absently, then, he gave a sudden jerk, and focused his eyes on me and said, 'What chicken?'

'That chicken, you know. The one he stole from your party on Saturday. He didn't finish it all. He threw the rest of it into the dam.'

Dura looked quickly at me, and then away. He moved as if to get away from me. I followed him.

'He wanted me to bring the uneaten part of the chicken to you so that you could ask your mother to give him the neutralizing medicine.'

'What are you talking about?' Dura said, his voice a trifle shaky.

'The poisoned chicken. You told us about it.'

'I don't know of any chicken ...'

'We can ask the boys here,' I said. 'They were there. They heard you.'

'Ask them. I don't know of any chicken. You are making it up. You are lying. You just want to get me into trouble with my mother.'

'But you said he stole a chicken at your ...'

'There was no chicken stolen from anywhere.'

'You said ...'

'I didn't!'

'You said ...'

'I didn't!'

I looked around for witnesses from his gang. They were all backing away. None of them wanted to be involved.

'You ...'

'I didn't!'

I pushed him, hard, on the chest and he fell into the shallow water. His gang scattered. He tried to get up out of the water. I pushed him back in again. Then he grabbed me by the ankle and pulled. I fell on my back into the water. We splashed about and then I was sitting astride him on his chest and his head went under the water. He gurgled and hiccuped. He couldn't even scream. His glasses cracked and slid off his face and fell into the water and his weak eyes were wide, rolling and unfocused in fear. His hands were raised and groping, his fingers clawed at the air as his head went in and out, in and out of the water. A sharp stinging clap stopped me deaf and blind. I felt strong, rough hands hauling me up and out of the water. My eyes were closed, my ears ringing. Then a sharp voice hissed fearfully, 'Do you want to kill him?' I opened my eyes.

I saw the figure of one of the divers wading out of the shallow water towards us. In his arms he carried the limp body of Pamba. I saw how Pamba's head drooped back unnaturally, how his arms and legs, bent at the knees, hung down, water dripping from them. Intense light was shimmering off the boulders on the green tree-fringed opposite bank of the dam. A lone white bird stood stock still on one of the large grey rocks along the water's edge as if supervising the events on our side of the water.

A single female voice pierced the silence of the afternoon,

'P–a–mb–a–a!' shattering my vision of the man carrying Pamba's lifeless body into many rainbow-edged images and then the wailing began, low at first and climbing higher and higher into a deafening crescendo. Beyond the head and shoulders of the figure carrying the body, the white bird rose into the air and flew up-river, over the shimmering surface of the water, emitting a weird quawk-quawk sound.

Another horrible sound near me made me turn my head. Dura was on his hands and knees, vomiting – retching, groaning and heaving up spurts of clear water streaked with a sickly yellow fluid.

I walked away from Dura and his friends. I walked towards the man holding Pamba's lifeless body who was standing just out of the water, his head bowed, holding Pamba in his arms as if he were making an offering of him to the people. Then he gently laid him down on the grass at the water's edge, stepped back and stood looking down at Pamba. One of the women came forward, unwrapped her *zambia* and spread it over the body. She stood back and started to sing a popular hymn for the dead. We all joined in: one strong powerful voice.

Something caught in my throat. I could neither swallow nor spit it out. Blindly, I walked away from the crowd. I went into the bush, up to our rock. I lay on my back on the rock and looked up into the infinitely blue sky. I imagined Pamba's soul making his journey out there, travelling on and on and on, further and further away forever and alone.

Pamba is King of the Hill –
Who says 'No' he will kill

Then I cried.

I cried for the whole of the next two days as people came and went in and out at the Dengus' house. There was a huge gathering. Singing and wailing and the ceaseless thudding of drums. I didn't go to school for those two days. It was the first time I had decided on my own not to go to school. Neither Father nor Mother said anything. I could see that they were avoiding looking me straight in the eye. Their voices were very low and gentle when they spoke to me.

I looked over the hedge into Mrs Gwaze's yard. Dura was nowhere to be seen. I only saw his mother once, when she took a bag of mealie meal to the Dengus' house. She didn't stay for long. I heard later that she had had to go to hospital where Dura had been admitted with a severe attack of pneumonia. When she passed in front of our house, I looked at her. Her head was down and I didn't know if she was pretending not to see me. I didn't say good morning. I was sure she knew that I knew what she had done to Pamba. I was certain she could see the hatred in my eyes, a hatred that she must have felt burning a hole in her heart.

The day after Pamba had been buried at the Seke Cemetery, I saw a huge removal truck parked in front of Mrs Gwaze's house. Men in green overalls were lugging furniture from the house to the truck. After everything had been loaded onto the truck, it drove off, followed by a smaller car with a strange man at the wheel and Mrs Gwaze sitting beside him. I couldn't see Dura anywhere. I hoped he was still in hospital. Mrs Gwaze didn't even say goodbye as I stood at our gate, watching them leave.

Next door, in the Dengus' house, there was an ominous dark silence which we all felt pressing down over the neighbourhood, and which grew heavier and heavier.

Then one evening, Mrs Dengu walked out of the gate, carrying a huge trunk on her head and a smaller suitcase in her hand. She walked out and walked down the street without looking back, or saying anything to the people who looked at her from their gates on our street. I never saw her again.

The evening following Mrs Dengu's departure, Mr Dengu brought some bottles of beer in a carrier bag to our house. My father was home. They sat on chairs in our verandah, drinking. They drank until very late, talking in very low, subdued voices. At one point I heard Mr Dengu saying in a tear-choked voice, 'Tell me, Claver, what wrong did I do?' I didn't hear what my father said because at that moment I felt something as big as a boulder blocking my throat and I heard myself saying, 'You killed him! You killed Pamba!'

Mother, who was doing the dishes in the kitchen must have heard me. I was in the lounge kneeling on the sofa below the window that opened onto the verandah. Mother shouted at me in a very dark voice, 'Damba–a!'

I didn't answer her. I left the lounge and went into my room, banging the door so hard that the whole house shook. My hands were clenched into fists so tightly they hurt.

The Empty House

Gwizo Maneto had gained some notoriety, but not a lot of money, with his paintings. That was before he got married. While other people his age had graduated from college or university to become teachers, lawyers, doctors, accountants or were pursuing some other such prestigious career, Gwizo had dropped out of high school to devote his life to painting. Gwizo's father, Mark Maneto, a prominent Harare businessman, was very disappointed – so disappointed with his first and only son that he wouldn't talk about him in public. (There were two girls – one before and the other after Gwizo – but as Mark Maneto put it, both of them together didn't weigh as much as the boy.)

'What is your son doing?' friends and colleagues would ask.

'What son are you talking about?' Maneto would retort in a tone that silenced them immediately.

Art, among Maneto's people, was a foreign thing, a disease, something you didn't want to be associated with. It was like syphilis or some mental aberration. If, occasionally, they seemed to tolerate it, then it was in the same spirit that they tolerated children's games at twilight hour: watching them was just a way of passing aimless time. Art? For fart's sake!

'What work do you do?'

'I paint.'

'You paint? What? ... Houses?'

'No. Pictures.'

'You mean as a pastime? But I mean what's your profession? How do you earn your living?'

For some time after he had embarked on his painting career, Gwizo had begun to doubt the wisdom of his choice. He didn't want to refer to his painting as a career. A career was something you put on and took off, like clothes. Painting for him was a sacred calling, an inseparable part of his life like an arm or an eye.

Then he had married. He had married late in life, or so his family and relatives said. At thirty-two, other people would already be thinking: no more children.

Thirty-two, Gwizo often said ruefully, was just a year short of the age at which they crucified Jesus Christ.

'I won't allow any blasphemous talk in my house,' his father had shouted at him once, shocked to hear Gwizo saying this to Synodia – the elder of his two sisters –

who had mentioned that his delay in finding a wife would mean that he would still be worrying about things like nappies and school fees long after everyone else his age was building the house in which they would die.

'You're going to die a pauper,' Synodia laughed at him.

'And don't ever think that you're going to get a cent from me,' his father, not for the first – or the last – time, shouted from the lounge.

As a self-made man, who had also found God through his own personal efforts, Mark Maneto had become as stiff and unyielding as a slab of concrete, Gwizo told his friends. His heart was now so hard, it could only break, he said; a change of heart would be impossible. Gwizo's friends didn't take him very seriously.

They said that he could afford his directionless lifestyle, because he knew that his old man would leave him the transport business. But Gwizo understood that his father would rather sell the whole company – at a loss – to his worst enemy than leave it to him. As time passed, however, and as his views on girls – and women in general – mellowed, Gwizo's father began to entertain thoughts of leaving at least part of the business to his first daughter, Synodia, who had shown that she could take on any man by becoming one of the very few – if not the very first – women civil-engineers in the country.

'Why don't you give your degree to Gwizo?' Mr Maneto had said to Synodia on her graduation day. People had laughed but those closest to him knew that Maneto was serious. Maneto never ceased to worry about what he called his son's treachery. In his world, only sons were entitled to inherit their father's wealth.

Gwizo met Agatha MacFarlane at the first exhibition of his paintings at the National Art Gallery. Agatha had just come out to Africa from the United States of America on some cultural exchange programme. She was in fact so vague about it all that Gwizo was never quite certain about what had really brought her to Zimbabwe. The first thing she told him as they sat on a bench in Harare Gardens, behind the National Art Gallery, was that her informants on Africa had been wrong.

'They told you we were still living in trees?' Gwizo asked her.

'Well, not exactly, but something pretty close to it.'

'Do you mind ...'

'I am afraid it wasn't very complimentary.'

'We are immune to ...'

'No ways!'

She looked at him half teasing, half serious, putting out feelers to gauge how deep and how far she could go. And he seemed to give in too easily – her look softened, as if she were discovering something new, something her informant in the States had omitted from his briefing.

That first encounter in the National Art Gallery and the conversation, while eating hamburgers, Gwizo's idea – Agatha would have preferred something 'Zimbabwean' or at least 'African' – had led to other, longer and more intimate, meetings in different places all over town: cinemas, bars, restaurants, night clubs; walks in the park or through the high density suburbs, short-cuts down the dark, often dangerous, sanitary lanes; and endless hours in Gwizo's studio or his bed-sitter in the avenues, listening to his favourite music: Afro-jazz or Zimbabwe Chimurenga. Agatha resented the fact that Gwizo seemed to prefer to spend the daylight hours in his room or his studio, only venturing out after seven in the evening. She quickly pounced on this, confronted him with it, and almost succeeded in getting rid of his embarrassment at being seen walking with her in public.

'What's wrong with me?' Agatha asked.

'Nothing.'

'No. Don't give me nothing, Mister. You act as if I was something that crawled out from under a rock. Something you feel you must apologize for. What's wrong with me?'

And Gwizo preferred not to answer her, having realized, even in those early days of their relationship, that this would only entangle him further in nets that he had begun to sense that Agatha was putting out for him. He resented – even hated – her for always putting him on the defensive: everything had to be explained. Oh, God! Yet he secretly, almost guiltily, enjoyed being with her. He felt rebellious, adventurous as if he were headed for a place from which he would never return. Yet still, deep down, guilt lurked, a sense of betraying his people – as if he had an unfair advantage over them. Guilt clung at the edge of his mind, as he felt people pointing him out.

'We should get you out of the country one of these days,' Agatha said. She believed that Gwizo was still racially vulnerable since he hadn't yet been exposed to the more liberated international scene.

'I thought you mentioned that in the USA, racism was still ...?'

'In the backwoods, punk!'

He didn't quite believe her. Then he took her to meet his family. He had delayed doing this until he couldn't stand her asking any more. Of course, Sinikiwe, his younger sister, was ecstatic. She oohed and aahed at the sight of Agatha. She sat at her feet, unashamedly gawking at the white girl and Gwizo could see Agatha visibly ripening!

'Sinikiwe, for God's sake!' Gwizo shouted at her.

'Aah, *Bhudhi*. It's rare we get such a visitor in our family. Tell me, Miss MacFarlane ...'

'Agatha.'

'Sorry, Agatha. Tell me: Is it true that M.J. had facial operations to anglicize his face? Did O.J. really kill Nicole and her lover?'

Synodia remained at the other extreme, cold, unimpressed. (She had never been terribly impressed with anything Gwizo did.) And he found her coldness just as exasperating as Sinikiwe's enthusiasm.

'What are my chances in Hollywood, Ms McFar ... Agatha?'

'Oh, shut up!' Gwizo said.

'Well, what do you expect her to do – watching all those movies and indiscriminately gobbling everything if it's from the USA?' Synodia said, rising and leaving the lounge for her – the girls' – room. Gwizo thought there was more than just a reference to Sinikiwe in the word, `indiscriminately'. He looked at Agatha. She seemed not to have heard, thank God.

Gwizo looked over at his mother, knitting at her machine in a corner. She could have been in another room for all the attention she gave the young people. Yet Gwizo had more than once caught Agatha stirring in her seat under the unblinking gaze of his mother.

After the introductions, Mrs Maneto had wrung her hands, not knowing what to do. She had been happy when her girls came in and she had retired into the background – her knitting machine in a corner of the huge lounge – leaving her daughters to take care of Agatha.

But from her corner, behind everyone else, she had the best view in the room to watch what was happening among the young people. Soon, Agatha was aware of Mrs Maneto's questioning eyes. Mr Maneto hadn't even sat down for the introductions. Yet it was Sunday and Gwizo had chosen this day with his father in mind. Gwizo knew everyone would be at home on Sundays including his ever-busy father. But, after the introductions, Mr Maneto remembered a little business he had not been able to conclude at the office, and apologizing to Agatha, drove off in his Benz. But – as Gwizo noticed – not without first taking a long appraising look at the white girl. Gwizo was a little surprised at the positive response Agatha seemed to provoke in the Old Man.

'Why not drop in at the office some time and I'll show you around?' Mr Maneto had said before driving off. 'Then you can tell me what you think of us?'

'Oh, can I, really?' The enthusiasm that Gwizo heard in Agatha's voice told him that she, too, had been caught in the Old Man's snare. People called it 'charisma' and Gwizo wondered whether he would ever understand what the word meant; if his father had it, then it must be the smell of an old man's sweat – something akin to soil.

'Isn't he something?' Agatha said.

'He is something, all right,' Gwizo said.

'I mean – he's so *alive*. He's all there – if you see what I mean.'

'I wouldn't be taken in, if I were you. He's a businessman, after all.'

Gwizo had a private interview with his mother, when the two of them found them-selves in the kitchen. Gwizo was roasting peanuts in salted water and Mrs Maneto followed him in, closing the kitchen door softly behind her.

'Are you planning to marry that … that …?' Mrs Maneto asked.

'Her name is Agatha, Mother. Agatha MacFarlane.'

'Are you going to marry her?'

'Is there anything wrong with that or with her?'

His mother raised her hands in the air, palms open, in a gesture he had come to associate both with the crucifixion of Christ, and with Pontius Pilate washing his hands. Being the other – lesser – half of Mark Maneto, had left very few gestures in her repertoire. She said, 'You will be the second man in the history of the Maneto family to sleep with a white woman.'

'Oh?' Gwizo hadn't heard about the first one.

'Your great-grandfather,' Mrs Maneto said. 'Haven't you heard your father swear-ing sometimes?'

'"I swear on the head of Chigiga Maneto whom the whiteman hanged?"' Gwizo remembered.

'That's your great-grandfather. They hanged him for raping one of their women.'

'I'm sure the woman asked for it,' Gwizo said, suddenly depressed.

'But did her men want it?' Mrs Maneto's eyes fixed Gwizo to the spot.

'It's almost the same as it is in the USA,' Agatha said when he told her about the story of his great-grandfather. He sensed that she was slightly disappointed.

'Look. I don't live with my parents now,' Gwizo tried to comfort her, feeling Agatha's unspoken criticism of his family.

'Everything looks so like a bad replay of everything at home,' Agatha insisted. Sometimes she would take issues so badly that it frightened Gwizo and he had learned that the best thing to do was to keep quiet. 'Every goddam thing bloody looks like a bad replay,' Agatha repeated. Yet she didn't take the next plane back, nor did she disappear into the encroaching bush. Instead, she moved into Gwizo's bed-sitter. She had been staying at a YWCA hostel with the other cultural exchange students on her programme. Her excuse for coming to live with him was her desire to learn his language. One day Gwizo had to drive three hundred kilometres to Bikita to see his grandmother, his mother's mother. Agatha insisted on accompanying him.

'There is nothing to see out there,' Gwizo had said.

'That means there must be something,' she retorted obstinately, in the hard-headed, self-assured way that so embarrassed and irked him when they argued in the presence of other people. At such times, he felt like strangling her.

In Bikita Communal Land, Gwizo stopped at Nyika Growth Point, five kilometres from his grandmother's home. Gwizo introduced Agatha to some relatives – distant aunts and uncles. They all wanted to be photographed standing next to her. It took over an hour before they were able to release themselves and resume their journey. Three relatives even offered to ride with them to Gwizo's grandmother's. They would walk back to Nyika.

Agatha fell in love with Gwizo's grandmother. The Old Woman made Agatha some peanut butter to take back to Harare. She also told Agatha that she should have a baby as soon as possible so that she could have the joy of holding it before she left to join her forefathers. She called them, Those who Have Gone Ahead.

'I would like to hold Gwizo's child in my arms before I leave this world,' the Old Woman said. Agatha was deeply moved by the way she talked of death and her pending journey to join her ancestors. She felt the importance that the Old Woman placed on holding her grandson's child.

'And you choose to live in the city,' Agatha later chided Gwizo.

'Are you serious?' Gwizo looked at her, amazed.

'I wouldn't mind living here forever,' she said and Gwizo prayed that she was only joking.

'You wouldn't like it here in the dry season,' Gwizo said.

'Wouldn't I? Try me.' Of course. Gwizo had read stories of how *they* came out here with half-baked romantic notions of `going African', even `going savage' or whatever term was in vogue at the time.

But then *they* didn't have to live the rest of their lives here. They had money, a return ticket and a country to go back to.

'You are, after all, still gripped by whatever they told you in the States.'

'And I wish they'd been right.'

Gwizo looked at her irritated. He said, 'I don't mean anything to you, do I? I'm just another commercial item you've picked up on your great romantic safari through Africa ...'

'Don't say that,' Agatha answered, pained. Because Gwizo's outburst had reminded her of the money they had started to make out of Gwizo's paintings. It had arrived like a tropical deluge, something that threatened to cause a flood. It was as if everything had been waiting for Agatha.

She had introduced a handful of her friends in the cultural exchange programme to Gwizo's work. Then, somehow, mysteriously, word had spread like a veld fire and Gwizo had been 'discovered'. In less than two months he had become the talk of the town – and beyond. Rich international art connoisseurs claimed that Gwizo's paintings were as great as – if not greater than – the Shona sculpture which they had been shipping to their home markets in their diplomatic bags.

Agatha seemed to have abandoned her cultural programme as she busied herself with arranging exhibitions, fixing meetings, negotiating deals and trips. She became, in short, his agent. More than his agent. There is a painting – the only one from this period of his life – that Gwizo did of Agatha. He reveals her as his Guardian Angel, Lucky Star, Muse, Mother, Sweetheart, Confidante. She is an explosion of benevolent expletives in colour and form, an ecstatic dance eulogizing liberated, liberating woman. And Agatha seemed to have found her mission in life.

In the confusion of all this heady excitement, Gwizo Maneto and Agatha MacFarlane got married. How it happened, Gwizo would never be able to explain. It wasn't quite a marriage, people said, although there had been a priest, a wedding ceremony and a party. People had come more out of curiosity to see the bride than to celebrate the beginning and addition of yet one more family to the Maneto clan. How could it be called a marriage when there had been no bride-price paid to the bride's people? And who had ever heard of a woman who got married in the absence of her own parents; wedded without her aunts to give her away to the groom and his people? It was really a joke and people had come to Gwizo and Agatha's wedding to laugh.

Gwizo's marriage had also been another big thorn in Mark Maneto's side. Just the thought of the potential colour of his grandchildren gave Gwizo's father heartburn. 'A wedding? What wedding are you talking about?' Mr Maneto said to his friends in his office in Harare's heavy industrial area on the day Gwizo married Agatha MacFarlane. Mr Maneto had ignored the invitation which would introduce him to the members of the American diplomatic corps who were standing in for Agatha's people.

'From this day on, I have no son,' Mark Maneto declared to his family and relatives.

'But, Dad ... ' Sinikiwe protested.

'But Dad what?' her father glared at her, his hand on the heavy metal buckle of his belt.

'How am I going to face my friends at the Mother's Union?' Mrs Maneto moaned, wondering at the same time whether they had turned up for her son's wedding. Whatever tradition might say about marrying across colour and culture lines, she was proud of Gwizo. Wasn't it the fashion these days to go to America and England for everything? So why buy them if they could be acquired simply by marrying into them?

89

Mrs Maneto was proud of her son. Although, buried deep in her heart, lay a great shame and an unexplained fear.

'Let them go and live in America,' Mr Maneto said but Mrs Maneto, who had after all lived with him for many years, thought she detected a false note. But whatever her father-in-law might say, Agatha was determined to do the right thing. She would have a full traditional Zimbabwean wedding, as she called it. She ferreted out of Sinikiwe and a reluctant Synodia how 'these things are done.' And so she found herself impressing everyone by going through the whole new-daughter-in-law ritual of delivering bath water to all members of the Maneto clan. Only Mr Maneto wouldn't accept her water and face-annointing oil. She even managed to get Sinikiwe to persuade Synodia to accompany her on the long drive to Bikita to deliver water and oil to Gwizo's old grandmother. The Old Woman danced and ululated and gave Agatha a nanny-goat heavy with young as a wedding gift to 'start you on your way into the Maneto fortunes'. Gingerly, the Old Woman stretched her hand and touched Agatha's flat belly and looked keenly but shyly into her eyes.

'Not yet?, she asked, seemingly disappointed.

'Very soon, *Ambuya*, very soon,' Agatha said, laughing tremulously, deeply touched. And at that moment Agatha decided tearfully that she would have children, lots of children, if only for the Old Woman's sake.

'Make it very very soon,' the Old Woman said. Gwizo was very much against the whole business of Agatha going all the way to Bikita and 'making a fool of herself'. Very few people paid any attention to that piece of ancient ritual. Also, the very idea of parading herself in front of all those rustics – Gwizo found it abhorrent.

'Do you know what you are doing?' he asked Agatha, embarrassed beyond words.

'Isn't this how it's done?' It was how it was done but not many people took any notice of these ceremonies any more. And he felt that she, especially, didn't have to do it. It just wasn't right. Not at this time, at least. What he meant was, a lot of things could go wrong: an accident could befall her.

Deeper down, he felt the heavy disapproval of his father. Throughout the ceremony he had been aware of the dark hawkish figure of the Old Man standing and glooming in the dark background, making the shadows darker, hurling curses at the shame and ignominy with which his own son had seen fit to crown his nights and days of labour. Gwizo might have been scared of his father, and felt his ominous presence, but Agatha seemed to think differently.

During the first two weeks in the Maneto household she felt increasingly convinced that the Old Man was the most likable of the lot. Masculine pride made him grumble and growl but Agatha knew instinctively that after some time a deeper understanding could be reached, like water in the wells round the huge garden. She was already a hit with Sinikiwe whose naiveté and frivolity she was beginning to find boring. Synodia held herself aloof, as if sitting in judgement. And most of the time she found the mother frightening. Her silence made her nervous, so nervous that she didn't dare do the dishes in Mrs Maneto's presence. Already she had broken three of her mother-in-law's most treasured china pieces: a teapot and two cups. Agatha hadn't liked the pieces, she had found them false and pretentious – unlike Mrs Maneto herself, whom she felt was made of more solid and durable stuff, but she had not meant to break them. She didn't know how it could have happened. She wasn't usually so clumsy.

'Oh, Mother. I am sorry,' Agatha had said, showing the older woman the broken pieces.

'Never mind,' Mrs Maneto winced, laughing.'Synodia and Sinikiwe have already destroyed half the china in the house. Those girls have buried me ten times over in my grave.'

'But if I go on like this, I will bury you another ten times,' Agatha thought to herself.

What Mrs Maneto called china made Agatha really sad. It was cheap and mass-produced as was the glass, most of the furniture and the plastic flowers on the dining-room table. Now she realized what she had found so disconcerting, everything was so like a cheap replay of the USA: the fast-food restaurants sprouting up all over the capital, the many high-rise glass buildings, the Coca-Cola adverts, the baseball caps. Sinikiwe's favourite soap operas were *Dallas* and *Santa Barbara*. Agatha felt desolate: she couldn't say anything, of course.

She realized she had come out to Zimbabwe for something else and that something she had found in some of Gwizo's paintings. Then she remembered how Gwizo's father had refused to wash his face when she took him the ritual, new daughter-in-law's bath water. This still hurt and rankled, despite his softening attitude towards her over other things.

'Do you think he hates me?' Agatha appealed to Sinikiwe. She wouldn't dare ask Synodia. They were all – the three of them – sitting in the garden one Sunday morning. She was reading and Sinikiwe was doing Synodia's hair. Mr Maneto had just driven off in his Benz. He had only nodded his 'Good morning' to her and Agatha had the feeling that she was the reason why he wouldn't now spend his Sunday mornings with his family. Gwizo was out at his flat in his studio. Or so he said.

'He seems to be running away from me,' she said to the girls, talking of Mr Maneto. Sinikiwe looked at Synodia and Synodia looked away laughing. Sinikiwe giggled.

'Do you know something I don't know?' Agatha asked. She could feel the heat rising in her face. She couldn't recall when last she had felt like this.

'He thinks you are very brave,' Synodia said, seriously.

'I am sure if you offered him that washbasin to him now he would accept it,' Sinikiwe said and Synodia gave her a playful dig in the ribs. Then both of them burst out laughing in a high-pitched tone that Agatha still found a bit vulgar.

She shut her book and left them. Loneliness had nothing to do with being with people, but being with people who didn't understand each other. She heard the two girls clapping their hands together and laughing even louder. Through one of the windows she now saw Mrs Maneto sitting at her knitting machine, looking out at her.

'It's the way you sit,' Gwizo told Agatha rudely when she asked him why his mother always seemed to be staring disapprovingly at her and why his sisters would sometimes not give straight answers to her questions.

'What's wrong with the way I sit?' Gwizo looked at her hard and then turned to walk out of the studio – Agatha quickly barred his way.

'You aren't getting out of here till you give me an answer.'

'You really want to know?'

'Yes.'

Gwizo pushed her out of the way and left the room.

Gwizo had inexplicably dried up after he got married. But he hadn't noticed as his paintings still continued to attract the attention of the rich international buyers. He enjoyed a secret satisfaction at seeing some of the so-called local chefs and cultural know-it-alls forced to buy his pictures which until recently they would hardly have looked at, let alone bought. Now, because America and Europe had opened their eyes to the treasure under their own noses, there was an indecent stampede to collect them. Sometimes Gwizo felt an almost irresistible urge to sell them a blank canvas with his signature on it. He thought they would probably buy that as well.

In private, Gwizo told his wife that she had brought him luck. Agatha had indeed brought him more than just luck – she had brought him fame and, most important of all, money. There was, suddenly so much money flowing through Gwizo's fingers and so much said and written about him in the galleries and the media that he didn't notice that he was spending more time among people, mostly strangers and admirers, throwing parties – Agatha's idea – than in his studio. He had no reason to doubt that he would go back to work – very soon. He needed the break. He was on honeymoon, he told friends.

And Agatha was so proud of him. 'Mrs Gwizo said' was the catch-all name women in her own circle of friends had given her from her habit of prefacing nearly everything she said with the words, 'Gwizo says,' as if she could not say anything on her own and feel she had said it right, or, if it were right grammatically, she couldn't vouch for it being culturally or politically correct, so she always had to bring in Gwizo's name.

'She's got him wound round her little finger,' the cynics among those who professed to be close to the Gwizos would say.

And indeed, in secret, her voice reiterating his name to other women was like music to Gwizo's ears. If he sometimes found her habit of beginning with 'Gwizo says' rather embarrassing, even tiresome, secretly he enjoyed the attention it brought him. By nature he was quite modest, a bit withdrawn – almost taciturn – to the point of being considered rude.

Whenever Agatha's friends were around at their house, or in the small open-air gallery Agatha had set up in the very small garden in front of their flat, Gwizo would quietly slip out into his studio, not so much to work as to have one or two glasses – usually more – of vodka just before slipping out through the back door to meet his own friends at the local bottle store. They were not really friends but hangers-on, vultures that had suddenly smelled raw flesh …

On the days that he drank in his studio, he would always have a blank canvas propped up on the easel in front of him. On such days (which, as he made more friends at the bottle store, became fewer and fewer), he felt as if at any time he chose, he could pick up his brush and bring out the one painting that he knew was still in him, the one he knew he had been born to paint.

And so he wasn't too alarmed when he woke up in his studio staring at the dusty blank canvas. Such dry spells happened to artists, he had read somewhere. (Agatha brought home books on artists, musicians, writers who lived for ten, fifteen, even twenty years without producing anything.) It was nothing new.

He also discovered that he liked to talk *about* paintings and painters. He had collected enough information on some painters to hold a group of ten or more art enthusiasts enthralled by his perceptions. Indeed he now found it easier to talk *about* paintings than to paint. He wouldn't mind going on a lecture tour of the States or Europe. There was easy money to be made.

Gwizo became his own best publicity agent.

And around him the beer flowed as he talked. They renamed his favourite drinking place after him. Local people who didn't understand his paintings or who had never looked at, let alone bought, any of his pictures, began to point him out to each other on the streets. Complete strangers would walk up to him and offer to buy him a beer. But it would all end up with him giving another lecture on art and his life and buying the strangers round after round of beer.

'I like your paintings.'

'Which ones in particular?'

'Oh, that one with ... the, with the ... Which ones did you paint by the way?'

So the days, weeks, months, a year, two years, passed with Gwizo drinking each day more heavily than the day before. At home, his people grew deathly quiet. Although they seemed to be laughing at him, they greeted him with respect: the presence of his name in the daily papers and on TV must, after all, mean something. But they couldn't help wondering about Agatha. Wouldn't a baby make her look less strained? Smoothen out her body and make it less angular? Wouldn't it make her look less hurried, harried and worried? She was making money for Gwizo – yes, that was accepted – but, still, she would be more respectable, people would take her more seriously if she had a child ...

'We are on our honeymoon,' Agatha joked, less easily now than during the first year of her marriage, trying to explain why she wasn't pregnant. She had really begun to be afraid of having a baby. And, afraid to face Gwizo's people and their unanswered questions, she threw herself into her work as if a demon was driving her. She buried everything in the promotion of Gwizo's art.

She pretended not to hear what they said about her, that she was growing thinner and thinner as if she wasn't eating normally. They didn't speak openly to her but she began to notice empty spaces opening up around her each time she entered a room in which Gwizo's relatives were gathered. At first, Gwizo had been supportive. He would comfort her, 'All they can think about is having babies,' he would say. But now she wasn't so sure any more.

'I have friends who would give anything to have a child by you. What is it you black men see in white women?' The way Synodia had said those last words, in Agatha's hearing, made the white woman feel that what Synodia really wanted to say was 'white bitches'.

Agatha wasn't sure of Gwizo any more. He seemed to be drifting further and further away from her. Not, she thought, that he had ever really loved her.

'Don't you think you should lay off the booze just a little?' Agatha cautiously asked him. One could never talk to men about their drinking habits, but Gwizo was rarely sober. And she had discovered – or was perhaps more ready to acknowledge – that he was capable of crude cultural barbarism that sometimes knocked the breath out of her.

'*Rega ndidye mari dzangu!*' he had barked, and the force of those words prematurely brought on her menstruation. And when Sinikiwe had told her what the words meant, Agatha felt, not for the first time, that she was a long long way away from Dubuque Street, Iowa City. She had promised herself that she would never again say anything about his drinking. But she couldn't just watch him sinking: he was going down fast.

'You realize this can't go on, don't you, hon?'

'What can't go on and on?'

'One of these days you've just gotta turn round and face facts, haven't you?'

'What the hell are you talking about, woman?' Agatha winced at the hate-loaded word. Now, she had become *woman*?

'Tell me, honestly,' she said, 'is there something I am doing wrong?'

'Listen. You just stop chattering and listen. Do you hear anything?'

'No. I don't hear anything. What am I supposed to hear?'

'That's right. You don't hear anything because there is nothing to hear. The house is empty.'

'I don't understand, Gwizo. Are you ...'

'You're afraid the kid will be a chimpanzee, aren't you? Just like the kids you see around you: chimpanzees, baboons, monkeys – all wallowing in shit and muck and clambering up and down trees. That's what's bothering you, isn't it? You're afraid you will give birth to a moron.'

'Please Gwizo. I only suggested that you visit Alcoholics Anonymous. They just might help you. They ...'

'Who are Alcoholics Anonymous? Your Mafia brothers, I suppose?'

'Look, Gwizo. Two can play at this game. All I'm saying is that if I'm going to have a child, I don't want it to have an alcoholic for a father. That's all. I had enough of that in the States, thank you.'

Agatha was crying. She was exhausted. She was disillusioned. If someone had come along at that moment and said: Come on, let's go home, she would have gratefully accepted the offer. She would have been glad to drop everything and take the next plane to Cedar Rapids. But then she had a brain wave. Whether it was instinct or just common sense, didn't matter. She did what any traditional Zimbabwean daughter-in-law would have done.

'I've been to see your father,' she told Gwizo one evening as he was lying sprawled on the floor of his studio, a full bottle of vodka in his hand, an empty one lying on its side at his elbow.

'What about?' Gwizo snapped at her.

'He asked me to pay him a visit at his office one day. Remember?'

Gwizo didn't remember and at that moment he didn't care.

But one day his father paid him a visit at his studio. 'Don't lose her, sonny,' Mr Maneto said after the preliminary greetings, the self-conscious throat clearing and the cough-coughing. All of which made Gwizo stop and look at his father.

'I thought you were against our wed ...'

'Forgive an old man's short-sightedness,' Mr Maneto said, 'Weddings, *lobola*, they can cost you a fortune when you can least afford it.'

'Father?'

'I was wrong about her. I have since got to know her a bit better. She knows what she wants and she is going after it. If we had two or three more with her enterprising spirit in Zimbabwe ... . Look what she has done for you ...'

'She hasn't done anything for me, Father.'

'You have always been stubborn, Gwizo. You're a wasted night. Cattle can do what you've done. Pile up a lot of dung. Without knowing how to carry and use it in the fields, do you think you'd harvest anything on your own?'

'Still, I think I ...'

'Shut up and do something about your drinking!' Mr Maneto's right hand fingers were playing a tattoo on the heavy metal buckle of his belt.

'Is that what she complained about? My drinking?'

Mr Maneto sighed and shook his head, 'You'd be a fool to lose her.'

'You mean she'd be a fool to lose *me*?'

Mr Maneto waved him away as if he were a fly. 'Don't make me laugh. What have you got? The trouble with you young people is that you take our politics too much to heart and then ask all the wrong questions. There is such a thing as compromise. We wanted our land back, now we want them to teach us how to develop it. That's all. The rest is ...'

'Did you tell her that?'

'What?'

'That she is here to help us develop the land?'

'Listen. If you don't use her she will end up using *you*.'

Then Gwizo did something that he had never dreamt he would ever do. He shouted at his father: 'Get out!'

And his father, too surprised to notice who had issued the order, went out. Gwizo was exultant. Things began to move fast.

Soon after the exchange with Mr Maneto, Synodia came to see Gwizo in his studio.

'I hear Agatha has got a job with father. She is his new secretary and helping him in his transporting business. He in turn helps her with the shipment of paintings, and so on, to her country.'

'She is very smart,' Gwizo said.

Synodia was quiet for some time, then she turned to leave. At the door, she turned and faced Gwizo:

'*Bhudhi* Gwizo, think about what I said about my friends,' she said gravely, curtsied, turned her dignified back on Gwizo and went out.

Then, one day, as Gwizo was leaving his studio through the back door, he bumped into a lanky, dreadlocked young man. Gwizo knew him as a budding graphic artist, one of a number of young men who took themselves so seriously you could hear their satchels crackling with rejected masterpieces. Gwizo was familiar with that gaunt, starved, red-eyed look.

'Hi, One-Picture Gwizo,' the young man said, clearly spoiling for an early evening fight.

Gwizo stared at him open-mouthed, wondering whether he had heard correctly.

'Oh, stop the posturing, man. We all know you. You are done for and you know it. It's sad, man. Very sad.

'Who are you trying to fool? You shouldn't have got yourself entangled with that useless piece of washed-out white shit. You know what? She came, she saw, she stole. Forget painting, man. You give Art a bad name. You look and sound like you could make a successful Mbare shebeen politician!' And, cackling the high, drug addict's laugh, the young man disappeared into the stream of honest workers returning home from work. He was gone before Gwizo could collect himself. He couldn't even remember the man's name. Gwizo knew that the young man's words were out of spite. The young man really envied Gwizo's luck. But something at the centre of the young man's words frightened Gwizo.

Gwizo turned back through the door into his studio.

He locked it and sat down before his easel, looking at the blank canvas which had begun to yellow and curl at the edges. He began to sweat. He put it down to the many vodkas that he had already drunk. For the first time, Gwizo became aware of his growing fear of that blank canvas. It seemed to have acquired a life of its own, to be interrogating him. It looked like a black hole through which he would disappear forever – a yawning mouth, waiting to reveal the final truth.

Gwizo didn't realize it then, but this was when he started to cut out his visits to the studio, preferring to start his day at the local bottle store (the one named after him), at eight in the morning, and then sail homeward on a sea of vodka, arriving at around ten in the evening. Or even later.

'When are we going to have the honour of viewing the next masterpiece?' This was another day, at the Far Lane Gallery (one of Agatha's brainchildren), and the man, whom Gwizo greatly respected, was Mr Rashid, his ex-art teacher in high school. They had bumped into each other at Ranga's graphics exhibition. (Gwizo had now recalled the name of the dreadlocked bearded youth in the alley behind his studio.) Ranga had joined the retinue of Agatha's most recent discoveries, despite all the abuse he had heaped on her. Gwizo had come in at an hour when he knew the gallery would be so full that his chances of being spotted or running into Ranga or Agatha were virtually non-existent.

'Teacher,' Gwizo was pleasantly surprised, although the man's question made him feel very uncomfortable.

'The question, Maneto,' Mr Rashid pressed him, 'answer the question.'

'Oh, very soon. A bit of a creative block lately but very soon.' Gwizo still respected Mr Rashid and he felt uneasy about telling him such a blatant lie.

'Hurry up, then. Forget that illusory block and give us another masterpiece,' Gwizo's teacher said.

At that moment Agatha passed by. She saw who was standing talking with Gwizo, made an abrupt turn and joined them. She greeted Mr Rashid -- with much gushing, Gwizo thought -- and hardly acknowledged Gwizo's subdued, 'Hi.'

After some small talk in which the teacher praised Agatha for the excellent work she was doing for the young artists in the country, he said, 'I have just been asking the maestro here when he is going to treat us to another masterpiece.'

'Oh? And what does the maestro say?'

'Very soon, he said. As soon as he has worked through his creative block,' Mr Rashid said laughing and Agatha laughed with him. Gwizo gave a thin watery grin.

'Oh, really? I didn't know he had a creative block,' Agatha said, her eyes sliding over Gwizo's face. She went on, 'But then the maestro doesn't confide his secrets in me these days. He prefers to shock me with surprises. Excuse me. I have to meet Ranga. Imagine! He's just sold four of his big drawings. That young man is going places.'

And she was gone, leaving Gwizo staring after her. It wasn't what she had said but how she had said it that took him by surprise. But as if it were not enough for Gwizo to realize that Agatha had another life in which he now had little or no part, he saw Agatha turn to greet another very familiar figure. They stood talking together for a few seconds, then they walked side by side towards the door and out into the street. Gwizo was so astonished that he forgot his teacher standing beside him.

'They make a handsome, international father-and-daughter-in-law couple, don't they?' Mr Rashid said in a low voice.

'Who?' Gwizo started. 'Oh, yes. Quite.' He was wondering how many people's tongues had begun to wag. Harare could, at times, be such a small claustrophobic place.

'I didn't know your father was into art as well,' Mr Rashid said.

'It's not really surprising, Teacher. He is, after all, a businessman.'

'I had almost forgotten your charming sense of humour, Maneto.' There was a moment of silence in which Gwizo watched his father and Agatha disappear down the street.

'So, how's the home front?' Mr Rashid asked.

'The home front?'

'Any little geniuses yet?' Mr Rashid inclined his head in the direction in which Agatha had gone.

Gwizo's heart skipped a beat. He smiled — it was an awkward smile and he felt sure his teacher would notice — and shook his head in embarrassment.

'Don't worry. Children aren't everything, you know.' Mr Rashid was quiet for a second, then, as if he too felt uncomfortable, continued, 'Plenty of time for that. I know you'll do it. I don't doubt you.'

Mr Rashid put his hand on Gwizo's shoulder and patted him. It was a very familiar gesture. The man had also occasionally taught athletics and he had used that pat more often than Gwizo cared to remember. After days of hard practice on the race track, he might scrape into sixth position, and then the coach would pat you on the shoulder, in exactly this way, and say, 'Well tried, Gwizo. Better luck next time.'

Gwizo felt dizzy. He left the gallery, took a taxi home and spent the rest of the day — and night — alone in his studio with a bottle or two of vodka.

It could hardly be called a quarrel — no, just a little early-morning exchange of words, the morning after the night that Agatha had brought Ranga home for dinner to celebrate their success. Agatha hadn't told Gwizo about this arrangement and he hadn't been prepared for it. He had told her so and she had answered, reasonably enough, that he had been even less prepared on other similar occasions.

'Or are we getting a little bit jealous?' Agatha had said, icily.

'Me? Jealous?' Gwizo said, giving the table, which had already been laid for dinner, a hard push. That had been the end of that dinner. Gwizo hadn't really meant to push the table over but when it happened, he suddenly felt elated and he bent down and picked up a couple of plates and sent them crashing against the wall.

It gave him a clean feeling of accomplishment. It brought back something that he had begun to feel slipping away. But later, alone, with a bottle of vodka, after Agatha had driven Ranga to a restaurant in town, after which, so she told him, they would go to a night club or to Ranga's place in Chitungwiza, Gwizo had felt sick.

A thought, or was it a realization, had crept up on him: *He would never be able to paint another picture again.*

He saw everything so clearly that suddenly the idea of taking his own life seemed very attractive. He thought of the different methods which might bring eternal rest. A razor blade, an open vein and blood all over the bathroom floor? Rather messy — and feminine. The traditional Zimbabwean cowhide rope round the neck and kicking off into space? There was something cowardly about that too. Also, he recalled stories of how in such a death, the sphincter muscles tend to loosen – Gwizo shuddered at the thought of the sight (and the stench) that would greet the first person to come upon his dangling body. No. That little mound of faeces would always point a finger at him even in death. A fistful of sleeping pills then? Or a phial of liquid pesticide? He had a vision of jilted pregnant housemaids, their wide-open eyes staring at forever-and-ever, a far-away heaven on the piss-besmirched kitchen floor. Or drown himself? There was a drought in the land and no water in the swimming pool in his parents' garden. And he didn't want to have to drive out to Lake Chivero or Seke Dam where some pedestrian – a fisherman, a herdboy or even a mouse trapper – would point a soiled finger at his bloated body bobbing up and down, among some reeds or cattails at the water's edge. There seemed to be no dignity or honour in death by drowning. Drive over the edge of a cliff (what cliff?) or smash into a tree? The car might burst into flames, leaving his half-charred body looking like some ancient log; or there might be a gash across his face and an eye bubbling out of its socket. No! What he wanted was a clean death, with his body intact, pointing at a heroic, dramatic end; a body that was in full control of itself right to its very last breath; a death that would make her pull up, stop and gasp and bring a lump the size of a cocked fist into her throat as she sank down on her knees in a cascade of tears. His legs would be stretched before him, head half-tilted back as if scanning the farthest horizons, his back resting against a wall, a thin, taut Clint Eastwood snarl drawn across his face, his hand firmly gripping the old *bhemba* stuck to its hilt in his guts just below the navel – his entrails ballooning out into his lap. *There* was a death with a future. Only the bit about the entrails ballooning out bothered him. He just might leave the old *bhemba* plugging the hole in the belly. But otherwise *there* was a death with a name. *Harakiri*. Trust the Japanese to come up with a vintage death. Strange, Gwizo thought. Then he felt very sad that even for a good death he had to go to a foreign country. He began to cry.

Then, as the fumes of the vodka lapped at the furthest shores of his inflamed imagination, he wondered whether there just might be, somewhere, in his dusty studio, some undiscovered, unfinished canvases that could be brought out soon after the announcement that he had died, died gloriously, something that would posthumously crown his career: The Unfinished Masterpieces of Gwizo Maneto. Or, better still, Gwizo Maneto's Last Testament. He didn't think he would have any such luck. She had cleaned him out. She came, she stole, she conquered ...

Agatha had returned towards daybreak. She found him sprawled on the dirty floor of the studio, before the blank canvas, a full bottle still clutched in his right hand, an empty one on its side by his head. Gently, Agatha prized the bottle from his fingers. She brought out a blanket from the bedroom and spread it out over him ...

The first thing he felt that morning was someone gently rocking him from side to side. He opened his eyes and saw Agatha's ankles and sandalled feet. He looked up and saw her looming above him, against a strange sky. His head buzzed with unspoken epithets and the light in the room seemed harsh. His mouth felt foul, a taste of ashes. He wanted a drink badly. He saw the empty bottle near him and lifted it to his mouth. Nothing. He threw it into a dark corner of the studio. It didn't even break.

'When are we going to see another masterpiece?' Agatha said, smiling and squatting down beside him. He saw the full bottle in her hand. He reached for it. She pulled it away out of his reach.

'Bitch,' he said.

'What did you say?'

'Give it to me, bitch.'

'Please,' Agatha said, bringing the bottle within his reach. He lunged for it. She pulled it away and he fell on his face, his arms stretched out before him.

'Please,' Gwizo pleaded. Agatha pulled his head up and let him take a gulp and then she forcefully pulled the neck of the bottle out of his mouth as a mother would her tit out of the mouth of a greedy baby.

'Please,' Gwizo said again. Agatha shook her head, saying: 'That's enough!' then she looked down at him for a moment and said, 'Ranga would like to see you. Just to see you. He really admires your work and all this time he didn't know how to approach you. You are his greatest inspiration.'

'Did you spend the night with him?'

'Yes,' Agatha said, kneading Gwizo's shoulder muscles, but her hand stopped moving and remained resting on his shoulder.

'What do you mean?'

'You know what I damn-well mean, bitch.'

Agatha's mouth fell open. For a moment her eyes blazed, then she bit her lower lip, slowly rose to her feet and straightened up to her full height.

'If you feel up to it, he's in the lounge. He's just got an hour. He is a very busy man.'

'And very active in bed, I presume?'

Agatha looked down at him, and then walked out of the studio. Gwizo watched her go as if she had been an apparition.

He tried to hold his head up but, slowly, it sank to the floor. He wanted very much to go back to sleep but he couldn't. The white heat that came with a splitting headache and self-lacerating words had been turned on.

He tried to think of Ranga but he realized that Ranga had nothing at all to do with it. Ranga was only an excuse, a scapegoat. Because ... because he found it hard to focus on the huge blurry image of the Old Man beside whom Gwizo felt himself to be a pale insignificant shadow ...

Gwizo's mother looked haggard and old, as if witches had been riding her for the past two nights. She was sitting at the dining-room table, drinking tea, alone, while her fingers pulled at loose threads in the jersey she had spent the previous night knitting.

'Tea?' she offered Gwizo as he sat down opposite her. Gwizo shook his head, no. They sat in a heavy silence. 'Your father is planning to go to America with your wife,' Mrs Maneto said, then after a sip from her cup: 'On business.'

'She is his secretary,' Gwizo said without enthusiasm. Mrs Maneto's mouth twisted distastefully. 'Did you know that I was your father's secretary, once? Before me, there were other secretaries – you're sure you don't want some tea?'

'No,' Gwizo said, shaking his head again.

'What have you brought into this house, Gwizo? I had begun to think that we had put all that behind us.'

'You sound as if it's all my fault, Mother.'

'Who said it's all your fault? It's only – only that – just that your father – it's just your father's insatiable hunger for new markets. And each new market takes him further away from home.'

'Well, it's the businessman's itch, isn't it?'

'You are certain you won't have any tea?'

'No, Mother.' They sat in silence. Gwizo noticed that his mother was plucking and pulling at a thread which was creating a long ladder in the otherwise well-knit jersey.

'Mother!' he exclaimed.

'What?' She blinked at him, then looked down at the jersey.

'Leave me alone. I have got a terrible headache.'

Sinikiwe was sitting on the old swing under the old *muonde* tree in the garden.

Gwizo came from behind her silently and gave the swing a sudden push. Sinikiwe started, gave a little frightened yelp and looked back at him, holding tightly onto the chain. She put her feet down and stopped the swing. Then she got off and started walking away. Gwizo grabbed her by the arm and turned her round to face him.

'Hey. It's me. Why is everyone suddenly treating me as if I were a criminal?'

'Let me go,' Sinikiwe hissed, her fists ineffectually pummelling Gwizo's chest.

'Don't you remember me?' Gwizo asked, flustered.

'I don't want to go to America, ever. It's a dirty, old ...'

'That's not what I asked.'

'Even if somebody gave me a million dollars ...'

'Shut up!' Gwizo shook her violently.

Sinikiwe began to cry. She wriggled free of his clutches and ran up the wide steps into the house. Gwizo looked up and saw his mother standing at the big front window looking out at them. And he remembered her standing there shouting down at them not to hurt each other as the three of them played on the swing when they were still young. And he realized that whenever she was angry or upset, Sinikiwe still behaved as if she were a child.

It was morning. Gwizo lay on his back in bed, smoking. Agatha came through in her morning gown. She had nothing on underneath. She had spent the night sleeping on a sofa in the lounge.

She went straight to the window, drew back the curtains and opened the window. A sheet of soft morning light leapt into the room bathing her in it. She stood for a long time at the window, looking out at the jacaranda trees along Livingstone Avenue. Birds were chirping in the trees. Traffic was roaring along the road. Children's voices. Agatha turned slowly to face Gwizo.

Gwizo gasped and held his breath. The exquisite shock of it – *Woman at Window* – the light behind her at the moment of her turning, outlining the profile of her face, her breasts, the warm curve of her belly, with the navel like a small sprouting horn, then the sharp descent into the dark depression below ... That was easy enough: what about the brief, piercing ache inside him? The thing that only comes once, never to be repeated? Because, he knew, even if she were to make that slow-turning movement a hundred times ...

'I thought I should tell you,' Agatha's voice cut through Gwizo's thoughts, her face now in shadow, towards him.

'I know already.'

'No, you don't. Listen. Your father has asked me to accompany him to the States.'

'On business. Is there anything else?' Gwizo said softly, icily, his eyes moving from her face, down to the little horn pushing through her delicate skin. Agatha followed the movement of Gwizo's eyes.

'I'd thought of getting rid of it.'

'Are you coming back or going for good?'

'Please, Gwizo. You are not listening.'

'I heard you. I said: Are you coming back or going for good?'

'Now I have decided to keep it.'

Gwizo was silent, studying her, in flames of colour where the light came into contact with her body: her face was in shadow.

'And what about my father? Are you going to give him the slip once you're in the States?'

'I haven't told him yet. But I'm not going with him.'

'You are going alone?'

'I have decided to stay.'

The cigarette dropped from Gwizo's fingers onto the blanket. He picked it up, his eyes not leaving Agatha's face. Now she was turning again to look out of the window. That ache: a box within a box within a box ... Now she had her back to him.

'I am going to live with Grandmother in Bikita,' she said.

Gwizo sat bolt upright in bed. He was about to ask, 'Are you out of your mind?' but her straight back, the erectness of her neck and the outward-looking stubborn head stopped him. He began to laugh. She remained very still, very erect at the window, bathed in the soft African morning light. And he suddenly stopped laughing. He coughed. He felt foolish in her dignified presence.

'And that ... that ... that?' Gwizo finally said, pointing at Agatha's belly with its soft bulge.

'The baby?'

'It's his, isn't it?'

'I did it for you.'

'It's his, isn't it?'

'He wanted an heir.'

'It's his, isn't it?'

'I have been to my gyno. A black man. Young, good-looking, soft-spoken, very fine, gentle hands. Doesn't poke things or fingers up one's ... He said it's a boy.'

'*It's his, isn't it?*'

She now turned to look at him. 'No, Gwizo. It's mine.'

Gwizo looked down away from the brilliance of her smile. He watched his own hand – his fingers – as he stubbed out the unfinished cigarette in the ashtray on the small table beside the bed. He went on putting out the cigarette long after it had been extinguished. He was fascinated with the play of his fingers, feeling the familiar itch slowly awakening.

'Bitch,' he said softly, under his breath. 'Bitch,' he repeated.

She stood at the window, with that wonderful light round her, smiling at him.

'Wouldn't you like to come with me to Bikita?' she said, slowly walking towards him. 'The play of light and shadow on the mountains there just about breaks my heart,' she said, sitting down on the bed beside him. She put her arms round his neck.

Gwizo stiffened, then relaxed as, slowly, in response he brought up his arms. Gently, his fingers encircled her neck.

'Gwizo?' Agatha asked, hoarsely, 'Gwizo.'

Of Lovers and Wives

In the middle of the night, in the midst of a very pleasant dream involving some children and some men, Shami shook him violently and asked him if he was dreaming about Peter. Chasi woke up. Shami was leaning on her elbow, looking down at him. She held the bedside lamp so close to his face the light hurt his eyes.

'What is it?'

'You are dreaming about him, aren't you?'

'Who?'

'You were calling out his name, smiling.'

'My God, Shamiso. You are not serious, are you?'

'What were you doing? Making love?'

Chasi sat up in bed. All of a sudden, he wanted to go to the toilet. When he came back, his wife's eyes followed him right from the door until he tucked the blankets under his chin. Chasi closed his eyes and pretended to fall asleep. She was staring at him. He could sense the intensity of her look through the thin skin of his eyelids. He turned the other way, but her eyes bored through the back of his head. Chasi stretched a hand out of the blankets and switched off the light. Shamiso switched it back on.

'Shami, please.'

'You haven't answered my question.'

Chasi looked at her hard. If she wants to suffer, let her, Chasi thought. 'Yes,' he said, 'I have been dreaming that we were making love.'

'I thought so. How was it? Better than when you make love to me?'

Chasi just stared at her.

'Can we have the light off now, please?'

'No.'

He hated it. He pulled the blankets over his head to keep out the light. But this only kept him awake. Even completely covered, the light somehow found its way into his head. Married for eighteen years, Shami knew very well that he could not go to sleep with the light on.

She was still on her elbow, looking down at him.

'What do you want from me, Shami?'

'Nothing worse than what you have already given me.'

'Look, if it galls you ... '

'If it galls you, he says! Will you just please listen to the man! If it galls you!'

105

Chasi sighed and let his head fall back on the pillow. He picked up a book from the headboard and tried to read. But, too tense to concentrate, he threw it on the floor, unable to read a word. He switched the light off, turned his body away from Shami and once again pulled the blankets over his head.

But Shamiso knew that he couldn't sleep. Neither could she.

It was so hopeless, Shami had to laugh. To tell God's honest truth, she was out of her depth. Chasi had managed to surprise her in a way she had never thought possible. Chasi? Her husband of all these years? And just when her daughter was engaged to be married.

Peter, on the other hand, she felt she could understand. She felt that his personality was so dark and ambiguous that nothing was impossible. Besides, having been a part of their lives for the last eighteen years, Shami had come to accept that Peter never seemed completely at ease with women. She had once asked Chasi if Peter was all right – biologically – and Chasi had told Peter this. The two of them had laughed at her so much that she had never again raised the subject.

Of course, they had assumed that she understood what they were laughing about. And now, looking for someone to blame, she knew she only had herself, realized with shocking clarity that the two men hadn't hidden anything from her, but that she had been blind to what was going on right under her very nose.

However, the surprise, when she stumbled on the truth, had been more of a shock for Peter than for herself. Peter couldn't believe she hadn't known that the two of them had been sharing Chasi for all these years. It was even more galling for Shami to realize that she had found Chasi already in – a spade is a spade – Peter's arms when she married him. So, she had been the fool all this time. She had loved Chasi so much that she had accepted Peter as part of her life without question. There hadn't been any talk about him living elsewhere when Shami entered Chasi's life and home as his wife.

And when their daughter, Kathy, came along, Peter naturally became the uncle that Kathy didn't have on either Chasi's or Shami's side of the family. Not that they weren't there. They just didn't seem interested in becoming part of their lives. Now Shami suspected that their relatives had sensed what was going on under their roof – Shami had previously put it down to the fact that no one on either side of the family had ever really approved of their marriage.

Shami had got pregnant in Form Four and her parents, strict Salvation Army members, had written her off as a bad investment. Chasi, on the other hand, had had to abandon his studies at University to get a job. His parents – a lawyer and an educationist respectively – had given him up for lost. Maybe that was the reason why it had been so easy for Peter to remain part of Chasi's life, and become such a close member of the young family? Or maybe both Chasi's and Shami's families knew what kind of man Chasi had been before he married Shami? They had known and kept quiet, waiting for Shami to find out for herself! And she had – eighteen years later. So she couldn't very well go and cry on their shoulders. She had made her bed, their silence seemed to have implied all along.

Shami had stumbled on the truth after Peter, a chartered accountant, had decided to form his own company.

'Would you like to join me, as a secretary?' Peter had asked.

Shami had been ecstatic. And Chasi had been more than encouraging. It was only then that she began to notice the late meetings and heavy silences in Peter's office whenever Chasi was present. And the office door that would be silently closed whenever she happened to pass by to and from her office and reception.

Of course, her few women friends seemed to have known about the situation as well. For a long time afterwards she hadn't been able to penetrate the screen of pity which lay between them. Why did they refer to her as 'Poor Shami!' behind her back? She now felt she understood the sudden silences, the glances exchanged – not hostile but wry. Why hadn't she bothered to find out the reason why? Or had she simply been afraid, afraid of their patronage or scorn?

Peter had made a lot of money, there was no denying it. More than she and Chasi had made jointly. And he had shared it with them. At first Shami had felt a sense of guilt, as if they were sponging off Peter, but Peter had characteristically laughed off her anxiety.

'I'm an orphan,' he'd said. 'You are my only people.'

It wasn't that Peter had to spend more money than was really necessary even in a normal family relationship: food when his turn came, rent, the bottle of wine or crate of beer for special occasions, a present for someone's birthday, then the Christmas or Easter treats. What she should have questioned was the way Peter spent money on more intimate presents for Chasi: expensive silk shirts, ties, socks, underwear. But she hadn't. Peter seemed like Chasi's younger brother, and Shami was thankful that she could then use their own combined salaries on the things the family really needed: a deep freezer, say ...

Chasi was the more bewildered of the two men when Shami confronted him with the truth. He couldn't see what bothered her. Peter, of course, took umbrage and retreated into silence and work.

Shamiso's first reaction was that both men had taken advantage of her. She didn't know what she would have done if they had told her right at the beginning. She tried to sound out Kathy on this and Kathy's response was to laugh. Shami was shocked. Could it be that the seventeen years between herself and her daughter had formed such an unimaginable gap? Had the world moved so quickly and so profoundly that she was now isolated? Kathy seemed her senior by generations! She couldn't bear to imagine what her own daughter must think of her!

She wanted answers to certain questions but no one seemed prepared to give them. Chasi was still bewildered, he couldn't help it. Peter, Peter seemed now to be living in a world of his own. It wasn't that he avoided her. He just wouldn't talk. But after weeks of total silence, Shamiso had to make a decision.

'You know we have to talk, don't you?' she said to Chasi one day in bed.

'What's there to talk about?' Chasi said.

Shamiso turned to him, genuinely surprised. He looked so innocently back at her that she wondered if she hadn't made a mistake – if people weren't just a little mistaken in thinking there could be something wrong in the character of people like Chasi and Peter.

'It isn't natural,' Shami said lamely.

'What is natural?'

The way Chasi asked the question, Shami knew, they were getting nowhere. She had been asking the same question and getting the same answer for the past month. Peter had simply taken refuge in silence.

'There is nothing natural or unnatural about it,' he had said. 'Once upon a time, the fact that the world was round was considered unnatural by the highest human authority in the world of that time.'

Peter hadn't bothered to go on, but Shami understood the implication.

It was, in fact, Peter who finally rescued them from the impasse, seeming to suggest, with an invitation to dinner, that there could be, after all, an answer to their joint problem – if problem it was.

Peter had arranged that after dinner they would go on to a party at a friend's restaurant off Chinhoyi Street when they would be joined by Peter's friend, Chegato, and his friends, for a drinking binge.

They met at the restaurant called 'The African' at five thirty in the evening. Peter told Chasi and Shami to relax as this was going to be a very long evening.

At first, Shamiso remained on the edge of their conversation as Peter and Chasi seemed to be talking about experiences in a world which Shami found hard to imagine. She realized with renewed shock that they had always engaged in this sort of unintelligible conversation and banter ever since she had come to live with them. Always, it seemed to Shami, the subject of their conversation threatened to disappear the moment they tried to bring it to shore. Again Shamiso had the exasperating feeling, and even more intensely this time, that she was the outsider, the intruder, the uninvited gate-crasher.

'Can't we discuss something we all understand?' Shami's voice was shrill after two double gin and tonics. She had become somewhat reckless with her drinking soon after discovering that for the past eighteen years she had been a stowaway on a boat bound for an unknown destination.

Chasi and Peter looked at her patiently. Patronizingly, she thought angrily. 'At least it can do no more harm than what's been done already,' she said, signalling the waiter for another gin and tonic.

Then Shamiso began to talk. Something in her mind seemed to have been let loose and she couldn't stop, except to gulp down her drink.

Chasi seemed to be suffering. Peter listened, his eyes never leaving Shami's face. Without realizing it, his hand hunted for Chasi's fingers and the two of them held hands on top of the table as Shami talked on. Whether she saw their entwined fingers or not, neither could say.

Shamiso said, 'I can't keep it all bottled inside me. It's driving me mad. When you're talking to each other, on the phone, I'm aware of the things you don't say, the things just between the two of you. I'm not part of your lives. I've been pushed to the periphery, to the place where the light ends, to the edge.

'Or like that day. We were in the middle of something intimate and he, Chasi, called out your name. I mean, he forgot me and I was right there, staring at his face and he forgot me! I couldn't believe it. I don't think he even noticed it because he went to sleep right away. I couldn't sleep. Over and over again, I asked myself what was happening to me and of course there were no answers. No, just more revelations.

'One day I came into the office and there were you two with your heads close together — your noses were almost touching — deep in conversation. You, Peter, saw me crossing over to the reception and you put out your hand and pushed the door shut. I stopped. I felt terrible. It hit me there and then how little I meant to you both. I had become the unwanted third.

'Since then I have watched you two talk together. I can see the way you look into each other's eyes and I have caught myself thinking: this is how it should be between husband and wife. But I couldn't imagine talking to *him* like that! I don't know how to talk to *him* like that. But I'm the one he accuses of being shallow, frivolous ...

'Or sitting at the dining-room table, I have always wondered how you seem to know each other's needs — a drink of water, a salt shaker. I notice how your fingers meet when you stretch to reach for something...

'It's possible I'm reading more than I should into such incidents but why should I apologize? I'm a stranger in my own house. I can't go on pretending that nothing has happened between us. I can't. I can't let go. I can't relax. I've told myself over and over again that I can't think of you this way ... It's wrong and it's not healthy, least of all for me. It is different now I know and it's tearing me apart but what the hell can I do?

'I think ... I keep on seeing you together, you know ... in those moments only meant for a husband and wife ... I see you then and I imagine you sharing experiences which Chasi will never share with me. Say Chasi has an accident? He won't think of me ... It's crazy. And I can't stop thinking like this ...

'I'm trying very hard not to blame anyone. But I think marriage and things like love and so on have to be worked for, they don't just happen like rain. I can't go on pretending that we're still together when ... when ... things are like this. I mean, it's hypocritical, isn't it, Chasi? Peter? Our lives are a lie?

'I mean sometimes I think it's time we thought, really thought about things like love, marriage ... Can they still exist or are they just arrangements put together, built out of our fear and loneliness because otherwise we wouldn't survive, we wouldn't ...'

Shamiso suddenly stopped talking. She didn't look at Peter or Chasi. But Peter could hardly take his eyes off her. And then he realized that he and Chasi were holding hands.

Shami looked at their hands, fingers entwined, on the table. She said, ' I just can't see how I can go on living with you like this, thinking these thoughts, seeing these things between you ... Someone has to be reasonable, someone has to stand up and say: Enough! No more pain, no more ...'

Peter couldn't stand it any more. He let go Chasi's hand and put his hand on Shami's shoulder. He said, 'You just have to trust us, haven't you? There is no other way. Can you think of any other way, Chasi?'

Before Chasi could answer, Chegato, Peter's friend, the owner of the restaurant, waved a bottle of whisky at them. He was making his way towards their table. Then somehow the bottle of whisky slipped from his hands and fell with a loud explosion on the floor.

There was a moment's silence, everyone looking down at the waste. Then Chegato shrugged his shoulders and said, 'It's only a bottle of whisky.'

But although they had another bottle of whisky, which they drank to music and danced until four in the morning, that first bottle seemed to Shami to symbolize that something more than just a bottle of whisky had broken.

In fact, they danced as they had never danced before, the three of them. At first Peter danced with Shamiso, but she seemed to prefer dancing with Chegato which left Peter and Chasi to themselves. Shamiso became reckless and hinted that she could go with Chegato, if she wanted to. But she knew that the two men knew that she couldn't do it.

When the telephone call came later that morning, it seemed that something which Shamiso had been expecting all her life. Somehow, the news had such a fitting rightness to it that she didn't feel grieved when she rang Chasi to tell him that, 'Peter has just had an accident. He died on the spot. If you are driving out there, could you come and pick me up?'

'Where did this happen?' Chasi asked almost beside himself.

'A few kilometres out of Chegutu. He drove into Mupfure River.'

That word, 'drove' seemed right, too. There could be no question about the rightness of certain situations, under certain circumstances. And when Chasi decided to leave town after Peter's funeral, preferring only to visit his wife occasionally during a weekend, Shamiso felt that that too had its own fitting rightness.

The Slave Trade

He was getting drunk, she could see that. He had begun to talk a little louder now, non-stop, not listening to them at all. And, Ravi felt, they were listening to him keenly, dangerously attentive. She saw how their unblinking eyes were fixed on him, how their shoulders were hunched, their heads pushed forward as if they didn't want to miss the slightest movement of his face or a word he said. It was too late now to tell him that they should leave for home — thirty kilometres on the other side of town. She had let that opportunity pass when they forced the first glass of whisky on him.

Still, she felt she too was to blame. He had looked at her, as if to ask for permission to continue. She had looked down and then he had shaken his head three times no. They had looked at her and she had only smiled, unable to say anything, and, of course, they had laughed — having uncovered their little family secret — and then, including her in a huge conspiratorial wink, they had asked her if she would let him — just today.

We are all friends here, Tim had said and Marara had grinned guiltily, sheepishly accepting the glass that the man, Tim, held towards him. And she, Ravi, had smiled — thinly — realizing that the day was already lost but unable to do anything about it.

She shuddered to think of the damage that he could do in this state if she tried to oppose him in any little way. Things like: You see — she thinks she should have been married to someone better than me. Or, she is ashamed of me because I am not dressed in a suit. He would of course later deny having said any such thing, saying that she always took advantage of him when he was drunk. And then he would go into a sulk for a week. She had learned to put up with these moods. Even to forgive him. But it was hard. He just didn't know what hurt other people. Even when not drunk, he often succeeded in saying something that hurt her. And now he was saying a lot that must hurt their hosts although they were trying to hide it — laughing a lot and winking at her, saying: Isn't he brilliant? And they kept on refilling his glass while they hardly touched theirs.

Ravi found it hard to feel at home in Tim and Joan's house. They had insisted that she call them by their first names but she found it almost impossible to break through hundreds of years of a law that forbids its subjects to refer to each other by any name other than their tribal totem or family name. So each time she found she had to mention Tim or Joan's name, Greene or Jones presented themselves. This was the first time that Tim and Joan had invited her and Marara to their house for a let's-get-to-know-each-other dinner, as they had called it on the invitation card. They had just had the dinner, it was the first time she had ever been invited to dinner by white people. And these were not just any white people. Mr Greene and Miss Jones were her husband's new employers.

We are not your employers, they had said. We are all colleagues working together. Marara had seemed euphoric but she had reminded him to remember himself. He was excited by the fact that he had been the first man they had approached since they came into the country – from, was it Zambia or England? – to open up a new company, one of the many companies that were being set up with emphasis on manpower development for the newly independent nation. They were not promising Marara a lot of money, they said, but he would be getting four times what he had been getting under the old colonial régime. And Marara would be one of the directors. Ravi had welcomed the money when Marara told her about the offer. She would be able to buy a stove, a fridge, a ...

He had been working for them for only three weeks and here he was – talking and talking and talking and accepting a further – fifth or sixth? – drink and they were looking at him so intensely, never letting their eyes off him as he rolled on, all brakes loose, an unharnessed cart going downhill. It wasn't the job that she was worried about now. The dinner she had just had seemed to stick in her throat. Tim and Joan seemed to be interested only in names of the big people and Ravi felt that Marara had let slip a little more than enough for one evening.

'Don't you think we should be thinking of going home?' Ravi said in a very low voice, leaning across the table towards Marara.

'Oh, come on Ravi,' Tim said. 'Tomorrow is Sunday, isn't it?'

'He doesn't beat you up when he is drunk, does he?' Joan said, winking first at Ravi and then at Marara. Had she been among her own people, Ravi would have told Joan never to speak to her like that again. Marara might drink himself blind but he would never ever dream of raising his hand to her. She realized she was getting angry as Joan went on to talk of some friends of theirs in Mozambique who would start a fight in their front yards, advance onto the veranda, right through the lounge, farther on into the bedroom where later on you would hear noises which you couldn't exactly call wife-bashing or husband abuse!

Again, Ravi hid behind that thin, sickly smile she brought forth when she was confused, when words failed her. She tried to convey her helplessness to her husband but Marara was in his element now, laying all his grievances at his new employers' doorstep, splashing mud and dung all over the place. Inwardly, Ravi gave up any little hope she still had about the job and felt relieved. Better get over with it now than later.

'He needs to rest,' she said, looking at Marara.

'Don't worry, Ravi. There is a spare bed in there,' Tim said.

'Or if you prefer a hard, reed mat ...' Joan offered.

'There are things to be done, things that we have to do,' Ravi said, slowing down, breaking off when she realized that they were not paying any attention to her, their eyes bulging, giving each other knowing or surprised looks, sometimes laughing that flat, dry, contrived laugh that makes the jaws ache, for their guests' benefit, to show that they were not offended, that they were enjoying all this, even hinting that the drinkers that they knew, where they came from, could out-drink or out-talk a hundred Mararas any place, any time. This was the kind of frankness, the openness, that should always be there among friends, their winks seemed to be saying.

Whatever they might have thought, Ravi now only saw how Marara's head seemed to have a loose nut in it. She heard with burning ears how fluently he could now speak their language, how the 'fucks' and the 'shits' were competing with the spittle that flew off his foam-flecked mouth onto the table and into the faces of their hosts. Some time earlier on in the conversation – at the sixth or seventh glass? – Tim had asked not exactly unpleasantly:

'Do you know what "fuck" means, Marara?'

'The word or the act?'

'The word, of course,' Joan said, laughing in spite of herself, Ravi thought.

'It means that I can't say it in the presence of old white ladies with a weak heart or of Victorian sensibilities, that's what it fucking means,' he said.

Marara went on: 'We also have forbidden words where I come from. Certain words or acts cannot be mentioned in front of elders or in mixed family gatherings, but we do have one hell of a fine day when you can say anything under the sun and get away with it. The *rukweza* threshing feast. On this day son can tell father what a cuckold he is and the father is not allowed to take any action against his son. I can tell my enemy that I know he is planning to send lightning to destroy my home and he can only answer by saying something better or pretend he hasn't heard.

'The threshing floor is where you say all and no one may use what you say on the threshing floor in court or to start a fresh feud. And the language used on the threshing floor – well, it would make a sailor green with envy.'

'Have you ever seen a sailor, Marara?' Tim cut in quietly.

'Or a ship?' Joan added with a little smile.

'Do you even know what a canoe is, Marara?' Tim rounded off, looking at Joan, and Ravi could only look down at the remains of their dinner, the names of whose components she had now forgotten except for the one dish to which they had set a match – *flame* something or *flamb* other. And Marara shook his head sadly.

'Can you imagine?' he said. 'At my age, thirty-three, I haven't even seen the sea. But I can imagine how it looks from reading Dana, Monsarrat, Conrad and Hemingway – *The Old Man and the Sea* – I think I can imagine what it feels like ...'

'We should take him to see the sea, shouldn't we, Joan?'

'And Ravi too,' Joan said aware of Ravi's heavy silence, then a little guiltily: 'You haven't seen the sea, have you, Ravi?'

'If you could call the duck pond on my father's farm a sea.'

'Yeah I think we should take them to see the sea, Tim.'

'What I would really like to see,' Marara said thoughtfully, his eyes turned inside himself, his voice very low, 'what I would really like to see is the ocean. I can only imagine distantly the restlessness of so much water. In our lessons in geography they taught us about the Bering Straits, the Straits of Gibraltar, the Straits of Magellan, Hawaii, the warm Gulf current, the cold North Atlantic current and a thousand and one other more or less useless facts. They made us write exams on all this – most of us came out with As but not one single one of us had ever seen a mass of water bigger than his bath.'

He now looked at them, stunned at the profundity of what he had just said, realizing for the first time the absurdity of it, seeking explanation from Tim or Joan. Tim and Joan looked blankly back at him. They seemed uneasy. Marara wouldn't take his eyes off them.

'Can you imagine it? Sakala, a friend of mine, committed suicide on the day he got his results. He couldn't have known that all that garbage wouldn't have rescued him if he had fallen into a disused mine the following year. There was no way he could have known that for the real game of living, nothing of what we were taught would help us. And this is what no teacher would tell us. And here, here I am ... '

Ravi tried hard not to look at her husband's lower lip. It was the least manly part of him. She said, 'We really must be getting back now. Thank you for the dinner er ... Miss Jones, Mr Greene.' She was getting on her feet.

'We will take you in the car, Ravi. It's only ten o'clock. We don't go to bed till one,' Tim said.

'When did we go to bed last night?' Joan asked.

'Can't remember. Must have been two or three.'

'Three, I should say,' Joan said.

'The children,' Ravi said lamely, sitting down.

'You went to bed at what time?' Marara said.

'Three o'clock. We invited a couple of businessmen for a drink and they wouldn't leave. Went through a whole bottle of gin, two really.'

'And you kept on saying my best London Dry, my best gin.' Joan laughed.

'They began by asking for Beefeater and I told them I didn't drink Beefeater.'

'Then they said give us what you have. And at first you gave them the local.'

'Then I felt guilty and brought out a bottle of London Dry.'

'You could have let them drink the local. I don't think they would have noticed the difference,' Joan laughed and Ravi looked at Marara laughing with them and she realized that he hadn't heard what Joan had said.

'Then they began to sing ...'

'And the dogs began to bark ...'

'Probably thought somebody was attacking us.'

'And our neighbour,' Joan leaned towards Ravi, reducing her voice to a whisper, 'our neighbour, he's white, loves his horses more than his workers ...'

'You should see where his poodle sleeps, Marara!' Tim shook his head.

'Anyway, he called us on the phone and threatened to blow us to hell and gone with his shotgun.'

'What must have really pissed him off was seeing these two huge black men in suits drinking and dancing with white people '

'He wears his racism on his sleeve.'

'And the dogs – Rhodes and Jameson – wouldn't stop barking and he kept on saying stop those dogs or I'll shoot them! And I couldn't tell whether he meant the real dogs – Rhodes and Jameson or Gara and Stones, our guests.'

'What did you say the dogs' names were?' Marara asked.

'Rhodes and Jameson,' Tim said.

'This would have come under history in your lessons Marara,' Joan said.

'They introduced the dogs to us when we came, remember?' Ravi said, prodding Marara with her eyes.

'Rhodes and Jameson – that's bloody good! Yes, and now I remember looking up the gender of the dogs when you said meet Rhodes and Jameson ...'

'Marara,' Ravi said softly.

'Yes. I remember saying: But the bloody dogs are bitches!'

'And so were they all, honourable men,' Tim said, making a mock stage bow.

'But Rhodes and Jameson is bloody good! I'll drink to that. Another whisky, Tim. Let's drink to their Cape to Cairo dream. If it hadn't been for Rhodes ... Oh, if it hadn't been for Rhodes and his gang ...'

'Oh, not another song, please,' Joan protested.

'Whisky, Tim. We will drink to those gentlemen of fortune – Cecil John Rhodes and Leander Starr Jameson.'

'Don't give him any more to drink,' Ravi said, looking at Tim who was about to pour a generous tot into Marara's glass.

'Come on, Tim. She thinks I don't know what I'm doing.'

'And I don't think you do either,' Tim said, withdrawing the bottle.

'You call this drinking? At home this would only be the beginning, the drums warming up by the fireside, getting taut and tighter, and you wait till you see the dancing ...'

'I think we had enough singing and dancing last night, thank you,' Joan said.

'Who said I am going to dance?' Marara glared at her.

'Well, you sounded as if you were about to.'

'He isn't going to dance,' Ravi said.

'You hear that? I'm not going to dance. You afraid I'm going to smash the furniture? Break up the elephant-foot stools and blacken the ivory? Or maybe get the wrong set of fingerprints on your pa's portrait?'

After a pause he began to sing: 'If it hadn't been for Cecil John Rhodes and his gang ... ' And Tim joined in: 'You'd still be up in your tree, picking at your fang,' as he splashed whisky into Marara's glass. 'Tell me when to stop,' he said.

'You shouldn't have done that,' Ravi said to Tim.

'The man wants to drink, doesn't he?' Tim retorted and Joan looked at him uneasily.

'Gang and fang,' Marara was saying, as he raised his glass to the level of his eyes and looked at it. He held the glass aloft like a trophy for some time, his face trying to compose itself so that it could better reflect the solemnity of the occasion.

'To Rhodes and Jameson, the best bitches in town!'

And the glass was empty in no time and neatly sitting on top of the table. He let out a burst of whisky fumes, shivered and they saw the glitter in his eye.

'Yes. Fang rhymes with gang. The thing that will never cease to amaze me with you English, is that ...'

'I'm Canadian,' Joan said.

'English-Canadian. Not French-Canadian — there is that nationality difference. The one thing that never ceases to amaze me is how throughout your history your kings and queens would knight you for some of the most atrocious crimes ever committed. Take Sir Francis Drake, for instance, who was a pirate of the first order ...'

'I can't sit here and listen to all this,' Joan said.

'I am simply returning his 'fang' for my 'gang'. Remember the threshing floor? None of this is supposed to be used as evidence in a court hearing, nor is it to be taken as the basis of further vendettas. Now, your Rhodes and Jameson — knighted for what? What has history got to say for them today?'

'Are you going to sit there and listen to this shit, Tim Greene?'

'Go and lie down, Joan. You've had a hard day. The man should have his freedom of speech.' Joan made a sound inside her and Ravi intercepted the look that Tim gave her.

'If you will excuse me,' Ravi said, standing up. 'You said the toilet is ...?'

'Oh, the bathroom. Through that door, down the hallway, turn left, first door to your right.'

'Thank you.'

'Where is she going? Where is my wife going?'

'She's not gonna leave you here, thank God,' Joan said.

'Where was I? Oh yes. Sir Francis Drake. And then the slave trade ...'

'How much history do you know, Marara?' Tim suddenly asked.

'As much as the white man taught me – and all of it twisted.'

'Have you ever realized that there are some of us who no longer believe in the history you are talking about?' Tim looked Marara straight in the eye.

'People who have given a lot for the liberation of your own country?' Joan added with emotion.

'Did you ever fight for the liberation of your own country, Marara?' Tim asked, accusingly.

'I didn't handle a gun, if that's what you mean.'

'What did you do?'

'I sent money to three of my brothers who were fighting in the bush. None of them came back after the war.'

'For three years we sent money and clothing to our brothers in the bush. Several times Marara tried to cross the border but he was sent back each time. The fighters told him he should help in the villages,' Ravi was approaching the table at which the others were sitting.

She went on as she sat down, 'There was no way you could live in our village and not be involved in the struggle – whether you liked it or not.' Ravi looked at Tim and Joan, then addressed Marara, 'We really ought to go now.'

'You hear her? That's the truth. You just couldn't afford to pass by the gate like a stranger and say: How are things in there? like you fellows did ... please don't misunderstand me: you are the first white people I have really ever talked to and who have really ever listened to ...'

'O, my God,' Joan said, looking away and closing her eyes.

'The good people want to sleep, Marara,' Ravi said.

'They are my friends, aren't they? They said so. We don't have to look at each other with pangas in our hearts. We should, in fact, invite them to our home and kill them a goat.'

'Where I come from goats are pets,' Tim said.

'A cow, then. We will slaughter a cow for you but you have to hear this first. I don't deny that you have helped in our struggle. I have read the books that you have written in and for our cause. But I still maintain that you are the third wave of missionaries.

'What do you mean?'

'You are here for what this land can offer – bounty, comrades, treasure, adventure, the T.E. Lawrence syndrome. The books you write will identify you with this land for ever but really ...'

'Let's go, Marara,' Ravi said touching his elbow.

'The books you write give your opinions about us, they will never give our point of view. So, you are still sending ships back to the old homeland with black cargo ...'

'How do you live with him'? Joan asked Ravi.

'Nothing has really changed – deep, deep, deep down ...' Marara said, sadly.

'Do you hate us that much?' Joan said.

'Who – me? Oh, no. I am simply puzzled by your twisted way of thinking and the blindness of your arrogance: We have come here to help you. Who gives you the right to say that? What about yourselves? You seem to be more in need of help than us ...'

'You know what, Marara?' Tim said. 'I think I should really treat you like the little turd that you are and give you a real hard thump on the nose.'

'Darling,' Joan said laying her hand on Tim's arm.

'There are people who really fought for this country, people who are still struggling to make it a good place for everyone to live in and here is this little ungrateful piece of ...'

'Why don't you just take them home, Tim?'

'The man is a bloody racist!' Tim shouted. He banged his hand on the table. Marara looked at him uncomprehendingly and shook his head. Then, shrugging his shoulders, he planted both his hands on the table for support and heaved himself up.

'I'm sorry about that. Anyway, I didn't think you could stand up to or understand the threshing floor ritual. You are not supposed to take things personally.

'Here, Ravi. Let's go. You see, in the slave trade, the African chiefs who sold their own people for a bottle of whisky were even more to blame than those who bought the slaves. The costumes and circumstances may have changed but the relationship still remains the same. You do not come to us in peace and good will. Thank you for the dinner, Mr Green, Miss Jones.' A long, sad pause, and then. 'Goodbye and good luck.'

From the way he stood up to say his last words, Ravi knew from previous experience, that her husband had made a very important decision about their life.

Sacrifice

Three weeks after they buried Chemai, Nhata's four-year-old daughter, Chizema told his own daughter, Tayeva, that she wouldn't be going back to school: not this term, nor any other term of any year of her life. This was the end of her education. Stunned, Tayeva had been unable to speak. She had looked across at her mother, busy at the fireplace cooking their evening meal of *sadza*. She expected an explanation but Ketiwe, her mother, only looked into the fire, preferring not to know. Tayeva had left the room and gone to her own room. During the weeks that followed, Tayeva had watched her uncles – Mungofa and Nhata – who came every day to talk with her father. She realized that her uncles' visits were connected with her father's decision.

She could see them now, through the tiny triangular aperture that served as a window in her small round hut – her living-room, bedroom and private world – she could see the men: her father, Uncle Mungofa and Uncle Nhata, seated on wooden blocks at the *dare*, dwarfed by the tall, green wall of maize in the field beyond them, just at the edge of the yard.

As always, Uncle Mungofa and her father talked with lowered voices. You could pass within a yard of them and you could hardly hear what they were saying. Nhata was the exact opposite. From his raised voice, Tayeva was able to pick up a few words. It was the story of the family. It was the human skull in the Mutunga family's granary. Tayeva knew about it through bits of conversation.

From the time that Tayeva had become conscious of the big adult world of the complex extended family in which she was a member, she had sensed that all was not well with the three smaller families that made up the larger Mutunga family. Throughout her childhood, as far back as she could remember, she had lived in the middle of quarrels, accusations of witchcraft, finger-pointing, and doors slammed in the face of others. There had even been death threats and the village elders had been called in more than once to try and bring peace among the three Mutunga brothers and their families. Tayeva had got used to all this and she had learned, as her mother had advised her, to pay little or no attention to it, to distance herself from it all. And that was what she had done: looked at it all with a child's other-world eye, uninvolved, detached, a waking dream that had nothing to do with her.

But her mind had begun to catch up with her. Memories she wanted to keep down began to pop up. Questions began to demand answers. For instance, there was no way she could avoid being aware of the deaths in their families, her own and her uncles'. One of her games as a child involved paying visits to the family graveyard and counting the number of graves. And each year, sometimes every six months, she counted one or two more than there had been at the last count. Three of these graves, she had been told, belonged to her three elder sisters. She remembered them dimly. They had been a comfortable presence in her awareness and she could still remember the ache when suddenly they were no longer there. She remembered asking her mother: 'When are they coming back?' All three had been swept away and drowned crossing a river in flood.

There was yet another family grave in the graveyard: that of her younger brother. He had died only a year ago, aged four. His death, when Tayeva was sixteen years old, claimed the only other surviving child in their family and it left a chill, an indelible fear of death in Tayeva's mind. Whenever she heard an elderly person say: 'Death can come to anyone at any time,' she, Tayeva Mutunga, knew in her bones how too true that was.

With the death of her little brother, Tayeva also began to see and understand the pattern of a story, the Mutunga family story, in the quarrels, accusations, death threats and the endless courts held among the three families. Slowly, the bits and pieces that she had picked up throughout her life from different members of the family at different times, in different places and circumstances, began to adhere together like grains of sand and bits of dirt on a dung beetle's ball.

But it was still a story, something out there, in the larger family's past, just one of those folk tales her mother used to tell – and still told her:

'Kusema and Kanhondo were friends. Kusema fell in love with Mavhu, Kanhondo's wife. One day, while Kanhondo was out in the bush, hunting, Kusema paid Mavhu a visit during the night. VaZviripi, Kanhondo's mother, had also paid her son's family a visit on that day. (She had heard rumours about Mavhu her daughter-in-law and Kusema, and she wanted to find out for herself). Now, at some time around the second cock-crow that night, VaZviripi thought she heard a man's voice in her son's bedroom. She knew that only Mavhu was supposed to be in the bedroom, alone, as her husband had gone hunting and wouldn't be expected back home for another day or two.

'So the old woman went out to investigate. She stood outside Mavhu's room for a long time, listening. When she was certain that indeed there was a man in the bedroom with her daughter-in-law, in anger, VaZviripi pushed the door open and the old woman received a spear deep in her chest ...'

The story had always ended, as it still did, with the spear in Old VaZviripi's chest.

Years later, after Tayeva had started reading literature in her third year at secondary school, it hadn't been hard for her to substitute the name Mutunga for Kusema. But still the story had remained somewhere out there, the story of the Mutunga family and that particular ancestor hadn't made a meaningful impression on Tayeva's mind. He was just something ugly and mysterious that flitted from shadow to shadow at the periphery of her imagination. Even the deaths in the family hadn't brought this shadowy ancestor any closer to Tayeva.

But now-now, with the death of Nhata's daughter and these meetings daily, Tayeva had a feeling that the story of this shadowy ancestor might be closer to her than she had suspected ...

She knew that whatever the reason for her father's decision, it wasn't lack of money to pay school fees. They were not any poorer than the poorest family in the village and she was the only child her parents had to look after. She was also certain that it couldn't be that her father had suddenly begun to believe, like Uncle Nhata, that educating a girl was money thrown into Munyati River. Most of her father's stories were about him hunting for an education and for better-paying jobs – from Southern Rhodesia right down to Cape Town in South Africa. Her father always spoke, with regret, of how he could have been somebody, if he had had a little education when he'd been working in Cape Town. And when he was feeling particularly lightheaded he would say, 'Maybe you, Tayeva, might have had a different face from the one you have now.'

That long-gone unknown ancestor had to be the reason, Tayeva felt now as she looked out through her window at the three men seated at the *dare* on the edge of the maize field ...

They were sitting round the fire in a triangle with Uncle Mungofa, the eldest of the three, at the apex and the other two, as always, addressing their words to and through him. Tayeva's room was a little too far away for her to hear Uncle Nhata's words. But she could almost tell what he was saying from his gestures: he waved his arms in the air, slapped his knee with his open palm, pounded the ground with his clenched fist, pointed at God in the sky and their long-gone ancestors deep in the Earth, and ran his index finger across his naked neck in a throat-slitting gesture. All this while her father, the youngest of the three, arms folded across his chest, head bowed, stared into the fire, and Uncle Mungofa, pipe in mouth, eyes half-closed (from her daily observation), seemed to be contemplating the wall of green maize swaying in the breeze before him. Then, as she looked at them, Tayeva saw Uncle Nhata springing up and in the same movement, grabbing his axe and raising it in the air and the word KILL exploding from his mouth towards her in the sultry heat of the summer evening and Uncle Mungofa's hand quickly (she was reminded of the speed of a cobra striking) grabbing and wresting the axe from Nhata's hand and throwing it away into the gloom of the maize plants. Nhata jumped away from the fire, fists cocked, hitting his chest with his right hand: *'Come on! Kill me!'* (Tayeva heard his words) and, seeing that no one rose to his challenge, Nhata's arms fell to his sides, and rather embarrassed, he went over into the maize returning a few minutes later with his axe on his shoulder. Without looking back at his brothers, Nhata took the path to his home and left. The other men didn't even glance at him as he left.

At the edge of the yard, just before he disappeared into the bush, Tayeva heard Nhata shouting, *'Chew on it, Chizema! Tomorrow she leaves this home!'*

Throughout all this, Tayeva realized that Chizema, her father, had remained very still, without making the slightest movement (something Tayeva hated him for) his arms folded across his chest, staring into the fire. He was like that now as Uncle Mungofa removed the pipe from his mouth and spoke to him. Tayeva could only see Uncle Mungofa's left hand moving, from the wrist, as he leaned towards her father. Then he straightened up again, silent, as if waiting for her father to say something.

Her father seemed to be taking a long time to answer. Then, slowly, he shook his head, from side to side, like a tired ox, and, uncrossing his arms, slapped his knees with both open palms and (Tayeva heard him): *'NO!'*

At that moment Tayeva heard something like the roar of a distant river in flood coming towards her and in that instant she knew that she was earmarked for sacrifice. She turned away from the window and just stood there, leaning against the wall. Slowly, she slid down to the floor and rested her head on her drawn-up knees. She remained like that for a long time, listening to her heart beating in her ears. Then she raised her head and looked at her room as the light faded from it: the rush and reed mats and goatskins spread out on the clean cowdung-smeared floor; the three ragged blankets neatly folded on one of the mats; the beer-bottle candlestick and her favourite piece of furniture in the room: the varnished wooden bookshelf which had won Rambai (oh, Rambai!) first prize in his carpentry class and which he had given her as a present (for being the most improved girl at the school — Rambai's own words) on their last day at school last December. (Now she would never see Rambai again.) There were a few books on the shelf, mostly textbooks from her three years in secondary school, some used-up exercise books and three tattered romantic novels she had borrowed from her friend, Tabitha.

The walls of her room were bare except for her four dresses, two of which were old school uniforms, her grey school jersey and blue blazer, all of them suspended from a wire hanger on a nail sunk in the wall behind the door. When she opened the door into her room, the same motion also shut her wardrobe so that whenever she had visitors in the room she always kept her door open. Right now the door was closed.

There was a cough outside. 'Yevai?' her mother called.

Tayeva didn't answer. 'Are you in there, Yevai? Shall I bring your food?'

'I am not hungry, Mother.'

'You haven't eaten a thing since morning.'

'Please, Mother. When I want to eat something I can get it for myself.'

'I'll talk to your father. He'll let you go back to school ...'

Tayeva didn't say anything.

'Yevai?'

She didn't answer. There was a long silence. Then she heard her mother's feet as she shuffled away. Tayeva remained seated under her window until the room got so dark she couldn't see any part of herself.

That night Tayeva's mother brought her blankets into Tayeva's room. In silence, she spread them out and stretched herself beside Tayeva. She tried to make conversation but Tayeva kept a stony silence. Three times during the night she woke up and knelt on her blankets and said some very long prayers. Each time she woke up, Tayeva heard her.

With the rising sun, Tayeva's mother rose from her mat, folded up her blankets and sat on top of them for a while, her legs stretched out in front of her, her cheeks in her hands, looking at Tayeva. Tayeva was also awake but still in bed, lying on her back and looking up at the thatched roof.

'You will get soot in your eyes,' her mother said.

'The candle hardly makes enough smoke to build up into soot.'

Her mother looked at her, surprised and pleased that she had spoken, cleared her throat and said, 'I thought you said the Virgins of Veronica held their meetings every Wednesday ...'

Tayeva nodded her head yes without looking at her mother.

'Shouldn't you be getting yourself ready to go?'

'I am not going to the meeting.'

'Why? You have always been a keen and active member of the Union of Veronica's Girls. You used to attend every meeting and function. Why do you want to stop now? You should go and see your friends. You haven't seen them since schools closed, have you?'

Tayeva turned on her side and looked at the bookshelf, away from her mother. Her mother lowered her eyes, sighed, stood up and carried her blankets out of the room.

Tayeva looked at the brittle, smoke-yellowed books that were dusty and had cob-
webs, flies and other small insects squashed in between some of their leaves. She had
read all, or almost all of them. Now she would never read another book again. Not in
school anyway ...

They had sung on the bus to school in the rain every January. The boys always liked
sitting at the back of the bus. Some of the senior boys would be drunk, shouting
obscenities, telling jokes, laughing raucously, stamping their feet on the floor of the
bus and pounding its sides with their fists and open palms, in time to the music.
Sometimes it was hard to get the boys to sing but once you got them going, it was
hard to stop them.

They had shared – there was always sharing on those buses to school – sweets,
biscuits, boiled maize cobs and salted nuts which her mother had prepared for her.
Her parents couldn't afford pocket money so that she could buy such things as sweets
and biscuits but none of her schoolmates had ever made her feel that she was any
different from them, or that she lacked anything ...

And then they would arrive at the school: red corrugated-iron roof, very high redbrick walls. Many jokes were made behind those walls. And there was Rambai. Rambai
the Clown, everyone called him. Rambai was well known for disrupting unprepared
teachers' lessons. He could make the whole class laugh continuously for forty minutes. Tayeva would always remember how Rambai once ruined Sister Immaculata's
Divinity lesson.

'Tell me, Sister Immaculata. How do you explain the mystery of eating the body and
drinking the blood of Christ as opposed to what the early missionaries described as
pagan cannibalistic practices in what they called darkest Africa? Don't you think that
basically the concept is the same?'

Sister Immaculata had gasped, her hand to her breast, and broken down in tears.
Rambai had been stopped from doing Divinity for the rest of the term. So, each
time Sister Immaculata walked into the classroom, Rambai walked out to go and dig
in Father O'Reilly's flower garden. 'Let the smell of God's flowers cleanse thy
abominably stuffy heathen thoughts,' Father O'Reilly, the school principal had said.
And so each time Sister Immaculata came in to teach Divinity, Rambai would don
his pitch-black sharp-horned paper hat and, imitating King Kong grunts, shuffle
and tread heavily towards the door, trailing a long black spike-ended piece of jute.
But, Tayeva felt that Rambai sometimes took his clowning too far. Somehow she
saw through him. As on Sundays, when he put on his oversized, navy-blue jacket,
shiny black at the collar, the bird's nest stuffing in the shoulder pads peeking through,

his sleeves rolled back; and his perennial farmer shoes – the tops held to the soles with bits of electric cord – people thought that *that* too was funny! Sometimes Rambai could go too far ... But he had never been able to fool Tayeva ... And he respected her for it.

Tayeva had excelled at netball and the egg-and-spoon race; she had taken leading roles in school plays and sung a beautiful soprano in the school choir; and, at the end of the year, she had walked away with first prize in English and History. The year had, as always with her, come round again to its end without her really being aware of the passing of the time. And again there would be singing on the bus, this time in the December rain, and it would be even better than it was in January as they all knew each other well, having been a whole year (or more) together. And for some, it would be a sad time as they wouldn't see each other again the following year or maybe, as usually happened, ever. But, they were happy all the same because this was December and they were going home for Christmas. And while Christmas didn't mean much to Tayeva, she was happy because she had good news for her parents, especially for her father. She had done well in her lessons and had won some prizes ...

Tayeva sighed and slowly turned her head towards the half-open soap-box door. She looked outside. The mango trees rocked and rustled, swaying with the heavy fruit in the gentle morning breeze. Across the open sandy yard, her eyes fell on the green shifting shimmering sea of maize, and the hazy blue hills in the distance. Beyond those blue hills her dusty ghost haunted the empty corridors of St Michael's Secondary School, rattled on metal doors, dissolved through redbrick walls and floated across the now overgrown netball field. A feather fell through the red iron roof of the church building onto the red wax-polished floor below, silently floating past the wooden statues of Joseph, Mary and the Holy Child, past the shining bronze candle-holders, the fourteen Passiontide pictures of Christ depicting the stations of the cross on his way to Calvary or was it Golgotha? She couldn't quite remember. On, along the long central aisle her ghost glided, then, at the huge clock, turned right and opened the wrought iron door into the Holy Name Chapel where the Host was kept and the light was never put out. She knelt down to pray with the white-robed pale-faced white sisters of the Holy Name who didn't pay any attention to her but some of the Chita *chaJesu* sisters out in front, dark-skinned, dressed in blue, raised their heads from their holy books and smiled at her and later returned to their bibles, although she could tell that some of the older sisters were lip-reading what they remembered from years of repetition – if you opened an unfamiliar page they would fall as silent as a church mouse. Tayeva felt ashamed of

127

this unkind thought about the old palsy-head-shaking sisters who couldn't read any other text than those they had committed to memory. She felt even worse when she tried to pray and realized that she had forgotten most of the prayers she used to know. Except for the Lord's Prayer which she now repeated over and over again, rather desperately, clinging to the rhythm of the words. She prayed for herself. At school — two months or was it three months ago? — she would have prayed that she do well in her examinations; she would have prayed for her mother to be given strength to bear in silence her suffering over the death of all her children; she would have prayed that her father rely less on medicine men or *n'angas* and turn to God instead; and she would have wound up her prayers by asking for the repose of her little brother Kufa's soul, and the souls of her sisters whom she could hardly remember. And, as always when she prayed long and sincerely for herself and the people she cared about, she would feel a sudden sharp stab of pain in her heart, pain for her little brother. And she would know, rather guiltily, that she didn't feel such pain for her sisters and she would ask — rather insincerely, she felt — when the feeling was translated into words: 'Why did they have to die, Lord?'

But now, she prayed only for herself, and, without the heart to remember or make any prayers of her own, she kept repeating the Lord's Prayer and sincerely hoped that He would remove the snags in her way and drag her out of the mire. She prayed fervently: 'Let this bitter cup pass from me, Oh Lord'.

Once again, Tayeva sighed. She stretched out her right hand and pulled out one of her old textbooks, whose leaves, stiff and brittle, crackled and broke like a wafer in her hand as she carefully opened its pages. Then she quickly closed it, removed its cover which once had been a poster for a commercial advert: AFRICA: *LAND OF SUN-LIGHT*. She crumbled the cover which dissolved in small particles of white dust, went out into the bush at the edge of the yard and squatted in the tall grass.

Emerging from the bush, Tayeva picked up her hoe and, without washing or brushing her teeth as she would have normally done, or rinsing out her mouth with a warm salt-and-water solution, she took the path to the fields.

From the doorway to her kitchen, her mother watched and shook her head. Tayeva went to the field furthest from their home two kilometres away. She wanted to be alone. She didn't return home for the afternoon meal. Her mother had to bring it to her.

'Are you all right, Yevai?' her mother asked, putting the basket with the lunch down on the ground. She sat down on some uprooted weeds beside Tayeva.

'I am quite well, Mother.'

'You look ill. If you are ill, tell me. Don't work. You will only make things worse.'

Without a word, Tayeva took the covered plates of food out of the basket. She took off the cloths that covered the cold pumpkin, *sadza* and thick sour milk prepared the way that her mother knew she liked it. Tayeva began to eat in silence. She found she had no appetite. She covered up the plates and put them back in the basket. Her mother looked away, in pain.

'I saw Tabitha yesterday,' her mother said. 'How healthy she looks.' Then she waited for Tayeva to say something. Tayeva didn't say anything.

'But you looked a lot better than she did when you came back from school. What did they give you at school?'

'Beans.'

'Beans?'

'Beans, beans, beans, meat and vegetables ...'

'We have those huge white beans. Do you mean those?'

'Yes.'

'Would you like me to make them for you? I think they are good for you.'

'Don't bother, Mother. I can make them for myself when I want them.'

'Why? Do you think I can't cook them well enough for you?'

'I don't mean that, Mother. I just don't like them.'

Her mother fell silent. She felt slightly guilty. She had heard that in jail they give the man they are about to hang any kind of food or dish that he asks for, no matter how expensive it may be.

'Yevai.'

'Mother.'

'Why don't you tell me what's eating you? Do you think a mother shouldn't know? It just can't be school. I said I can talk to your father so that he can let you finish your education ... '

Tayeva didn't answer or look at her mother. She picked up a stick and began to dig a hole in the ground. Her mother watched her as she dug. Tayeva scooped the soil out of the hole, she plucked a fresh, blood-red flower from a weed, laid the flower in the hole and covered it with soil. She made a little oblong mound of soil and stuck a tiny cross on the heap of earth.

'Please Tayeva, don't do that,' her mother said in a voice constricted with pain and fear.

Tayeva levelled the heap of earth with her hand.

After a short pause, her mother asked her: 'Are you afraid?'

'Afraid of what?'

'I don't know. Like your time of the moon.'

129

Tayeva threw her mother a short sharp look and began to dig again.

'I said don't do that. You make me nervous!'

Tayeva laid the stick down, looked at her mother for what seemed a long time, and then she looked away at the bush at the edge of the field. She said, 'I know what happened to Kusema's children.'

'What Kusema's children?'

'In that story you are always telling me: Kusema, Kanhondo, Mavhu and VaZviripi. You always stop when VaZviripi is killed.'

'That's all I know.'

'But it's not really the end of the story, is it?

After VaZviripi was killed Kusema ran away with Mavhu. They went to a far-away land where no one knew them. They had six children, three girls and three boys. Their children grew up and married. Kusema and, later, Mavhu, died. After their death, the spirit of VaZviripi began to haunt and harass the families of their children. It wanted to be avenged. It began to kill off all the little children born to Kusema's children. The carnage wouldn't stop until it was appeased.'

Tayeva stopped and looked at her mother. 'Isn't that so, Mother? Isn't that how it is, how the story continues?'

Her mother looked at her strangely, surprised: 'Who told you all this Yevai?'

'Isn't that how it is?'

'Is this what's bothering you?'

'Isn't that how it is, Mother?'

Tayeva fixed her mother with a look, a look that wouldn't let her go.

'It's bad manners to look at your elders like that when they are talking to you,' her mother said, shifting her bottom uneasily as if she were sitting on thorns. Something flickered briefly in Tayeva's eyes as she watched her mother, then she turned her eyes away towards the blue mountains in the west. Her mother sensed an emptiness falling between them and she stretched her hand out to touch Tayeva's knee. She spoke softly: 'I will talk to your father. He will listen to me. He has to listen to me. You are the only one we have. You will go back to school. You will see.'

Tayeva, her eyes still averted, said, as if to herself, 'How did they stop old VaZviripi's spirit from destroying their families completely ?'

There was silence, then her mother said, 'You don't think I can help you, do you, Yevai?' Her voice sounded very small.

'I didn't say that, Mother.'

130

A short pause, then her mother said: 'Look at me.'

Tayeva turned and looked at her mother, her eyes lowered.

'Smile at your mother please, Yevai.'

Tayeva forced a thin self-conscious smile, which provided just a glimpse of her small, even, white teeth, a 'beauty gap' in the upper row, and then she closed her mouth.

'There. That's better,' her mother said. 'Don't look so sad. You frighten me. Every day I wake up, and I tell myself that even our worst nightmares must end, one day. Don't make me lose hope.' She stopped, her mouth still open as if there was something more she wanted to say, but all she said, was,' Will you be all right if I go now?'

Tayeva nodded her head without saying anything. Her mother picked up the basket with the uneaten food and slung it over the crook of her left arm.

'Have you seen Tabitha since you came back from school?'

'No.'

'Don't you think you should go and say hello to her? She was asking about you the other day.'

'If she wants to see me, she'll come.'

'She is your friend.'

Without realizing what she was doing, Tayeva began to dig another little hole in the ground. She saw her mother looking at her and immediately filled the hole up and smoothed the soil over it.

'I am going now,' her mother said, rising to her feet.

Tayeva didn't answer. Her mother didn't move.

'I am going now,' her mother said again, taking a step, then two steps and then just as she was about to turn her back on her, Tayeva sprang onto her knees and threw her arms round her mother's waist. She buried her head in her mother's back.

'I don't want to go, Mother! Can't you please do something to stop them, Mother? Why, why, why mother? Why me? I am still too young. I want to go to school. Please don't let them make me go, Mama!'

Her mother stood very still, her eyes closed as if she was feeling the movement of a very sharp pain deep inside her. Tayeva's arms loosened from her mother's waist and dropped to her sides. Still kneeling, she bent forward so that her forehead was touching the ground. She brought her hands up and buried her face in them.

Her mother squatted in the sand and put her arm round Tayeva's shoulders and buried her face in Tayeva's hair.

'My daughter. My one and only daughter. I don't want ... I won't, let you go,' she murmured, stroking Tayeva's shoulders and back, over and over again, repeating the same words until Tayeva was very still.

131

Then, at that moment, in the sultry stillness of the midday heat of a summer's day, they heard the raised voices coming from the direction of their home, two kilometres away. They both recognized Uncle Nhata's angry voice. Only Nhata's voice. No one else's.

'Let's go home,' Tayeva's mother whispered. 'I can't leave you alone here. I will go and call Tabitha to come and keep you company.'

Tayeva didn't move for some time. She might have fallen asleep for all the movement she made. Then, slowly, she raised her head and her mother helped her up.

As they walked out of the field the sky was preparing to let loose one of those late-afternoon mid-summer downpours that usually last until early the following morning.

As they entered their yard, they found Uncle Mungofa and Uncle Nhata sitting once more under the huge *musasa* tree at the edge of the yard, talking to Tayeva's father.

Uncle Mungofa was holding Nhata's axe, the end of its handle planted in the ground between his feet, his chin resting on his hands which lay on the head of the axe. Nhata was half-sitting half-crouching on his stool, shouting at Chizema, who sat opposite him, his eyes on the ground endlessly tracing patterns in the sand with a twig.

'Your medicines, son of my father,' Tayeva heard Uncle Nhata saying. 'Your medicines have finished off this whole family. But I am not going to sit here on my potatoes and watch the soil swallow one after the other of my children when I damn well know that *you* know what's eating them. Is she an angel, that daughter of yours? Is she more important than the rest of the family? We don't eat beauty. You listen too much to your wife, son of my father. When she has got her witch's legs round your waist, her witch's hands cupping your potatoes and her witch's lips whispering in your ear ...'

'Nhata!' Uncle Mungofa didn't quite shout but the force of his voice stopped Uncle Nhata in mid-sentence.

'Nhata what? Every time it's Nhata! I am right and you know it. You think I hate him? Hate my own brother? I hate what he is doing to the family. I hate that coiled witch's tongue which whispers into his ear in bed at midnight every ...'

'Leave his wife alone, Nhata. Ketiwe is not part of the Mutunga family. She doesn't sit in the courts of the affairs of the Mutunga's family. No Mutunga blood runs through her veins,' Uncle Mungofa said.

'She sits in the court of what goes on in his head. She is the magistrate in there.'

'You talk as if he and she haven't already lost their children to the Earth.'

'Then why does he refuse to do what we say he must do? Tayeva is now the oldest in all our three families. For years we have been told what to do and for years we have begged him to let her go to save the family – who does he think he is? And, listen *Babamukuru* Mungofa – remember: he is not really a son of our own mother. I want you to remember that ...'

Uncle Mungofa didn't say anything after Nhata had said this. Ketiwe dropped some faggots that she had picked up on the way onto the firewood stack. The sound made the men turn their heads and notice the women's presence.

Ketiwe and Tayeva sat down in the sand near the firewood stack, a little distance away from the men.

'Good afternoon, *vana baba*,' Ketiwe said clapping her hands.

'Good afternoon, *Mainini*. How has been your day?' Uncle Mungofa returned Ketiwe's greetings, as innocently as if they had been discussing preparations for a feast.

'As usual. Lots of weeds in the fields,' Ketiwe said, playing along.

'Lots of weeds? But you are doing quite well. Look at the maize behind us. You would think it grows on a special kind of medicine, which only you know about.'

'You think so, *Babamukuru*?'

'I don't just think so. Anyone can see for themselves. It's as if it only rains here in your fields and in no one else's. How many families can boast of such a healthy crop of maize?'

'Your own fields are not really barren, *Babamukuru*.'

'My fields are all right, I agree, but yours are greener.'

'Tayeva,' Nhata called out.

'Uncle?'

'Uncle? Did you say "Uncle"?'

'*Baba*.'

'That's better. You haven't said "Good afternoon *Baba*" to me. May I know why?'

'I have been waiting for Uncle Mungofa to finish talking with Mother. I didn't want to disturb their conversation ...'

'Liar! When you came back from school did you come to greet me?'

'Leave the child alone, Nhata,' Uncle Mungofa said, shaking his head.

'Leave the child alone? She is my daughter! I am as much responsible for her manners as any man here.'

'We all know that ... Tayeva, go into the kitchen and get on with your work,' Uncle Mungofa said, waving his hand in the air as if he were fanning away a bad smell.

Tayeva went into the kitchen. When her mother came into the room a few minutes later, Tayeva had already swept it out, kindled and got going the fire, and put on a pot to boil water in preparation for the evening meal. She was now sitting on one of the goatskin mats, cutting up the *mowa* leaves before washing and boiling them.

Ketiwe sat down beside Tayeva and put her head in her hands. Tayeva finished cutting up the bundle of *mowa* and put them into a metal basin. She poured hot water over the vegetables, added cold water and began to rinse them, leaf by leaf, getting rid of every tiny grain of sand through the feel of her fingers. She threw away the dirty water, washed out the basin, put the *mowa* back into it, and poured some water over the leaves to give them a final rinse before lifting them out, handful by handful, and throwing them into the pot to cook. Then she covered the pot, wiped the basin dry with a clean cloth and put it away. She mopped away all the water that had spilt on the floor, wrung the mop outside and put it away. She took the lid off the pot to check if there was enough water in which to cook the *mowa*. Satisfied, she covered the pot, and began to do the morning and afternoon dishes which were all piled up in a jug of soapy water, sitting by the fireside while keeping an eye on the cooking pot.

It would be an hour, or just under, before the *mowa* was properly cooked.

'Mother,' Tayeva said in a near-whisper.

'Yevai?'

'What did Uncle Nhata mean when he said Father is "not really a son of our mother"?'

Ketiwe remained very still. Then she sighed and said, 'Your father had his own mother. Your grandfather was really wild. There are more children by him out there than we will ever know. Your father's mother died when he was still a little boy and your grandfather gave your father to Mungofa's and Nhata's mother to bring up. This is something none of us are supposed to know but you know what your Uncle Nhata's mouth is like. Please don't ever tell anyone that I've told you this.'

'But why, Mother, why didn't you tell me before?'

'What difference would it have made, my daughter?'

'So you don't think it ...' Tayeva's voice had gone a little higher.

'Yevai, *please*!'

'I am sorry, Mother,' Tayeva said, putting her hand lightly on her mother's knee.

After a long pause, without wiping the tears from her cheeks, Tayeva's mother continued with the story of Kusema and Mavhu as if she had been narrating it only a few minutes before.

All the n'angas *and diviners they consulted told them that the spirit of the Old Woman, VaZviripi, would not rest until it had wiped out Kusema's children and his children's children from the face of the earth, starting with the little ones still suckling at their mothers' breasts to the last of the hoary-haired elders until there was nobody left, not even to bury the last of the very last of them. Everything that answered to the name of Kusema – cattle, goats, sheep, chickens and dogs – all would have to be buried in the earth before that Old Woman's spirit was satisfied. Unless ... unless Kusema's children paid the Old Woman's people ten head of live cattle and a girl, a virgin, who would bear children among the people of the wronged woman for the rest of her life. This girl's mother or parents would receive no beads nor have a goat nor a cow killed to thank them for giving these wronged people a wife ...'*

Ketiwe stopped.

A shadow fell across the doorway. Tayeva's father came into the room. He sat down on the earthen bench against the wall. Tayeva didn't look at him directly but, from under her eyelashes, she could see that he wanted to say something. He seemed almost desperate under the weight of what he wanted to say but his tongue seemed to have been cut off.

Finally, he spoke, as if to himself: 'They have daughters in their families, more daughters and children than I have and yet they still insist that I provide the ...'

He stopped. His eyes wandering above the heads of his wife and daughter.

'If my daughter goes,' Ketiwe said quietly. Tayeva realized, from the weight and tone of it, that it was a full sentence. And she realized at that moment, the distance at which her parents now lived from each other. She had never been allowed to see this before and she was lost.

'Do you think I want her to go, woman?'

And he stood up and Tayeva wanted him to sit down, just to sit down there with them, even if they had nothing at all to say to each other any more. But she was only a child. Her father went out of the room.

Tayeva looked boldly at her mother. Her mother saw the look but once again, she preferred to look away.

Tayeva couldn't bear it. She said, 'Mother ...'

'He is also a man, Tayeva!' Ketiwe almost, but not quite, shouted. At Tayeva or herself? Tayeva couldn't remember any time in her life when her mother had used this version of her name. It sounded so cold and she hated it.

Without a word, Ketiwe stood up, picked up her waist cloth, wrapped it firmly round her, and left the room.

For the first time since her mother had taught her how to cook, Tayeva burnt the *mowa* to cinders. She thought of going to her room and leaving the preparation of their evening meal all together, but unconsciously she found herself washing out the pot with the burnt vegetables, cutting up some fresh leaves and putting the pot back on the fire. Her mother came back an hour later with Tabitha and two other girls whom Tayeva had only seen from a distance once or twice before. The girls, who called themselves by the biblical names of Maria and Marita, were itinerant preachers and they had been going about preaching in the area for the past three months. Tabitha had once told Tayeva about them but Tayeva hadn't paid much attention to her. Tabitha was looking for a man to marry her and that was why she was infatuated with them, Tayeva thought.

Maria and Marita said they were married to Jesus Christ. They didn't belong to any particular religious congregation or denomination. The elderly – religious – people of the village spoke of them with a kind of awe, tinged with a little fear, Tayeva felt. The two girls – who said they were virgins – were reputed to cast out demons, remove curses, sniff out witches, Tayeva had heard. They also made the blind see, the lame walk and the barren bear healthy children. But they were still girls, of Tabitha and Tayeva's age. And they were not very popular with the young of the village who loved going to the local Growth Point to dance to popular hit songs. Among the young, Maria and Marita had become a kind of huge joke. Married to Jesus? Young wives, watch out!

When Tayeva saw Maria and Marita in the light of the fire in their kitchen-living-room, she thought they were twins. Maybe it was the living together every day that had made them look alike, Tayeva thought.

'Maria and Marita,' Tabitha introduced them to Tayeva.

'And this is Tayeva,' Tabitha went on. 'I have told you about her.'

Tayeva looked sharply at Tabitha, and then at her mother. The two didn't allow their eyes to meet Tayeva's. But Maria and Marita beamed beatifically as each in turn shook hands with Tayeva. Tayeva thought they seemed very polite. They spoke in low sing-song voices that, to Tayeva, suggested moonlit nights in bush clearings rather than candlelit altars in incense-filled churches. They looked beautiful despite their drab habits – long, plain dresses, like cassocks; big sisal- and baobab-fibre satchels hung from their shoulders.

'Maybe you would like to take them to your room, Yevai?'

Tayeva's mother said this in a voice that she knew wouldn't be refused. 'Don't bother with the dishes tonight. I'll attend to that myself,' Ketiwe said; then, smiling to the other girls, added, 'You wouldn't want me listening to your stories, would you?'

In her room, Tayeva asked Maria and Marita to make themselves comfortable on the reed mats and goatskins. She remained on her feet and, after a while, said, 'Tabitha, can I see you for a minute?'

Tayeva led Tabitha outside. They walked a little distance from the hut and stood under a mulberry tree at the edge of the yard.

'You told Maria and Marita about ... about ...?'

'I had to. Your mother was in tears. She ...'

Tayeva was suddenly very angry. She felt as if she had been stripped naked in front of the whole village.

'You're a nice friend, Tabitha. A very nice friend.'

Tayeva turned to go back into the hut. Tabitha quickly grabbed her by her arm.

'Don't be angry, Yevai. Your mother is very worried. She is afraid that you might think ... do something bad to yourself. She thought it might help if I talked to you.'

'And you went and told your Marita and Maria?'

'Please, Yevai. You should listen to them. They are great. They have helped a lot of people.'

'It's probably all over the village by now: Tayeva Mutunga is going to be given away as ...'

'Please, Yevai. Maria and Marita are not those kinds of people. The village has its own ways of finding out about such things.'

Tayeva gave a short derisive laugh. 'Of course they have their own way with you at the water hole and at the washing place on Nyamhere River ...'

'Yevai, Yevai. I'm your friend. Don't you trust me? Wouldn't you have done the same for me?'

Tayeva looked at Tabitha, and then walked back to the hut. Tabitha held her back again.

'You will at least let them say a little prayer for you, won't you?'

'What do you want me to say? Do I have a life of my own to do as I wish any more?'

'Don't say that, Yevai. Please don't give up. Things will work out fine, you will see. You just give them a chance to say their little prayer for you.'

'Let go my arm ...'

'Yevai, promise ...'

Tayeva shook off Tabitha's arm and entered the room. Tabitha followed her in. They sat down opposite Maria and Marita who were reading their bibles in the guttering light of the smoky paraffin lamp which they had lit. They went on reading while Tayeva and Tabitha looked at them in silence. Then Maria raised her head and smiled at Tayeva and Tabitha. Maria seemed to sense the tension between the two girls. She cleared her throat, closed her bible and put it back into her bag. Then she spoke.

'We don't do anything without the concerned people's consent. God's grace is a freely flowing gift and a very subtle and delicate thing. Whenever it meets the least resistance, it is hindered and flees away. We did not choose for ourselves to do what we do and sometimes I pray to God to take away this gift from me. I don't want it. She doesn't want it. But who are we to choose?' Maria fixed her eyes on Tayeva. Tayeva looked at the floor.

Maria went on. 'We see you are troubled in your heart and we wouldn't like to add salt to your hurts. When you are ready for us, Tabitha knows where she can reach us,' Maria finished talking, and, slinging her bag onto her shoulder, stood up. Marita closed her bible, smiled at both Tayeva and Tabitha, put the bible into her bag and stood up too.

'Give us a chance,' Tabitha said, holding them back with her eyes.

Maria and Marita looked at each other, then at Tabitha, then at each other again.

'Just one chance,' Tabitha said, looking from one to the other of them, now on her knees, she held her hands together as if in prayer.

'Nothing will help her if she doesn't want it,' Marita said. 'She has to accept in her heart of hearts that prayer can work. There are no miracles except deep down inside us.'

'Tayeva is too distressed right now to know what she wants,' Tabitha said. 'But I know her. She is my friend. I know her better than I know anybody else, here or anywhere else. You just can't leave her like this. She is in trouble and she needs your help more than anyone else you have helped.'

'Helped?' Maria looked surprised. 'Have we ever helped anyone, Marita?'

'Not anyone that I know of,' Marita said, shaking her head and added, 'Only God helps us.'

'Only God helps,' Maria repeated after Marita and added, 'We are only his tools.'

'He does with us what He wills,' Marita said.

'We are his vessels,' Maria said and Marita said, 'Amen.'

Both fell silent for a minute, then Maria said, 'Let's hold hands.'

All four of them joined hands to form a circle. Maria and Marita closed their eyes. Tabitha closed hers too. Tayeva looked at them. They remained like that for quite some time. Tayeva felt certain that she could hear Maria's thoughts. If not her thoughts, then *something* that made her silence not just any silence. Tayeva felt herself getting warm and she felt the individual parts of her body letting go, and relaxing, slowly, deeply.

'Do you ever pray, Sis Yevai?' Maria asked gently, conversationally.

'Sometimes.'

'Not always?'

'I find myself lacking the strength.'

'That's when prayer is effective. When we lack the strength. That's when we should pray harder. Otherwise it wouldn't be prayer if we only prayed when we had the strength or when we felt like it. It is hard at first but it becomes easier with practice. Later, it becomes part of you, a very necessary part of you like air, water and food. Later on you can't imagine life without prayer. It's like returning home after a long absence among strangers. Out of ignorance, people laugh at people who pray. They used to laugh at me. They still do but now I don't mind them. I know one day, something will happen to them. When it does, they will be the first to tell me that they are surprised that people who don't pray are still alive! You see, prayer is like breathing. Praying is living.'

'And that's the truth,' Marita said in a voice that didn't seem to belong to her and immediately she began to sing.

Tayeva hadn't heard the song before and she was sure Tabitha hadn't either although she could see her lips moving and hear her voice singing along. The song seemed shapeless yet Tayeva found herself moved by it. They sang on for a long time, singing in a manner that Tayeva likened to a wind moving through grass and trees, stirring them a little at the beginning and getting stronger and stronger until the grass was almost flattened to the ground and the tree branches threatened to break: then, just before the branches broke, they stopped. They stopped on a sudden high note that was like a clap on the ears. Tayeva felt: *Something has to happen*. Marita said, 'We will do a prayer for Yevai so that wherever she is going ... '

'I am not going anywhere,' Tayeva said in a voice that surprised even herself in its vehemence.

Marita continued as if she hadn't heard Tayeva's screaming protest, ' ... she may go well.'

'I am not going,' Tayeva said again with rising hysteria, trying to free her hand from Marita's.

'We are all going where He leads us and we are going all the same even as our bodies and minds scream against Him,' Marita said soothingly but with a strength that cut down anything that Tayeva felt coming out of her. She went on, 'Whether you go or not is out of our hands. Only God will tell you what to do and that's all that matters. What God tells you to do. Everything you do, here or anywhere else, is, finally God's will.'

'Shut the door, Tabitha.' Maria said.

Tabitha rose and went to shut the door and then came back to join the circle.

'Repeat after me,' Marita said. 'Thy will be done.'

'Thy will be done,' echoed the others.

'Thy will be done,' Marita chanted.

'Thy will be done,' chanted the others.

Tayeva didn't know how long they chanted this but when they stopped, she, too, like the others, was swaying. Marita was sweating profusely. There was a silence so deep that Tayeva couldn't believe it existed in this world. She felt something rising in her chest, something that threatened to explode inside her and burst out. It left her shaking, tears cascaded freely down her cheeks.

Marita prayed, 'If the road is long and hard and thorny and I feel so exhausted and tired and weak that I just want to flop down, lie down even in the mud and give in and give it all up; or if the words of the people of this world come flying at me from all sides like so many barbed arrows and threaten to rip and tear me apart; let me not give way to anger and despair. Let me stand erect like a rock in a storm and shout with all my strength: Thy will be done!'

Marita's last line was so powerful that Tayeva didn't hear it as words but only as a very strong yearning feeling that forced her, without realizing it, to shout with the others:

'Thy will be done!'

There followed a stillness, a silence that, to Tayeva, seemed to want to speak and what it said was only tears, tears and more tears that also somehow threatened to turn into a big laugh.

'And now, Sis Yevai,' Maria was saying, 'we will have some tea.'

'We don't have any tea or sugar,' Tayeva said and burst out laughing. For some reason, this, which she should have found extremely embarrassing, seemed so funny that she repeated, 'No tea, no sugar.' And she fell to the floor, laughing.

And the others joined in her laughter.

'I mean it,' Tayeva insisted. 'We have no sugar or tea in this house.'

Maria laid a warm hand on Tayeva's knee and said, 'Dear Yevai don't worry. God provides. He knows our hearts so well He always provides. But I am sure we can at least get some hot water?' And as she said this, Maria produced from her bag two packets: one of tea and the other of sugar.

Later, as they sat drinking black tea, Tayeva couldn't move her eyes from Maria and Marita. She thought there was something wrong with them, wrong in an innocent and extremely lovable way. They chatted away about inconsequential things, giggling and laughing and pinching each other like mischievous little girls. As they prattled on, in a private language of their own, they did not once refer to why they were there, or what they had just done, nor did they give any indication that they knew who Tayeva was. And Tayeva found herself laughing with them although she didn't understand their obviously very private jokes. And, all too soon, Maria and Marita announced that they were leaving. They wouldn't even let Tayeva or Tabitha see them out of the yard. And when they were gone, Tayeva found that she missed them intensely.

Tabitha stayed behind with Tayeva. They talked of other things and did not refer to what had just happened. When Tabitha said that she had to go home, Tayeva's mother begged her to stay the night and keep Tayeva company. What she didn't tell Tabitha was that *she*, Ketiwe, needed company. She had begun to be afraid alone with Tayeva in the house. She wanted someone with her, another woman, 'to handle' Tayeva, although she didn't know exactly what she meant by that. It was like the wish for a more experienced midwife during a difficult birth. Tayeva's mother had never felt so lonely in her life. It wasn't what might happen to Tayeva as much as what might happen to herself. All of a sudden, things had become loose inside her and they threatened to leak out of every pore in her body. Her husband had long gone to bed without having his supper. As had often happened in the past few weeks, she couldn't bear the thought of spending a whole night with him in the same bed.

'You wouldn't mind if we all slept in here tonight?' Ketiwe asked Tayeva but looking at Tabitha.

So Tayeva brought the blankets from her room and spread them out on the other side of the fireplace opposite her mother.

Tayeva and Tabitha lay under the same blankets, Ketiwe lay on the other side of the fireplace.

A smell of something burning woke all three of them during the night.

'What is it?' Tabitha asked in a whisper.

'Something burning,' Tayeva said, getting out of the blankets.

'I can smell it too,' Tayeva's mother whispered from the other side. But she wouldn't get up.

Tayeva went to the door, opened it and looked out.

'What is it?' her mother asked in a fearful voice.

'Looks like father,' Tayeva answered from the doorway. 'He is burning something at the ashpit.'

Both Ketiwe and Tabitha rose and went to stand beside Tayeva at the door. They looked out over Tayeva's shoulders.

'His medicines,' Ketiwe said in a whisper.

They watched Chizema outlined against the night sky, throwing things from a bag into the fire. Whatever it was he was burning seemed to strangle the flames so that, instead of rising higher, only a dark acrid pall of smoke rose into the air. There were dull explosions, hisses, splutterings and sometimes something leapt into a bright flame but died instantly as if dampened by the surroundings.

'The smell,' Tayeva said, holding her nose.

'His medicines,' Tayeva's mother said, in a dull voice. 'First, the bible. And now, his medicines,' she added, then she went on like a conductor reciting the names of the stations passengers would pass through along their route.

'His roots, leaves and tubers; oils and powders; his rhino horns and elephant tusks; all his lion's claws, porcupine quills and eagle feathers; the crocodile bile and dried owls' eyes and hyena shit; the otter's fur, snake skins and monkey's paw; his black, white and red beads, his black-and-white *retso* cloth ...'

As she enumerated these items, tears rolled down Ketiwe's cheeks.

'All the things – the talismans and amulets – that were meant to guard and protect his family; all the things that he has gathered and collected throughout his life against death – now death has forgotten about them and where is his family now? He . . he ...' but she stopped and, like the two girls, just watched. Then she turned back into the room.

At the fire, Chizema seemed to have finished what he had been doing. He was standing there, very still, arms straight down his sides, the fire was dying down.

Chizema turned round. He stood looking towards the living-room. Tayeva thought that her father seemed almost naked, she had never seen him look so helpless before. He didn't even seem to see them as they stood in the doorway.

'Shut the door and try to get back to sleep,' Tayeva's mother told the girls as she stretched herself under her blankets.

Somewhere in her sleep, towards dawn, Tayeva thought she heard a cow lowing so close to the house that she started and quickly sat up, throwing the blankets off her. She looked through the cracks in the door and saw that it was already very light outside. Birds were already singing in the trees.

Tabitha, feeling the bite of the chilly morning air, also woke up.

'What is it?'

'I thought I heard a cow mooing.'

'A cow?' Tayeva's mother said, pulling her head out of the blankets. 'Where?'

'Just outside,' Tayeva said, rising.

But her mother had already opened the door and looked out. From the doorway, Tayeva's mother began to laugh. She laughed so hard and so hysterically that Tayeva knew something very bad had happened. Whenever things went bad, her mother laughed in that same way – before the ear-splitting wailing began.

142

'Mother!' Tayeva called out as she, too, rushed to the door. Then Ketiwe flopped down, still laughing and shaking her head in a manner Tayeva knew was her way of accepting defeat.

Tayeva looked outside.

She remained rooted to the spot, her mouth slightly open. Then she felt Tabitha pushing her aside.

'There just might be something worth saving,' Tabitha said, rushing out towards the maize field.

'The heartless, me-alone, shit-eating, devil-worshipping monkey-faced son-of-a-witch!' Tayeva had never, in all her seventeen years, heard such foul language issuing from her mother's mouth. 'Let them finish it! Don't drive them out. Let them finish every little bit that's left.' Ketiwe was saying as Tayeva followed Tabitha across the yard into the devastated maize field.

Throughout the field, from one end to the other, over thirty head of cattle were wreaking havoc on the almost ripe maize: ripping off the big green cobs from the stalks, crunching and munching them in their too-small mouths, long silvery-green threads of saliva drooling from the corners of their jaws, while under their hooves they broke and trampled the still-standing plants into the earth ...

Tayeva saw Tabitha ahead of her, hitting at some of the beasts with a thick stick. She stopped for a moment, realizing that there was also someone else at the other end of the field, driving the cattle out. She recognized Uncle Mungofa's voice.

Tayeva picked up her hoe, removed the metal blade, gripped the thick smooth wooden handle tightly and went into the fray.

'This is terrible,' was all that Uncle Mungofa said when he and the two girls finally managed to drive the cattle out of the field and into the pastures beyond the village. They drove them a kilometre into the grazing grounds and then turned back homeward. They didn't even greet each other.

Uncle Mungofa, walking ahead of the two girls, shook his head and continued his monologue loudly, 'I don't know what's got into Nhata's head. This is murder. We don't do this even to our worst enemies. This is the work of someone with the heart of a witch.'

As they entered the yard, Tayeva saw her father sitting on an upside-down mortar against the wall of the kitchen, his arms folded on his chest, looking at the destruction. Uncle Nhata was standing beside him, smoking a hand-rolled cigarette, his axe leaning against the wall beside him. Tayeva could hear her mother, now talking, now laughing, somewhere in the field but she could not see her. She was laughing so hard that more than once Tayeva looked at Tabitha. If she heard her, Tabitha did not show it.

143

Uncle Mungofa went straight to the *dare*, the men's fireplace, the place where courts were held. The old man sat on his usual stool, a huge *mutsamvi* log, and pulled out his tobacco pouch and pipe.

Nbata picked up his axe and went to the *dare*. Chizema was the last to go and sit under the huge *musasa* tree. None of them seemed to want to face the field which was once a shimmering shifting sea of green maize. The few plants that still remained standing were a sorry apology. Shorn of their fruit and leaves, they looked like grave markers in the aftermath of a fierce battle.

Tayeva and Tabitha sat against the wall of the kitchen, a distance away from the men. Here, they were soon joined by Tayeva's aunts, Mrs Mungofa and Mrs Nhata. None of them exchanged any words. It was worse than a funeral, Tayeva felt.

Somewhere in the field, they could all hear Ketiwe talking and laughing.

Uncle Mungofa didn't speak right away, he seemed to be waiting for someone else who still had to come, someone who must hear what he had to say. He opened his tobacco pouch and began to load his pipe, then deciding that the pipe wouldn't draw well, he emptied the tobacco back into the pouch, took out a small knife and began to scrape the inside of the pipe bowl. Then he dismantled the pipe and with a piece of wire, cleaned the inside of the pipe stem. As he was loading the pipe, Ketiwe came out of the field carrying a load of green maize ears in the front of her dress which she had turned up by the hem to make a kind of kangaroo pouch, leaving the tops of her thighs exposed except for an under-dress of very thin see-through black material. Everyone looked down and away as Ketiwe entered the yard.

Ketiwe made her way straight to the *dare* where the men were seated. Tayeva restrained herself from rushing towards her with a cloth to cover her mother's semi-nakedness.

Ketiwe approached the men, knelt in front of Nhata and unloaded the ears of maize at his feet.

She straightened up, and, kneeling, took a deep breath and spat into Uncle Nhata's face.

Nhata slapped her hard, on one cheek, then the other, in quick succession with the same hand. Ketiwe's head jerked like a doll's at each slap. She put the back of her hand to her lips and wiped them. She drew away her hand and looked at it. There was blood on it.

Ketiwe began to laugh, then stopped. She ran her tongue over her now bloody lips, *chuke-chuke-chuked* saliva round her mouth and then, taking careful aim, shot it out into Nhata's face.

The blood-stained saliva landed in one of his eyes and began to trickle down his face.

Tayeva only realized that she had been screaming at the top of her voice when she saw Uncle Mungofa holding her father tightly round the waist, both his arms pinned against his sides. She saw the axe — Nhata's axe — slipping out of her father's left-hand-grip to the ground. Uncle Nhata sat on his bottom on the ground, his right hand to his left shoulder, blood seeping through the fingers. Nhata's eyes and mouth were wide open, surprised. He took his hand off his shoulder and looked at it. He saw the blood, gasped, keeled over and was still. Tayeva saw her mother squatted a little distance from Nhata, her hands to her face, crying-laughing.

Tabitha and Uncle Mungofa's wife were having a hard time trying to hold down Nhata's wife.

'If he dies you are going to eat him, shit, piss and all!' she was shouting at Chizema.

'Water!' Uncle Mungofa roared. He had left Chizema (who quietly slid away), and was now kneeling by the side of Nhata.

'Someone get me some water, quick!'

Tayeva rushed into the kitchen and brought out two buckets — one in either hand — of water.

'What happened?' Nhata asked after Mungofa had poured the buckets of water over him.

'Get me something to bandage his shoulder,' Mungofa said.

Ketiwe stood up and went and knelt beside Nhata.

'Get me one of my clean dresses, Yevai,' she said over her shoulder.

'If he dies...' Nhata's wife was struggling under Mungofa's wife and Tabitha.

Tayeva rushed to her parents' bedroom.

But the door was bolted from inside.

Then Tayeva heard noises of struggling inside.

She screamed, 'Father!' and she passed out. She realized that she hadn't noticed before that the door of her parents' bedroom was pitch black.

Her last thought was that the colour was too ominous for a door on a house where people lived.

Later, that evening, all the members of the three Mutunga families were gathered in Nhata's house. The headmaster of the local school had brought back Nhata and Chizema and Muza, the village headman, from hospital. Nhata now lay in bed, leaning against a heap of blankets, with bandages over and under his shoulder and across his chest. Chizema's neck was badly swollen, elastoplast bandages covered the bruises made by the cowhide rope with which he had tried to hang himself. When Mungofa had finally broken through the door and cut him down, Chizema was unconscious and they had had to take him to hospital as well. The headman, Muza, had been asked to accompany the two brothers to the hospital in his capacity as the village arbitrator, an elder and a friend of the family. He would know what to say to the hospital authorities if they asked too many questions, or insisted on calling in the police. Nhata and his wife had screamed, demanding that the whole issue be treated as a police case. They wanted to see Chizema in jail. But a lot of elderly people, villagers with families and problems of their own, had finally made Nhata and Sosana, his wife, see reason.

'Who are the police?' the villagers said. 'A bunch of strangers who wouldn't know how to keep their mouths shut and who would say the wrong things to all sorts of passers-by thus exposing the family to even worse ill-wind. The police? Would they send your children to school or feed your family if you died? Your brother is your brother and no matter how great your differences are, he is bound by blood to care for your family.'

And now they were all here. The men, Mungofa, Chizema and Headman Muza, seated on the earthen bench along one wall, with Nhata lying on a mat at their feet. Opposite them, across the fireplace at the centre of the room, were the women: MaDube, Mungofa's wife; Sosana, Nhata's wife; Ketiwe and Tayeva.

Tayeva was the only child in the gathering. She had been asked to come in and sit with them and she knew very well why. She looked round at the grim faces in the light of the flames in the fireplace. None of the faces was fully lit so she couldn't see anyone's expression. But she could see that none of the people were looking at each other. Except for Headman Muza who was droning on as if to himself, talking of the ancestors and the rains and how things used to be in the old days. Sometimes Uncle Mungofa, or MaDube, his wife, would drop in a word or two of agreement. At times the headman's speech grew so impassioned that Tayeva would look up, sensing that the old man was going to cry. It was as if Muza was trying to puzzle out, to explain to himself, why so many things seemed to be going wrong. This was not the first time he had been called in to arbitrate in the Mutunga families' squabbles. Today he seemed very angry. He wished they would grow up and learn to face their problems squarely like grown-up men and women. Those graves scattered all over the big anthill under the huge *mutsamvi* tree were not maize seeds which they had sown hoping that they would sprout and give them a bumper harvest. Those were people, their children, their own family, mowed down by the red-clawed, large-toothed reaper, Death. And they had to wake up and do something about something before there was not one single one of them left to bury the very last Mutunga. Did they hear him? Were the children of his old bosom friend, Gandiwa Mutunga, listening to him? That was not *rukweza* seed broadcast under that *mutsamvi* tree from which they hoped to reap *matengu nematengu* to fill their granaries to the brim.

They were a running shame for all the world to see, like a pariah dog with running sores. Did they see all the other families with whom they lived? Did they think all was well with them? Did they see the daily smoke issuing from those roofs? Those sooty thatched roofs hid their own secrets but the people under them didn't climb onto anthills and hilltops shouting for all the world to come and see what was biting them. No they did not, not in the way the children of Mutunga did. If the ground could open then he would sink into it in order to hide from the shame that was now the family of his bosom friend, Gandiwa Mutunga. Next time a thing like this happened, he would refuse to come to help them. Did they hear his words?

Tayeva looked round at her people, her family. They were all deathly quiet, heads bowed down. Even Uncle Mungofa wasn't smoking his habitual pipe. The only break in Headman Muza's speech came when Mungofa and his wife clapped their hands: 'Don't rub it in, *Sekuru*. Those are harsh words for your poor unprotected children, *aSekuru*.' They understood very well what he was saying. They would try again, once more, to bring their heads together and straighten out what had to be straightened out. They would really try, *aSekuru*.

Then Mungofa said, 'We hear you, *Unendoro*. But this is a crime that was committed long long back by a great-great-grandfather. We are only children. We don't know where to go to find these people who were wronged. We don't even know who they are, what their name is ...'

Old Muza raised his walking-stick as if he would hit Mungofa. '*Iwe, iwe,* Mungofa! Mhofu! You are no longer a child with snot on your nose. You are now the father of all these people here and you open your mouth to tell me such ... such ... Mungofa!' Old Muza expertly shot a gob of phlegm from where he was sitting straight into the fire.

Mungofa clapped his hands and said, 'If we don't ask you for advice who else can we turn to?'

The rest of the family helped Mungofa with clapping of hands. That seemed to reduce Headman Muza's ire. He became calmer, a loving father, advising his

147

obedient children. 'Once you have got together and agreed to look into this thing and you have put everything required there on the mat, they will come. They will reveal themselves. Once you are ready, there will be a sign ...'

Tayeva found herself drifting off, half-awake, half-asleep, and she couldn't tell whether it was Old Muza's words she was hearing or someone else's:

'Her spirit will only rest when the offender or the descendants of the offender have paid the offended's people or descendants ten head of cattle and a virgin, a young girl who has not yet known a man. The girl will be given away as wife to one of the offended's male relatives or her descendants. No bride-price shall be paid to the girl's parents as she will be part of a payment or fine by her people to acknowledge the crime committed against these people by her own people... '

Tayeva woke up with a start. She didn't know how long she had been asleep but, on waking up, what she had to do was so clear to her that she wondered why she hadn't seen it this way before. She felt so certain of what had to be done, it was as if someone had whispered it into her ear. It looked and felt so right that she didn't feel any responsibility for making the decision. It was as if she were only carrying out orders, obeying someone's will. Tayeva felt a strange strength welling up in her, a strength that would brook no hindrance. She felt as if she were sitting higher up than the rest of the people in the room. She looked at Ketiwe, MaDube and Sosana; then at Headman Muza, Mungofa, Chizema and Nhata. She looked into their faces, one by one, as if auditioning them for a role she wanted each of them to play. They looked like frightened little children whom only she could rescue from this fearful curse that gripped them. She cleared her throat and coughed and all heads turned to her. It was as if she had spoken. Even Headman Muza stopped his endless monologue.

'Listen,' Tayeva said and she didn't know if that was her own voice or not. To her surprise, everyone clapped hands and it felt right that they should clap.

'I will go,' she said.

The room grew very quiet. Tayeva's words seemed to take time to sink into the heart of everyone. Their faces showed the relieved surprise and disbelief of people who had been waiting for rain for the past six years and here now was the very first drop.

'I will go,' Tayeva said again.

'I don't want to hear this,' Chizema said weakly.

Tears rolled down Ketiwe's cheeks.

148

'Let's talk about it some other day,' Mungofa said, confused, disbelieving and relieved but at the same time frightened of what he couldn't at the moment say. The sheer weight of the issue ... the ...

'There is no other day,' Tayeva said, 'I have made up my mind.' Then looking at her father, she said, 'I will still remain your daughter. You will have a son-in-law and grandchildren to play on your lap.'

'I don't want to hear any of this,' Chizema said, but his voice had become weaker.

Tayeva turned towards her mother: 'I will remain your daughter, Mother.'

'Yes, Yevai,' Ketiwe said. 'You will remain our daughter.' Her voice was very subdued but, in spite of the tears rolling down her cheeks, full of a strange new strength.

There was a silence in which no one dared to look at the other except for Tayeva, whose eyes now seemed to be flashing with an unearthly fire as she looked from face to face round the room. None dared look into her eyes except her mother who was searching her face as if to discover who this stranger could be.

Then Nhata gave a long rumbling groan which sounded like a tree being pulled up by the roots, rose to his full height and crashed face down in front of Tayeva, sobbing like an exile who has just put his foot on the motherland for the first time since the days of his great-grandfathers. The effort and the exercise brought fresh blood seeping through his bandages.

MaDube let out a wailing ululation that almost deafened everyone's ears and the whole room crashed into pandemonium: ululations, dancing, whistling and crying.

Mungofa silenced everyone by clapping loudly, rhythmically, in acceptance and submission to a new authority. The noise died down and Mungofa spoke as if he were addressing the spirit medium of a great-great-aunt of the clan: 'We will survive, *Ambuya*. We ...' He choked on his words and couldn't go on. He rose to his feet and made for the door blindly, ashamed to let the rest of the people, those who were now his children, see an old man's tears of relief and gratefulness.

But before Mungofa could open the door, there was a knock. He stopped frozen. All eyes turned towards the door.

The knock again. Mungofa turned to look at Headman Muza as if he were seeking advice on whether to open the door or not. Old Muza gave him a slight nod of the head.

There was a third knock. Mungofa opened the door and Tayeva heard a strange voice saying, 'Those who directed me here said that this was Gandiwa Mutunga's home?'

'This is it,' Mungofa said. 'Please enter.'

And into the silence of the room entered a frail grey-haired old man, almost the same age as Headman Muza. As he sat down, his eyes darted round the room, at the women, then seemed to settle without moving, on Tayeva. Tayeva saw it and returned his gaze. For a moment their looks were locked in silent battle. Then the Old Man seemed to hesitate, lowered his gaze to the floor, daunted by the fire blazing in Tayeva's eyes.

In a clear powerful voice, Tayeva spoke to the silent room: 'I am ready.'

The Little Wooden Hut in the Forest

A year after he had paid the larger part of the bride-price for her, and Keri had come to live with him as his wife at Damba Forestry Station, Gavi began to feel, a little uneasily, that he had been taken advantage of. It is possible that Gavi wouldn't have noticed or felt anything about his marriage to Kerina Mashamba if it hadn't been for the young men he worked with in the forestry orchards. They all knew Kerina and her family. Gavi tried to find out more about what they knew but they were evasive. They had a habit of huddling together and leaving him out whenever he approached them for a favour. So, left to himself, the sense of having been betrayed grew in Gavi. That's what he called it: betrayal. Had he known more of the world, he might have called it something else but, at nineteen, he knew no better. If anyone were to have asked him what he meant, he would probably have rolled up his sleeves – as often happened – and threatened to beat up whoever had dared to ask such a question. Words were a waste of time, Gavi thought. But he understood the meaning of betrayal.

When Gavi got his job at Damba Forestry Station, he had just walked out of the bush, unarmed, in rags and alone. He didn't know how he came to be where he was. He had presented himself to the foreman of Damba Forestry Station one drizzly evening and the foreman hadn't liked what he saw in those sunken, expressionless eyes. 'You will help the boys in the nurseries, until ...' the foreman had been vague about what he meant by 'until.' The job would keep Gavi's mind off whatever had driven him into the forestry station. It would give him a means of livelihood. It would help him chart out his future – if he still had any such thing left in his dreams. It was the first job that Gavi had had in his life. And a month later, Gavi would meet Keri and she would become his very first girl in his adult life.

Gavi had never dreamt that he would marry Kerina Mashamba. She had just been a part of everything that happened to him as it had been happening to him and people like him for the past three years. She had been there and he had been there and what had happened had happened. He had not even given the matter conscious thought. He felt it was perfectly understood, as for the past three years it had always been understood, that he would soon be going away and he wouldn't ever be coming back.

So he was taken by surprise when, after sleeping with Kerina, he heard people telling him that he was now a part of Damba. Gavi felt threatened, hemmed in. He felt that it wouldn't be long before the people round him would be forced to betray him, to sell him out.

Kerina had never been part of his 'mission'. As long as the word 'mission' was part of his vocabulary, Gavi had the feeling of being in transit. This feeling gave all his actions a sense of unreality – of impermanence. 'I'll be moving on. Nothing matters. I won't be here to answer for the consequences.' These words more or less reflected what Gavi felt about his relationship with Kerina.

He had met her one night at a wedding in the village. It had been so dark for him (although there was a full moon) and he had been so drunk that after spending the night in her arms in a nearby banana plantation, he couldn't remember who she was just ten minutes after she had left him to fetch the beer he had asked for early the following morning.

Gavi had other things on his mind when he let himself spend the night in Kerina's arms. He had been so self-absorbed that he didn't realize that he had set the whole village talking.

No one could remember when Kerina had last had a boyfriend, let alone a fiancé. Girls of her age-group now had their third or fourth baby. Kerina was slowly becoming the village aunt. Her problem was that no man would ask her to marry him. It wasn't that she was unattractive. She was, in fact, very beautiful. So beautiful that some elders considered that this was the reason why no man had ever taken her seriously. 'You are not born that beautiful without some other secret deformity,' they said.

A curse had been cast on Kerina Mashamba. Everyone in the village knew it. At first she had thought it was a joke but as, year after year, she watched girls fall in love, get married and have babies, she began to believe what people said about her: she was cursed. Before Gavi, Kerina was certain that she was doomed to die single, and probably alone, in a little thatched hut at the edge of the village.

So the night that Kerina slept with Gavi in the banana plantation became: The Night That Kerina Slept With Gavi In The Banana Plantation. It was a historical landmark in the life of Damba Village. Even the wedding which brought Gavi and Kerina together in the first place was remembered as the wedding that took place on the night that Kerina slept with Gavi in the banana plantation.

People thought it was a joke. Even Kerina didn't let herself think it meant anything. She was certain that Gavi would leave her the following day, or the day after that. But, somehow, Gavi didn't leave her. He heard what people said about Kerina but he was so sure that he would soon be going away, leaving Damba forever, that he didn't feel that the curse on Kerina would rub off on him. He felt himself protected by whatever powers had protected him for the past three years fighting in the bush – the powers that had led him to Damba after everyone else in his section had been blown to smithereens.

He thought he was in the hands of the ancestors but most of the young men in the village thought he was just in the hands of *mbanje*.

But, somehow, Gavi became aware of the talk around him. It slowly sank into him that he would be stuck at Damba forever. As the days grew into months and the months into years without any orders arriving from the front or from the rear, Gavi felt that something was bad. He had lost contact with the rest of his section. He was certain he was heading into an ambush. He was walking in treacherous terrain: he couldn't see what was in the thick bush around him. He wanted to get out and quickly. He felt trapped. He was miserable. And that made him difficult to get along with. It landed him in fights.

'I am thinking of moving on,' he told Kerina that week as he felt the hostility in the air around him.

They had been seeing each other daily for over a year, sleeping together for two hours, between two and four in the morning in Kerina's room behind Mr Barnes's house. Kerina was Mr Barnes's housemaid and nanny to his two small children. Mr Barnes was the overall boss at Damba Forestry Station.

When Gavi mentioned moving on, Kerina felt almost relieved. Things were taking their normal course. She was beginning to worry that Gavi might prove an exception. She wasn't used to those who stayed. Men had always moved on. At times she compared herself to a waiting room through which all passed – writing filth on the walls, pissing and shitting in the corners – but none staying long enough to claim occupation and ownership.

'I understand,' she said to Gavi. But then she also felt with a pang, as she had felt before … what's wrong with me? 'My friends say that you are just playing with me but I don't believe them. Are they telling the truth? Do you want me to believe them?'

This was the first time she had raised her voice to any man. And Gavi found himself unable to answer her questions. Indeed he found it difficult to conduct a simple conversation with anyone at all. So, most of the time, he found himself at a disadvantage. He always got the worst of any conversation. So, now, even while he felt that he had been taken advantage of, he found himself unable to answer Kerina's questions: her large eyes wandering over his face, as if searching, grappling for a foothold, like a child lost in a swamp. When she was like this, at quarters as close as this, Gavi felt himself disintegrating into the depths of her eyes. He would panic, look away, and pretend that he had other, more important matters to attend to. More often than not, he would become blindingly angry with her.

'I am thinking of moving on,' Gavi said again one day.

Kerina knew that this time he meant it. And this time she knew better than to answer him herself. Instead she went to consult with her aunt. The older woman sympathized with her. She knew what losing Gavi would mean to her thirty-two-year-old niece. Three years was the longest she had kept a man and, although the rest of the family had given up on her, it was the duty of the aunt, no matter how bleak the chances might seem, to keep a flicker of hope alive in their hearts. Sometimes she was forced to lie to the family, but Gavi had come along just at a time when her stock of lies to the Mashamba family was almost exhausted.

Kerina's aunt tried to make Gavi see just how serious this thing was that he had got himself into.

'I don't know what you're talking about,' Gavi answered.

'Marriage, Gavi, is what I'm talking about. You don't just sleep with someone's daughter and then walk away from her the next day as if she were a piece of wood, a log you'd been sitting on.'

Gavi looked at her, surprised. 'We've never discussed marriage; Keri and I have never discussed marriage. And I think she is old enough to speak for herself. After all ... ' Gavi used his hands to complete the sentence which for him had been a long one.

'After all what, Gavi?' the aunt leaned towards Gavi.

'After all, there's a war going on. We don't know whether we will be here tomorrow or not. Marriage is out of the question, Auntie.'

'There is no war here, Gavi. And marriage is very much the question. I think I know about the rules of this war, the one you want to hide behind. I know about paying for what you buy in the struggle for liberation. I know about not looting the *povo* and working hand in hand with them. You wouldn't like your chefs to know about this would you, Gavi?'

'But I might die tomorrow. What would be the point?'

'Leave the point and all that to God. He knows why things happen the way they do. He understands the point.'

Two days later, Kerina's aunt brought four hefty men to Damba Forest Station Compound and introduced them to Gavi as Kerina's brothers.

'Shall we go for a walk?' the oldest of them, said to Gavi after the exchange of greetings. So they all walked down the long winding mountain path into the valley where some of Keri's people lived. And the brothers talked among themselves of things they had done to people who had disagreed with them. What Gavi learned about the fate of these people was that they were never heard of again. Then they stopped at the rim of Zvachose Gorge where, Keri's eldest brother told him, a lot of people had disappeared.

'How did they disappear?' Gavi felt obliged to ask, a knot in his belly. Kerina's eldest brother looked at his brothers askance and said, 'How did they disappear?'

'Some hadn't paid back what they owed others,' one brother replied. 'Some had stolen other men's wives,' another said.

'And some had slept with other people's sisters,' a third responded. 'Let's go,' the eldest continued. 'We would like to introduce you to part of our huge family. Do you mind?'

Gavi didn't see how he could mind being introduced to Kerina's family. After the introductions and the discussions which followed, he became a much-loved brother-in-law to Keri's brothers. They kept a close eye on him until he paid the larger part of the bride-price for Kerina. After that, they more or less lost interest in him.

And now, a year or so later, and Kerina eight months with child, Gavi found it almost impossible to live with her — or with anyone else at the station for that matter. The station foreman was blaming himself for having helped Gavi.

For after Keri had left the family, her brothers had nothing more to do with her. They were glad that there had, finally, been something that they had been able to do for her. Not that they had much time for Gavi, but she was no longer an embarrassing emotional family burden. Now it was up to Kerina's aunt to teach her how to keep her husband at home.

One day, Muto, the station foreman, said to Gavi, 'Um ... I thought I should give you some advice which you can take or leave. It is the traditional custom among these people for any young woman expecting her first child to deliver it under the supervision of her own people. I thought that since we have the Christmas holidays coming up, this might be the right time for you to take your wife to her parents for this very important business.' What the foreman wasn't saying was that he was afraid Kerina might have a miscarriage or even die from the daily beating she received from Gavi.

Of course, afraid of the shame of being separated from her young husband, Kerina would pretend that nothing of the sort was happening. And when, on a previous occasion, the foreman had asked Gavi about the noises he heard coming from their room every night, Gavi had raised his eyebrows and said, 'What noises?'

The foreman sent word to Kerina's brothers but they simply said that Kerina was now someone else's wife and it would be wrong for them to interfere. Anyway, they said, if Kerina felt she wanted to see someone, she had an aunt, didn't she? The foreman had known that Kerina's brothers wouldn't help. They believed that a beating now and again kept a woman in her place. They wouldn't even have raised a finger if Keri had had a rib or two broken after Gavi's beatings. And they would have laughed at Gavi if he had let Keri give him any shit.

Surprisingly, however, the foreman's advice prevailed and just a day before Christmas, Gavi and Keri left Damba Forest Station well before sunrise. They needed three hours to cross the plantation before reaching Keri's parents' home in the Choga Communal Land. Kerina's father and mother lived in another place away from the rest of their family in Damba Valley. They would have to travel slowly, on foot, with occasional stops to let Keri have a rest. When they started out from Kerina's room at Damba Forestry Station, a thick fog lay over the whole forest. And it seemed to Gavi that with each step the fog thickened.

It had been a terrible night. The idea of taking Kerina to her home for the delivery of her first baby had quite quickly begun to appeal to Gavi. If he played his cards right, it was something which would work in his favour. But Kerina noticed his enthusiasm and suspected some ulterior motive.

'You can take me to the clinic,' Kerina said. 'Delivery doesn't have to be at home anymore. They can as easily do the job at the clinic.'

'You are too young to know about the importance of these things,' Gavi said, and then regretted it.

Kerina laughed derisively. Then she said, ' Too young! I have helped many mothers deliver their babies. I know what I'm talking about.'

'No, you don't, We are going to your parents' home tomorrow.'

'You can go alone. I don't need to go home to deliver this baby. And you know it. You just want me there so that you can get rid of me. You are just going to dump me and then disappear back into the bush where you came from. You are going to leave me there and never return.'

'Don't be a fool. You know I wouldn't do such a thing. I just want you to have this baby in the correct manner. Only the mother of the woman giving birth knows what's best for her.'

'You sound as if it's you who is to give birth.'

'Say what you like. We're going! Even if I have to drag you there. '

'No! And no!'

And so they argued the night before Christmas Eve. It had been terrible. For the second time in their life together, Kerina fought back. She had tried to reason with Gavi but Gavi had never been one to use reason if his fists could settle the whole thing faster. So, in self-defence, Kerina had picked up a piece of iron and hit Gavi hard on the head, hard enough for him to fall unconscious – which might have allowed her just a few hours of rest.

But of course she hadn't been able to sleep. Instead she worried that she had killed him. And she vowed that she would never ever argue with him again. So, when he woke up in the morning with a horrible lump just above his right eye, and told her to pack, she had packed, thankful that at least he was still alive. She refused – absolutely – to think of what she would have done if he had died.

The fog was rising and swirling all round him so that he felt as if it was physically pushing against his eyeballs; and at other times he felt as if he were falling endlessly into a dark pit. Helplessness and weightlessness created a sense of silent panic.

They had started on their journey long before sunrise and now the sun was setting and they were still in the plantation. Gavi realized that they were lost when he recognized a stream he remembered having crossed before – more than once. Kerina didn't look as if it bothered her. She sat down on an old log and looked at something Gavi couldn't see, but whatever it was, it seemed to amuse her and her lips curled in a smile. Gavi suddenly became murderously angry. He felt she was playing a game with him. He felt betrayed. This was her home country. She must have crossed and re-crossed the plantation a hundred times and it was inconceivable that she should get lost in a place where she'd been born, reared and spent her life. The gurgling of the water in the stream made him feel even angrier ...

'You think this is fun, don't you?' he sneered. Kerina smiled and kept on smiling, her eyes taking in the trees, the forest, the stream ...

'I'm talking to you, Keri.'

'What did you say?'

'You were born here. You must know the way through!'

'Aha! Here at last!' Gavi whirled round. An old man emerged out of the mist like something that formed part of the landscape. He smiled at Gavi and Kerina, stretching out his hand in greeting.

He said, 'We got the message. But why didn't you tell us you'd be bringing her today? Welcome, welcome, daughter. Hello, son. Good to see you back again in one piece.'

As if in a dream, Gavi and Kerina found themselves shaking hands with the Old Man.

'Let's go into the house,' he said, leading the way. 'She's waiting for you. But, tell me: you usually come two days before Christmas. What happened?'

Gavi looked at Kerina; Kerina returned his look of puzzlement. Gavi said, 'Haven't you got us mixed up with someone else?'

And before the Old Man could answer, they were standing in front of a small neat grass-thatched wooden hut. An old woman stood in the doorway of the hut, smiling. She came forward and, hugging each of them in turn, said, 'We were expecting you

157

yesterday. Did you get lost in the mist? We got word that you'd be coming. Is this my daughter-in-law? Why didn't you tell us that you would be bringing us a visitor? You naughty boy, you ... But, look at me. Going on when you must be famished. Come right in. It's the same old home that you left – when was it? Where does she come from?'

Gavi and Kerina let themselves be led, without saying anything, into the little hut. A bright pine-log fire burned on the hearth in the centre of the room. The air was filled with the sweet smell of resin.

Gavi sat on an earthen bench against the wall with the Old Man. Keri and the Old Woman sat on goatskin mats on the other side of the room, opposite the men, with the fire between them.

'My! How beautiful she looks in the dark glow of the fire!' the Old Woman said. 'You must be very hungry. I cooked this yesterday. Your favourite pumpkin with milk.' She uncovered some earthen basins close to the fireplace and pushed them towards Kerina. She filled up another, much bigger, basin with water and handed it to Kerina again. She wouldn't take her eyes off Kerina. The younger woman felt embarrassed and uncomfortable as only people who know they are beautiful react to close scrutiny.

'Wash your hands and eat, *Muroora*,' the Old Woman said. Then she looked at Gavi and something about him seemed to strike her.

She said, 'And where is your gun, sonny?'

'This is not our Tongo, Mother,' the Old Man responded gently but quickly. 'These are just two young people I have been following all day in the mist. It was clear that they were lost and when I saw that they would not be going anywhere tonight, I thought I should bring them home. I thought it would be just like the old days when our own boy was here at Christmas.'

Gavi and Kerina looked at the Old Man.

'And here, *Muroora*. Do you like wild figs? Children in the village brought me these when I told them you were coming for Christmas. And here are some maize ears. Roasted just the way you like them. Remember how you used to fight your elder brothers over roasted maize? And how you would beat them all up although you were the youngest?' The Old Woman's eyes shone. 'And where is your gun? Do you think the war is over? Do you think ...'

'He's not Tongo, Mother,' the Old Man said, firmly but softly as if soothing a baby.

'Where's your gun, boy?' the Old Woman glared at Gavi.

'My gun?' Gavi asked, looking at the Old Man.

'It's all right, Mother. He hasn't got his gun. The war is over,' the Old Man said winking at Gavi. And then, looking at Gavi, he repeated, 'The war is over.'

'The war is over?' Gavi echoed, surprised.

'The war is over, didn't you know?'

He glanced complicitly at the Old Man. 'The war is over.'

'The war is over?' the Old Woman asked querulously. 'Who told him the war was over? Where has he been if the war is over?'

'I have been making my way here but I got lost,' Gavi said.

The Old Man smiled as if to say 'Thank you' and added, 'He has brought you a daughter-in-law. He has come home with a wife. He has come to settle down. He has come home to start a new life. The war is over.'

'Yes. The war is over,' Gavi said, smiling dreamily. The air was heavy with the scent of river fern, mud, and pine needles.

At that moment Kerina gave a piercing scream. She leaned back against the wall, holding her belly, her head rolling from side to side.

The Old Woman looked keenly at Kerina. Then she hissed, 'Both of you, get out, Quick!'

Before Gavi and the Old Man had left the room, the Old Woman had grabbed a blanket from a dark corner and spread it over the lower half of Kerina's body. Gently, she made Kerina lie on her back, her head resting on a padded wooden headrest. In movements too fast to follow, the Old Woman had put an old tin full of water to boil on the fire and was scrubbing her hands in a basin. She looked up angrily and shouted, 'I said get out!'

The Old Man stood up, picked up his stool and went out. Gavi hesitated. Keri's scream had brought with it the shadows of other screams and he was shaking, sweating, and scarcely able to move. It was only when a burning twig snapped that he seemed to realize where he was and moved outside.

There he found the Old Man making a fire in a grass shelter, at the men's traditional outside fireplace, the *dare*. Gavi sat down dazed and watched the movements of the Old Man's hands as he made a pyramid of dry twigs against a pine log. The Old Man looked at him several times, and then he said, 'Your wife is going to have a baby.'

'Oh, no!' Gavi gasped.

'Why not? Don't you want a baby? A child. Your own child. Maybe a son. Or even a daughter. God's own gift. A daughter. Better a daughter. Sons go away and never come back. Don't you want a daughter?'

The Old Man looked up and there were tears in his eyes.

Gavi didn't know what to say.

There was a scream in the hut. Gavi stood up. The Old Man pulled him down.

159

'Every woman goes through these labour pains. It's the one thing men never experience. That's why sometimes women can be terribly cruel, more cruel than men, if you cross them. And that's why it's taboo for a child to hit his or her own mother.'

Another, prolonged scream was heard. Gavi crouched down, panting.

'Your wife is in very safe hands,' the Old Man said, then added, 'Now you understand how every wrong a child commits against his or her mother hurts the woman? Some mothers, out of pain, kill their children at birth. Unknowingly, of course.'

Kerina screamed once more and said something obscene which cut right through Gavi's whole being. He was in the labour hut in two bounds. Then he bounced back out, warding off a burning firebrand that the Old Woman had thrown into his face. But Gavi had seen enough: Kerina's contorted sweating face, her abnormally wide-spread legs ...

'That's woman territory,' the Old Man chuckled as Gavi staggered out of the hut. 'You're lucky she didn't kill you. That's the shame – which, paradoxically, is also their pride – which they want to bear, or which they must bear, alone. In the absence of men. Here men are not, and will never be welcome.'

Not long afterwards they heard the unmistakable yowling of a new-born baby. There was ululation from the hut.

'*Makorokoto*! You're a father!' the Old Man said, grabbing and shaking Gavi's hand.

At that moment the little pyramid of twigs caught fire with a crackle and a tall flame shot up like an arrow.

An hour later, Gavi was looking at Kerina as she held the baby out to him. The fire in the hearth lit up her face. Gavi had never seen Kerina's face in that way before. And he did not think that he would ever see it like that again. Beside such a face, Gavi felt small.

'What are you staring at? Hold your daughter!' the Old Woman called out to Gavi. She was busy preparing maize-meal porridge mixed with medicinal herbs for the weak mother.

'Normally, I wouldn't have allowed you in here today. Who knows what curses you might have caught from other women?' The Old Woman shook her head. 'Men. They are such beasts.' But she was laughing. 'Come on! Hold her! You're a father! Come on! No, not that way! Yes, that way! Isn't she beautiful?'

A father? Gavi felt bewildered, small and insignificant, as if he were in the presence of something bigger, something that threatened to undermine him, but it wasn't the same feeling as being lost in the fog. He stepped forward, towards Keri, who, in the guttering firelight, now looked so painfully vulnerable, so mysteriously

160

beautiful, and so all-knowingly powerful that he couldn't stop the tears rolling down his cheeks as he knelt in front of her, to receive from her outstretched arms her gift to him, their first, his child.

As he took the baby in his arms, a hyena laughed in the forest. Instinctively, Gavi felt his arms tightening protectively round the baby, while being filled with anxiety that he might crush the poor little thing to death.

As he turned round to show the Old Man the baby, he saw other presences in the hut: behind the door, a cock stood on one leg watching over a roosting hen; between the Old Man's feet a cat sat hunched, purring; and in the doorway, a dog squatted on its haunches, looking into the hut. Beyond the dog's head, through the open door, Gavi saw the clear, star-sprinkled night sky.

His mind registered that the mist had cleared leaving an achingly deep blue-black serenity that went beyond words, beyond pain.

'Thank you,' he said to no one in particular, to everyone and everything present in the hut at that moment.

'Happy Christmas, Chenzira,' the Old Woman said, removing the baby from Gavi and with these words announcing both the day and the name she was giving the baby: Chenzira, she who was born on the road, she who will always be on the way.

Gavi looked at Kerina. Kerina looked back at him.

'You will have to kill her a goat. She must feed well so that she can also feed the baby well,' the Old Woman said.

'I don't have a goat,' Gavi said lamely.

'Listen to the idiot! He's probably going to tell his hungry wife: Die, I don't have a goat,' the Old Woman spat in the fire.

The Old Man smiled. 'Don't be hard on him, Mother. I'll lend him a goat to slaughter for his new family.'

'Another thing' the Old Woman said, 'She won't be able to take the baby out of this room for a week. '

'The child must be strong before she can face the harsh world outside,' the Old Man explained.

'Do you mind if I – if we – stay on here for a week?' Gavi said. It occurred to him that if they were to leave, he wouldn't know where he could take his new family. He felt a strong reluctance to leave the peace of the little hut in the forest, with its smell of river fern and the scent of pine resin that now seemed so familiar he was almost convinced that he had lived here once before.

'We have lived here all our lives,' the Old Man said, his voice inflected in a way that indicated to Gavi that an offer was being made.

161

'I am sure she and the baby will like it here,' Gavi said, quickly adding, 'Thank you,' to ensure that the Old Man did not change his mind.

'Sh,' the Old Woman said, index finger to her lips and throwing a sharp reproving glance at the men. 'Let her rest now, she's come a long way.'

Looking at Kerina, Gavi noticed that her eyes were closed and she seemed to have fallen into a very deep sleep. It struck him that this was not the first time Kerina had slept in this little room, in this place, with the Old Woman sitting exactly where she now sat looking down at her in exactly the same way as she was looking at her now, probably with the smell of river fern, wet clay and pine resin in her nostrils ...

'Look at the fool,' the Old Woman nudged the Old Man, pointing at Gavi, 'Just look at him. He comes home and he's crying.'

Glossary

The Hare

Ambuya/Mbuya	Grandmother or Aunt (mother's brother's wife)
Asekuru/Sekuru	Grandfather or Uncle (mother's brother)
Amainini/Mainini	Mother's younger sister
Amai/Mai	Mother
dovi	Peanut butter
daga (as in pole-and-*daga*)	Mud, clay
marufu	
hacha	
hute	} Different kinds of wild fruits
nzviro	
maroro	
Muchacha ndipe hacha	Plum tree give me plums
Muhute ndipe hute	Waterberry tree give me waterberries
Muonde ndipe maonde	Fig tree give me figs
	or
	Childhood song for learning names of different wild fruit trees
Jaja mandure	} Nursery nonsense ditty
Mandure mandure	
Zambia	A length of cloth wrapped around the waist by women which is said to originate in Zambia
derere	Okra
Mupedzanhamo	Second-hand clothing market in Mbare (colloq. all such markets) Literally: putting an end to suffering
mazitye	Second-hand clothes sold at such a market
Mai vauyawo-ho	Children's welcome-home song
hozi	Granary
E-e, veHarare	A form of greeting (which depends on the place the person being greeted is coming from)
titambire	Another form of greeting (receiving) the gifts the visitor has brought

Muroora	Daughter-in-law (may be used as form of respect by an elderly person to any younger woman)
sadza	Thick mealie-meal porridge (staple food in Zimbabwe)
huku	Chicken
nhodo	A game played with small stones or marbles

The Homecoming

hozi	See above

Did You Have to Go That Far?

mbambaira	Sweet potatoes
nyimo	Ground nuts
Iwe!	You! (As in Hey you!)
sadza	See above
musasa	One of the indigenous deciduous trees of Zimbabwe
Zambia	See above
Mukoma	Brother
Tinoadhaura mashizha *Ahe-e nd'o zvinoapatisa*	} Nonsense song
muti	Medicine (also tree)
kurasirira	To pass on a curse
Mhai!	Shout for Mother! or Ma! (responding to a call by one's mother)
nengozi dzakumba kwavo	Evil spirits from their house

The Empty House

Bhudi	Brother (Ndebele)
rega ndidye mari dzangu	Let me do my own thing (lit.)
bhemba	Home-made metal strip matchete
muonde	A kind of fig tree (Zimbabwean wild fruit tree)

The Slave Trade

rukweza	A Zimbabwean staple grain (from which beer is usually brewed)

Sacrifice

dare	Open-fire outside sitting place for men (also a court, where complaints etc. are heard and settled
sadza	See above
musasa	See above
Babamukuru	Father's elder brother (also elder sister's husband)
Vana baba	Fathers (form of respect in addressing men)
mowa	A kind of edible vegetable
retso	A piece of cloth in black-and-white colours worn for spiritual well-being
mutsamwi	A Zimbabwean tree
rukweza	See above
matengu nematengu	Expression to emphasize a 'bumper crop' – 'baskets upon baskets'
Iwe!	See above (can also be used as a warning – watch out!)
Unendoro	A man of the Ndoro totem

The Little Wooden Hut

mbanje	Zimbabwean form of hashish, *dagga*, etc
Muroora	See above
dare	See above